I0782134

HOW TO TAME A HELLHOUND

Hellhounds of Paradise Falls
Book 3

Shannon Mae

COPYRIGHT

Formatting by Tammy, Aspen Tree E.A.S.

Editing by Shannon, Aspen Tree E.A.S.

Cover design by Tammy, Aspen Tree E.A.S.

Page edge design by Painted Wings Publishing Service

BLURB:

Aiden

Apparently, the trauma from being kidnapped doesn't end when you're rescued, although I'm doing better. I have a roommate who has become family, and we've been adopted by a pack of otherworldly creatures who protect us. I'm still a little jumpy, and most people make me uncomfortable, but baking, therapy, and my daily walks are all helping. The sweet guard dog who follows me around in the woods helps, too. I can tell him anything I want—even how scared I am of my own family. I'm afraid to bring trouble to my new family's doorstep, but I can't end up caged again.

Atlas (aka Fluffy)

I have never belonged. I never knew my parents, and I grew up with a pack of wolves. (Yes, I was literally raised by wolves. Believe me, I see the humor in that too.) Wilder found me and adopted me, and I have a pack and a good life. People still make me uncomfortable, though, unless I'm torturing and killing them (only hellbound people—I'm not just some random serial killer). I just like solitude. But there's something about Aiden that calls to my hellhound, and I can't help wanting to protect the sweet human. I'll even put up with being nicknamed Fluffy so long as I get to stay close to him. When I find out he's in danger, I know I can't sit back any longer. The only problem? How will my traumatized human react to finding out I'm not just a guard dog?

Tags: Both characters have tragic backstories and need lots of comfort; Aiden loves cuddles and Fluffy is totally cuddle material; Atlas kind of likes being called Fluffy by his human, but he'll maim anyone else who tries it; there's torture and death (but only of really bad people); hellhounds have tails, and they know how to use them.

ACKNOWLEDGMENTS

For Maeflower - my strong, resilient, beautiful daughter. I love you.

Thank you to all my usuals—Scott, Tammy B PA, Ellie Ash, Avril, Mona, Jennifer, and all the readers who support me and send me such wonderful messages.

A special thank you to my Patreon, as well. They were there for every step of this book—they helped me name characters, gave me ideas on plot points, and encouraged me. Writing a book is a difficult process, and I inevitably think I'm doing a horrible job when I hit the halfway point. My Patreon encouraged me, and their feedback kept me going. Thank you to all of you—you helped make this book what it is.

READER WARNING

This book is intended for mature audiences. It is a dark(ish) romance that discusses torture, death, and maiming (but only of very bad people). There are characters who have traumatic backstories, as well. These things occur, for the most part, off page, because I'm squeamish and can't watch horror movies without covering my eyes.

There are also some very steamy times between men. Those definitely take place on page, in full detail. All sex acts are completely consensual and fully enjoyed by everyone involved. And (as always) there's a tail, and the hellhound knows how to use it.
 For a complete list of content warnings (including spoilers), please check the next page.

Content Warning

- Discussions of torture (torture occurs off page)
- Discussion of past trauma, including violence and sexual assault
- Past kidnapping (main character)
- Past abandonment (main character)
- Toxic family
- Violence
- Implied abusive relationship (secondary character)
- Consensual biting, knotting, and tail play

A Note Before You Begin

This book has been edited multiple times, but sometimes we miss something. If you notice a typo or grammatical error, please contact me! Sending it through Amazon is unfortunately not the easiest way to manage it. Feel free to email me at authorshannon mae@gmail.com. Thank you!

Chapter 1

Atlas (aka Fluffy)

I lay crouched down in the leaves, patient in my hunt. My regular hellhound form was not subtle—all darkness and flames—but when I'd been young I'd figured out how to mute it and look more wolf-like. It felt vaguely uncomfortable—like clothes that were just a little too tight—but then most clothes still felt weird to me. I preferred nudity, but humans were odd about such things. Even my hellhound packmates all wore clothes in their human form.

I mentally shrugged, sniffing the air silently.

He was coming.

I could smell him, and I could also sense his presence. But I was patient. I would wait. I was exceptionally good at waiting.

I heard his footsteps, and still I waited. *Patience*, I told my hellhound. He was itching to get up and run, to find our prey, tackle him to the ground, pin him down, and cover his face with licks.

Yeah, I know, not what you'd expect. But Aiden wasn't just any prey. He was...

Ours, my hellhound filled in.

Yes, I supposed that was enough. He was ours.

Smells good, my hellhound added.

He did. Like sweetness and joy. Like wild blueberries growing in the warm sun, all ripe and warm.

Only he didn't always smell like joy. Often, he smelled of sadness.

Hurt, my hellhound corrected. He wasn't wrong. Aiden was a wounded thing. I knew that. I knew that he had what the humans called trauma. I understood that, but my hellhound... Well, my hellhound thought it was something that could be fixed, like a thorn in our paw or like our loneliness before we'd found a wolf pack to take us in as children. My hellhound thought that we could fix Aiden, but I knew better.

Which was why I waited. Which was why I hadn't taken him off to our lair and kept him until he smelled of nothing but warmth and happiness. Because he needed the human things he liked, like his therapy...

He talks to us, my hellhound insisted. *Doesn't need "therapy."*

I rolled my eyes. I knew he did need therapy, even if my hellhound didn't. Hells, I probably needed my own therapy.

My hellhound made a snorting sound at the thought.

I wasn't exactly "normal," even for a hellhound. Most hellhounds didn't talk. We weren't technically separate entities; we were one being. I think the humans would call it multiple personality disorder or some such thing, but I enjoyed talking to my hellhound. For a long time, he was the only one I had to talk to, and I wasn't going to banish him to silence just because I now had a pack of hellhounds who I could actually converse with.

The footsteps were drawing closer, and I stood up in anticipation. I made a bit of noise by pawing at the leaves on the ground.

I had been silent at first when I stalked him as he walked, but he'd noticed my presence. Rather than being afraid, it had seemed to set him at ease. Then it seemed like he actually looked for me when he walked, so I made sure to be there.

Then he started talking to me. It was... odd. I didn't usually like small talk. What was the point? Humans liked to babble on about their days and what they did, and it was all so mundane. But I looked forward to hearing about Aiden's day, about what he baked, about what his roommate was up to. I enjoyed it when he shared his random worries with me.

I'd gotten closer and closer to him, and after a couple weeks, I was practically rubbing against his side when I walked next to him. And still, he wasn't nervous.

Touch, my hellhound growled. *Want pets. Want to rub against him.*

Yes, I wanted Aiden to touch me, and my hellhound wanted to lean into him and feel his warmth. But I wouldn't force it. He would touch me when he was ready. I heard a soft whistle—that was my cue. I trotted through the woods toward him, announcing my presence by being nice and loud. I was almost to him when I sensed distress. I tried to hold back my growl. Something had upset my Aiden.

"Fluffy!" he called out when he saw me, and I trotted closer until I was within a few feet of him. I expected us to continue walking then, only Aiden sat down on a rock that was jutting out of the ground.

I tilted my head. This was new. Aiden smelled agitated, though. He was breathing quickly, and his beautiful hazel eyes were wide. His heart was racing—he hadn't been running, so it shouldn't have been.

Scared?

I didn't think so. Not of us, anyway, because he wouldn't have sat down. I stepped closer cautiously, unsure what to do.

"Hey, Fluffy," Aiden murmured. He blew a breath out. "Rough night."

I crept closer, cautious and unsure.

Cuddles, my hellhound insisted. *Fluffy want cuddles with Aiden.*

I paused then. I knew Aiden called us Fluffy, but...

Fluffy? I asked my hellhound.

Like having name. Not just "my hellhound." Fluffy.

Well, ok, then. If my hellhound wanted to be named Fluffy, I wouldn't judge. Maybe I should have given him a name. But then again, he was me, so his name was Atlas, because that was my name.

Fluffy, he insisted again.

It was a ridiculous name, and my hellhound and I both knew it, but if he wanted to be Fluffy, then Fluffy he would be.

I resumed slowly stalking forward. Aiden had put his head in his hands, so I made lots of noise as I walked so he knew I was getting closer. His tree-bark brown hair had been very short, barely grown in, when he'd first come here, but it was slightly longer now. He was still thin, but he didn't look like he was hungry anymore. Still, I longed to cuddle his little form under my arm and make sure he was eating.

When I was close enough to touch, he slowly lifted his head. His heart was still racing, and he was breathing fast, but he seemed a wee bit calmer. He reached a hand out, tentative, like he was afraid I would bite him or something.

My hellhound scoffed at that notion. *Afraid we will run away. We never run from Aiden.*

That reassured me, and I crept closer, giving his hand a tentative lick.

He tasted like warmth and sunshine, and I wanted to lick him all over until his sadness was gone. He kept his hand out, and I walked closer, ducking my head until his hand was on top of it.

Fluffy want pets, my hellhound grumbled.

Yeah, so did I, but we had to let Aiden go at his own pace. He seemed sort of frozen though. I looked up, and his eyes were wide.

"You're so soft, Fluffy. I guess I named you well," Aiden whispered.

Yes. Good name.

I resisted the urge to grumble, and I moved a little closer still.

Aiden rubbed my head gently, and then he gave a little hiccup that sounded like the start of a sob. I moved closer and pressed against his legs, and then suddenly I had a human wrapped around my body in a hug.

It was very nice, and Aiden's scent was wrapped all around us, only he was also crying, and that was *not* very nice, because we did not want Aiden sad.

Fix him, my hellhound demanded.

But I was at a loss. I couldn't exactly turn into a human and ask him what was wrong. I thought that might be a wee bit terrifying. Aiden didn't seem to trust humans much, and I couldn't blame him. I didn't trust them either, so we had that in common.

"I'm ok," Aiden whimpered.

I realized I was softly rumbling against him. I tried to control it, hoping he didn't think I was growling at him.

I let him cry on me a bit—my fur would soak it up—and when a few minutes had passed and he was still crying, I decided we needed to do something.

My hellhound seemed to have the best idea, because we moved a bit and Aiden easily let us go. Then we started licking his tears off his face.

"Fluffy!" Aiden giggled wetly. He was still crying but also sort of laughing.

We could work with that. More kisses it was. We licked up all his tears, and he giggled a bit more and eventually stopped crying. Then he just sort of pet our fur and held us close.

It was nice.

"I don't know what came over me. I just... Liam gave me some bad news the other day, and I guess I haven't really let it sink in. I've been baking like crazy and avoiding it, and I know my therapist would say I can't avoid my feelings forever, but I don't want to think about my family. And then I'm trying to give Q and Liam more space and not sneak into their bed every night, and I promised myself I wouldn't last night, but I ended up being awake half the night thinking about my family, and then I was thinking about how I left my family, and then I was thinking about being kidnapped. So I got up and baked at like 3 am." Aiden laughed wetly again.

I grumbled a bit. Aiden should feel free to go get cuddles from Q and Liam whenever he needed to, and I would speak to Liam about that. I didn't want my Aiden upset in the middle of the night. Or maybe I just needed to stay closer at night. I could hunt while he was at work. If he was sad, I could go in and cuddle him myself.

Yes. Cuddles all night with Aiden. Best idea.

It might be difficult to explain how I got into the house, but I'm sure I could think of something. Or I'd make Liam think of something. Yes, he would have words to explain it.

"My therapist wants me to talk about it all," Aiden said, continuing to pet me. "She said it's like lancing a wound and letting the poison out. And I've talked about a lot of it, but there's some stuff... I don't know. Talking about it makes it real, you know?

"And then there's my family, and I did talk a little about that with her. I didn't tell her who they were, just that they had money and were very set in their ways. It was why I left. I didn't want to be in that life. I didn't want my future dictated for me. I didn't want to be involved in all their strict rules, even for the money. And it was hard to leave. My family... I don't know. I don't hate them. It's not like I want anything bad to happen to them. I just don't want to be a part of it all."

My hellhound grumbled in annoyance, and I had to agree. It would definitely be easier if we could just kill them. Of course, I didn't even know if they were technically rotten souls, but still... Aiden not wanting them hurt probably meant not even a little maiming.

Aiden breathed out a sigh. "I'm ok. Let's take our morning

walk, because then Q and I are going to work. Some fresh air will help me feel better."

He got up, and we started walking, and if I pressed against his legs now and then, he didn't seem to mind. In fact, he often reached down and ran his fingers through my fur in response.

Ours, my hellhound rumbled.

Yes, Aiden was ours. We would protect him, and we would find a way to spend more time with him.

⁂

I was waiting in Liam's office when he walked in, and I knew it was just him in the house. He gave a little start at seeing me, and I suppressed a grin.

Hellhounds could smell and hear very well, but I was gifted at hiding my scent, and I knew how to be quiet. So quiet even my packmates couldn't hear me. Sometimes it was nice to remind them of that fact.

"Your bare ass is sitting on my chair, you uncultured mutt," Liam grumbled.

I did smile then. He was grumpy, which meant I had definitely surprised him.

He just grumbled at my smile and walked out of the room. I heard him rifling around, and he came back with a pair of sweatpants.

I got up and put them on. I supposed clothes were necessary. It was good to remember how to be in my human form, and I'd been hellhound a lot lately.

"Last hunt was rough?" Liam asked.

I grunted in response.

Liam sat down in the other chair and continued to stare, his eyebrows raised. I sighed. He wouldn't give up until I talked to him.

"Children in cages," was all I said.

Liam nodded his head, his eyes soft. He knew I had a weakness for children, and he knew that children being neglected was... traumatic for me. I had been abandoned as a child. I didn't remember much, and Wilder assured me that my hellhound father must not have known about me, because he said no hellhound would ever abandon a child. Give them away to raise, yes, but never abandon them.

I only remembered being hungry and cold and alone. Not completely alone, though, because I had my hellhound.

Fluffy, he rumbled.

He didn't talk as much when I was in human form, but the name was important. Aiden had given it to us, so it was special.

I could feel his impatience, though. He wanted us to fix Aiden.

"Aiden didn't sleep and didn't want to bother you," I said.

Liam raised his eyebrows. "Why would he bother us? He comes in and cuddles all the time."

I shrugged. "He said he's trying to give you guys 'more space.'"

"More space?" he asked.

I shrugged. Liam and I both looked at each other, slightly puzzled.

"Do you think I should order a bigger bed?" he finally asked. "I didn't realize he might be feeling smushed when he cuddles us, but I do know they make bigger beds." He turned around to start typing away on his computer. "I think a king-sized bed will fit in Quinton's room. I'll have to measure. Although there's also a California King. Why would a king-sized bed be different in California?"

"Humans are weird," I answered.

Liam nodded in agreement, looking at his cameras now to see the size of Quinton's bedroom. "Ok, I'll order a bigger bed today. There's definitely enough space."

"And my hellhound should be allowed in the house," I added.

Liam turned and looked at me, raising his eyebrows again. We stared at each other in silence.

"You sure about that, Fluffy?" he snarked, and I heard the mockery in his use of the name.

I was up and had him pinned against his chair faster than he could blink. He was growling low in his throat and so was I, my hellhound close to the surface.

No fighting packmates, I reminded my hellhound, and my hand relaxed a bit. I knew Liam could have escalated it, but my pack usually gave me a minute to control myself. They were good like that.

"Don't mock. Aiden named me that," I growled out.

"Interesting," he said, like I didn't still have a hand wrapped around his throat.

I let go and stepped back, shaking it off. Liam had only meant to tease.

"My Aiden," I said.

Liam just nodded again. "Ok. I'll tell him the... guard dog he walks with in the woods can come in the house. But Quinton will know. I don't know what he'll tell Aiden. It isn't right to lie to him."

I tilted my head, confused. "Who's lying to him?"

"You're not a dog," Liam responded dryly.

I nodded. I knew that. What did that have to do with anything?

Liam banged his head against his desk lightly. He did that sometimes. An odd human trait he picked up, I guess. He eventually stopped and looked at me.

"If I tell him he can let the 'dog' in the house, I'll be lying about what you are," he reasoned.

Ah, yes. That was true.

Fluffy, my hellhound insisted.

"Tell him he can let Fluffy in the house. No lies then," I answered. That was simple.

He looked at me, head tilted like he was trying to figure me out. "Isn't that still lying? You're Atlas."

"My hellhound is Fluffy," I answered, then I got up and walked out. He would take care of the space, and if Aiden needed company, I would go in the house and keep him company.

Immediate problem solved. I'd have to talk to Liam about the long-term problem of his family, but I needed more time in human skin before I had any longer conversations.

Chapter 2

Aiden

I was icing the last few cupcakes when Cass walked into the back room. I looked up, smiled, then looked back down to the cupcake. I was keeping it simple with a nice swirly top for this one, but I still didn't want to mess any up. Not that the staff complained when that happened, because Cass let them eat any of the ones I deemed imperfect for selling.

He waited until I was done before he spoke. "Those look new."

"Yup," I answered, taking the icing bag over to the sink. "Apple cinnamon cupcakes stuffed with real apples, and a vanilla buttercream frosting with a hint of cinnamon."

Cass walked over and took one, unwrapping it and taking a bite. His groan of pleasure made me flush with pride. I was glad they had turned out well; I'd tried a few different recipes before I'd settled on this one. I'd done them mostly at home, because I hated to waste Cass's supplies on things that wouldn't work for sales.

I finished washing out the icing bag and the frosting tip, and Cass finished his cupcake. Usually he left at that point, but he sat down at a stool by the prep table instead.

"Are they ok?" I asked.

"They're excellent. Perfect. They'll sell out in no time, and people will be clamoring for more. Just like they do with every-thing you make. You were really a five star chef at a pastry shop in Paris or something, weren't you?" he joked.

I blushed at the praise and shrugged. "No formal training and no classes. I just always loved baking, and I did it a lot before... you know. I like trying new stuff out, and believe me, it isn't always a success. But baking is sort of my happy place, I guess. And I watch a lot of baking shows, so I get tips from them."

"So, that's actually what I wanted to talk to you about. I hired you at a barista's salary, and you make the same amount as Q and our other full time baristas."

Yeah, he had hired me to work up front, but once I'd come in, I'd ended up hiding in the kitchen most days, and I'd sort of slowly taken over doing the baking from the assorted employees who took turns doing it. I basically never stepped foot out front now.

I blushed, embarrassed. "Of course, Cass, I get it. I'm not really doing the job you hired me for. Honestly, I don't think working out front will really work for me, so I get it if you need to cut my salary."

"No! That isn't what I meant at all!" he insisted, raising his hands like he was trying to stop me from running off.

I just laughed. "It's ok, Cass. I probably don't work as many hours as most of the baristas anyway, and I know I kind of make my own hours. If you want me on a stricter schedule or whatever—"

Cass cut me off. "Aiden, since you started baking for us, do you know what's happened for the shop financially?"

"Well, I do use a lot of supplies and order a lot more than before, so I'm sure your supply orders have gone up in price. But really, those pre-made cookies and that muffin mix wasn't that great." I made a face in memory. I guessed it had sufficed, and customers had obviously liked it ok, but I really hoped we weren't going back to that crap.

Cass looked up at the ceiling in exasperation before he focused on me. "Aiden, our sales for bakery items have more than tripled. In fact, our overall sales have skyrocketed. We *were* just a coffee shop. Now people think of us as a coffee shop and bakery. Do you know I've had people asking about special orders?"

I shook my head. I hadn't known that.

"Well, that's something we can talk about eventually, if you're interested, but my point is that you've been amazing for business. People adore your food, and the shop's profits have drastically increased since I hired you. Which brings me to your salary. You're making a barista's salary, but you really should be making a head baker's salary. I'd like to rectify that."

I just stared at Cass in confusion. "You want to pay me more?"

"Yes, exactly. I want to give you a raise," he said, smiling.

"But I don't think I should make more than Q," I answered.

Cass gave me a look. "Q makes coffee, purposely gets people's names wrong, and gives the customers attitude. You bake marvelous concoctions that have people flocking here."

I smiled. "I don't know. I hear the customer chatter. I think they flock here for Q's attitude, too."

Cass laughed a little. "Maybe so, but you deserve a baker's salary."

"I'll talk about it with Q," I answered.

I didn't know how he'd feel if I made more than him. Q's feelings were way more important to me than money. He had become my family in every way that mattered. Yes, we had trauma that bonded us, even if he thought his trauma wasn't as severe as mine. It didn't matter. We both knew there were horrible people in the world who would do horrible things to us. Maybe we started a bond with that, but we pushed each other to be better people, and we really loved each other. He was the brother I never had.

Besides, what did we even need money for? Maybe it was naive to think that way, but we lived in Liam's back house (which used to be a pool house) rent free (despite trying to pay rent). Liam or Jude bought us groceries half the time, and someone paid for our phones. I still wasn't even sure who. Maybe it was Cass and Kushiel, or maybe it was Liam and the guys. I almost smiled thinking about them arguing over who got the privilege of paying our bills.

Maybe my wealthy upbringing had made me cavalier about money, but I also had a few hidden stashes if I needed them for some reason. And I would share those with Q if he needed them, too. Not that I saw that happening. He and Liam were attached at the hip, and I got the impression that Liam had plenty of money.

Cass rolled his eyes. "Aiden, that isn't how this is supposed to work. You don't negotiate whether or not you get a raise. You negotiate how much of a raise you want."

"I'll talk about it with Q," I repeated.

"Q! Get back here!" Cass yelled.

Q made his way through the door, scowling. Before Cass could comment, Q said, "Listen, I don't know what that guy said, but I did *not* spit in his cup, even if he *deserved* to have his coffee spit in for that comment."

Cass rubbed his forehead.

"He was an asshole, and honestly, you don't need business from someone like that," Q added.

I laughed and Cass looked up to the sky, muttering to himself.

"Cass wants to pay me a baker's salary," I finally said.

Q raised his eyebrows. "Well, it's about damn time. You work your ass off. You should make more money."

Cass nodded his head. "See, I told you." He looked at Q then. "He didn't want to take a raise without talking to you."

Q just rolled his eyes, then Steph called his name from the front of the shop, and he scowled before storming out of the kitchen.

"I better get out there and keep them from killing each other," Cass said, but he was smiling as he walked out.

I had a feeling that I was going to get a raise whether I wanted one or not. I finished cleanup from the cupcakes, and just as I was putting the last of the dishes away, Q stuck his head in the kitchen door and told me that Jude was out front. Q had started work later, so he'd get a ride home later—probably from Liam.

I felt a little bad that the guys had to drive us around, and I thought again of getting a car or using one of theirs. I had a driver's license, and I assumed Q did as well. We were fully capable of driving.

But... I didn't really like to be alone. Which was ironic, because I didn't really like to be around people either. At least not around people I didn't know, and the thought of driving to work alone, parking, and walking to the shop by myself... Well, all sorts of things could happen to a person on their way to or from work. I knew that only too well.

I walked out of the kitchen, and Jude waved to me, coffee cup in hand. We walked out to the car and got in, and he pulled out and made what was probably an illegal U-turn.

"You're a menace," I said.

He looked over at me and winked before turning back to the road. "Baby, you wanna drive my car?"

I couldn't help the laugh that escaped me. It was always fun to figure out when Jude was quoting the Beatles versus actually just having a conversation.

I was quiet then, and he hummed along to the radio, which was, of course, playing the Beatles.

When we were almost home, he asked, "Rough day?"

I shrugged when he glanced over at me.

"Want to talk about it?" he asked as we pulled into the drive-way. He stopped the car and looked at me.

"I'm ok. Some days are just harder than others. I'll go bake some more then take a walk to clear my head," I answered.

We both got out of the car. It was cold, but not freezing. The sun provided some warmth.

"Want some company for the walk?" Jude asked.

I looked at him. He was just wearing a t-shirt even though it was maybe forty-five degrees out. I raised an eyebrow at him.

"What? I like walks!" he insisted. "I won't even sing the Beatles the whole time, I promise."

"You'll freeze in just a t-shirt," I pointed out.

He shrugged and took a sip of his coffee.

"Besides," I added, "I'll have Fluffy to keep me company."

Jude sprayed coffee out of his mouth, sputtering and choking.

"Wrong pipe?" I asked, patting him on the back.

He sputtered a little more before he choked out, "Fluffy?"

"Ah, yeah, sorry. Liam seemed kind of surprised by the nickname, too, but I didn't know what you named your guard dog, and Fluffy seemed appropriate," I answered, feeling a little nervous.

Fluffy had pretty much become my emotional support animal, and he seemed to really understand me, but no one ever talked about him. I reasoned that pets always did seem connected to us, but... what if he were, like, a figment of my imagination?

I knew I could just ask the guys and they'd answer me, and they wouldn't judge, but I was kind of afraid of the answer. If he was a figment of my imagination, I didn't really want to know.

Hey, if I was hallucinating and creating an imaginary friend, I figured a huge fluffy dog wasn't a bad thing as far as hallucinations went.

"Fluffy," Jude muttered again, looking at me.

I laughed self-consciously. "I'm sure his name is something like Terror or Killer, but he's really such a sweetheart, and he always walks with me. I hope I haven't offended you guys or something by naming your guard dog."

Jude was just staring at me, but not like I was crazy and had made him up. I stuck my hands in my pocket awkwardly. Was Jude angry? Was he going to... I breathed out. Jude was safe. Jude wouldn't hurt me.

"Hey, it's ok," he said softly, noticing my distress. "I was just... surprised. You can call him Fluffy if you want."

I nodded my head.

He chuckled a little, "Fluffy. That's kind of hysterical. I love it."

I felt my tension drain a bit, and I laughed a little. "Like I said, probably absurd, but..." and I just shrugged.

Jude smiled. "You ok?" he asked softly. "You want me to call Q?"

I breathed in deeply and then back out, focusing on myself. Was I ok? I had gotten scared for a moment, but I was safe, and I knew Jude wouldn't hurt me. I would go bake something, and then I would go take a walk and see Fluffy.

"Yeah, I'm ok. Thank you, Jude."

He nodded and started walking toward my door. I appreciated the gesture. He wouldn't come in if I didn't ask him to, but he'd make sure I got in and locked the door behind me. Not that I felt unsafe here. There were cameras all over the place, including in our apartment (but not in my bedroom or the bathroom), and there was a security system.

Liam was kind of... well, calling him psychotic probably wasn't nice. When it came to Q's safety, he was really overboard, but Q didn't seem to mind. It took some getting used to thinking about a camera in the living room, but Liam had turned the sound off, and he didn't watch it regularly. He was sort of like our roommate anyway, so I just thought of it as him being there watching tv or something and half paying attention. Probably weird, but oh well.

I understood why Q didn't mind the cameras. It made me feel safer too. If one of us went missing, people would notice. People would see who took either of us. I knew the guy who took me was dead, but I still worried. What if he had friends? What if someone was after Q? What if someone tried to take one of us again?

I felt safe here, and I felt safe with these guys. Most of the time, at least.

I got to the door and opened it, and Jude shot me a wave goodbye, obviously sensing I needed some alone time.

I breathed out a sigh and went to sit on the couch. The house was too quiet, and I felt lonely, but the thought of being with people was... exhausting. My life was ironically pathetic. Being alone in a room for a year... it had fucked me up.

Sure, I saw my kidnapper. But towards the end, he wasn't really interested in me anymore. He had moved on to stalking Toby, and he "broke up" with me. I had a mini-fridge, food, and an enclosed bathroom in the bedroom I was locked in, so I could be left alone for days before he'd bring supplies and spend time with me.

I had actually looked forward to his visits at the end. It hurt my chest to think that, but I had.

And now, the thought of being alone... it was terrifying. It brought back that room. I had spent so much time alone. But at the same time, being with people was just so utterly draining. They always expected something. I was always reading into every word, every nuance of body language, every shift in movement. My therapist said that was a normal reaction, because I had learned to do that with the guy who took me. She said eventually I would trust people again and wouldn't be so on edge.

It was exhausting, though. I put my head in my hands and breathed, closing my eyes. *Focus on things in your control. Find a happy place for yourself.* That's what my therapist would tell me. I thought about going out and finding Fluffy—he made me happy. I was planning to bake, though, and I thought that maybe I should try out a recipe for a homemade dog biscuit. It would be nice to give Fluffy a treat. He gave me so much without even realizing it, and I wanted to give him something back.

It gave me focus, and I got up and headed into the kitchen. I rifled through the cabinets, pulling out oats, peanut butter, and an unopened jar of unsweetened applesauce. We had eggs in the fridge, and I knew all those ingredients were safe for dogs. I opened up a drawer that had random baking supplies. Cass had gifted me a bunch of cookie shapes awhile ago, and I thought...

Yup! I pulled out one shaped like a dog bone. Perfect. I was sure I could come up with a good recipe for a treat for Fluffy. I turned on a playlist on my phone as I began assembling ingredients. I was looking forward to bringing my new friend a treat.

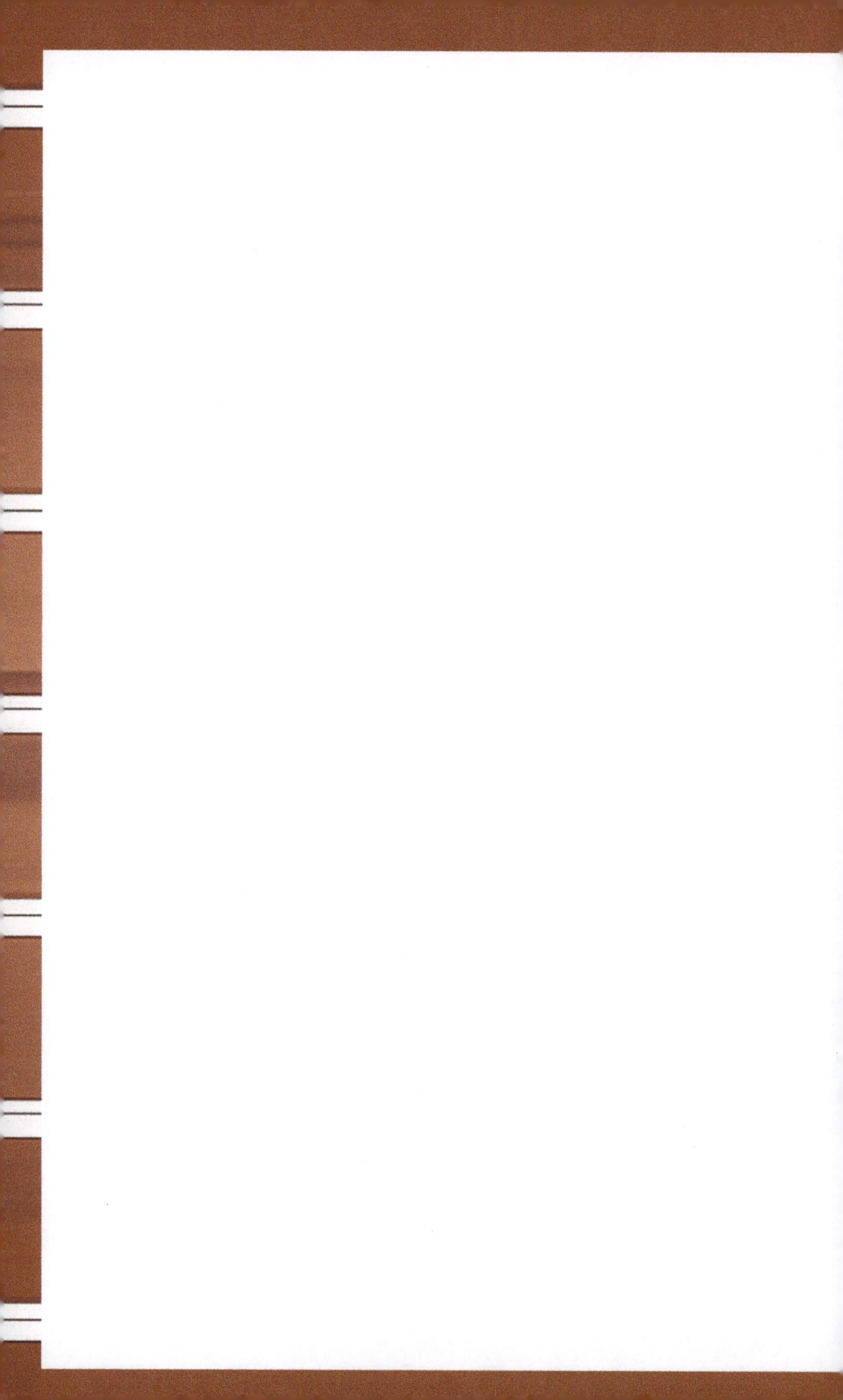

CHAPTER 3

ATLAS/FLUFFY

Aiden was home. We could be patient and wait for him to come out and walk, only there was a truck coming up the driveway, and Liam had left to go get Quinton.

I ran up to Liam's house, grumpily transformed into my human form, and went inside, picking up the spare cell phone he kept in a drawer.

He answered on the second ring.

"There's a truck," I said before he could speak.

"Oh, excellent. I put a rush on the bed hoping it would come today," Liam answered.

I heard Quinton in the background asking, "You ordered a bed? How come?"

"Aiden is home," I said.

"Ah, shit. I didn't think of that. We'll head straight home. I'll call Aiden and let him know, and then I'll call the delivery company and ask them to wait for us."

I hung up the phone, walked out the door, and transformed back into my hound. The truck was pulling up the driveway and straight toward Aiden's house. I heard his cell phone ringing just as the delivery truck stopped and two guys got out.

"Hello," Aiden answered.

I wasn't sure how good human hearing was, but if the delivery guys heard, they would know Aiden was home, and Liam was obviously just now calling him. Fuck. One delivery guy knocked on the door, the other standing a few feet back and looking at a clipboard. I trotted towards the house, starting a low growl in my throat.

Aiden was still on the phone, saying, "Yes, there's a truck here, and someone just knocked... Hurry home.... Yeah, I'm ok... No, you don't need to call Jude. I can wait for you."

I had mostly heard Liam's side of the conversation as well, but I tuned it out to focus on the delivery men. Neither was evil, but the one who knocked was definitely morally gray, as most people often were. I growled again, and the morally gray guy turned and saw me.

"Fucking shit!" he cried out, backing away from the door. "Hey, buddy! Come out and call off your dog!" he yelled.

The other guy saw me then too and froze. I continued walking towards the door, and the knocker slowly backed up, his arms up. I wanted to be in front of the door if Aiden came out.

Smart that the guys didn't run. I would have caught them.

"Hey, buddy! If I get attacked, I am totally suing!" morally gray guy yelled loudly.

I heard Aiden's footsteps inside. I was in front of the door, so I sat down and stared at the men, still growling.

Aiden opened the door. "Fluffy?"

I looked at him, gave my best doggie-looking grin, then looked back at the delivery guy and started growling again. I heard Aiden step all the way out of the door behind me.

"Listen, buddy, if he bites me, I'm reporting it," the morally gray guy said, arms still up. He looked towards his truck, but it was too far back for him to make it there quickly. "I suggest you call off your dog if you don't want him put down," the guy said.

The other guy was just standing still, so I mostly ignored him. He didn't smell happy about morally gray guy's threat, and he was a pretty pure soul. I did stop growling, though.

Aiden gasped in outrage and stepped forward, putting a hand on my head. "He isn't going to bite you! Fluffy is friendly!"

Smart guy who was standing back a bit snorted, and the other guy shot him a dirty look. "You wanna come up here and make friends with 'Fluffy,' asshole?" he grumbled.

"I mean, he's sitting now, and he's not growling," the other guy said.

Morally gray guy took a step forward, and Aiden's hand gripped the fur on my head. I could feel his nerves, so I started growling again. The guy could just fucking wait for Liam to get here.

He wisely stopped immediately and stepped back, so I stopped growling. Humans seemed to understand basic cues, and I could reward good behavior by not growling, since my growl obviously set him on edge. I didn't even look like a full hellhound, for fuck's sake. I looked like a wolf or hound. I didn't even understand what the big deal was, but as long as he stayed where he was, no one would need to lose a limb.

Aiden laughed nervously. "Uh, this is Fluffy. He's not... um... he's not mine?"

I growled a little at that, and Aiden's hand pet my head gently.

"I mean, I guess he's sort of mine, but I don't really, ah, know how to... umm, call him off?" he finished unsurely.

The smart guy in the back snorted again, and the morally gray guy opened his mouth to say something that was probably stupid, so I just flashed some fangs at him. He wisely shut his mouth.

Aiden went on, "But Liam, the guy who placed the order, he's on his way. He'll be here in like a minute or two, so if you guys could just, like, wait for him?"

My poor Aiden sounded very unsure, and we didn't like that at all, but the smart guy said, "Sure, man, no problem. We'll just step back and wait in the truck?"

"Sure, that's great," Aiden answered, breathing more easily.

They both backed up toward the truck, and I heard them

mumbling to each other as the asshole insisted on getting in first. Smart guy just rolled his eyes and opened the truck door for him.

Smart guy was nice. If any maiming was required, I'd definitely spare him. The other guy, though... eh, you didn't really need all your limbs.

Aiden breathed out a sigh when both truck doors were shut. I was going to seriously chew out Liam later for putting him in this position.

Speaking of... I heard a car driving rather quickly up the drive. Good.

Liam hopped out of the car, and Quinton followed after him. He did *not* look happy. He walked straight over towards us while Liam dealt with the delivery guys. Aiden gripped my fur tightly again, but I just looked up at him and gave a relaxing yawn. Of course I wouldn't attack Quinton. Silly Aiden.

Aiden seemed to relax at my yawn, and Quinton came forward. "Aiden, I'm really sorry about Liam not warning you. I had no idea. And what the fuck? Do we have a dog now?"

Aiden laughed. "This is Fluffy, the guard dog. He does a good job of guarding, too."

Quinton stared at me curiously, then he put his hand out, like he was waiting for me to sniff him or something. Liam was watching us closely even though he was talking to the delivery men. I almost rolled my eyes at him. I wasn't stupid; I wouldn't hurt his mate. Quinton was pack.

I also wouldn't stoop to sniffing him, though. I just stared at him, and he actually laughed. "He has about as much attitude as I do. What do you want to do while they bring in the delivery?"

Aiden's hand tightened against my fur before he let go. "I think I'll take a walk with Fluffy. I don't want to be inside when other people are in there. I just..."

"That's fine," Quinton said softly when Aiden trailed off.

"I'm just gonna run in and grab my coat and stuff, then I'll go walk," he said, then he looked at me, looked at Quinton, and turned and went into the house. I could hear him rushing about, and he was back outside in about a minute, like he was afraid I would leave.

Or maybe he was afraid I would attack someone. I gave a mental shrug. I definitely wasn't leaving, that was for sure.

Liam was still talking to the delivery men, stalling them so Aiden could head out. Liam looked over at us, and I bared my teeth in the direction of morally gray guy. He ought to be watched. I didn't like him. Liam nodded his head. Of course he would watch them both, especially with his Quinton here to protect.

With that, Aiden and I headed off into the woods.

Should've bitten off a finger, Fluffy huffed. We had been unified in our focus on protecting Aiden, but now that Aiden was calm and the danger had passed, my hellhound couldn't help a little snark.

Aiden was bundled up, although it really wasn't that cold. Humans were fragile, though, and I was glad he was warm. I wondered if Liam had talked to him yet about having Fluffy in the house? Although he hadn't even warned him about the delivery men, so my guess was that hadn't happened.

Peanut butter, Fluffy grumbled.

Yes, Aiden did smell rather strongly of peanut butter. That wasn't unusual, really—he often smelled of sweets and baked goods, but...

I stuck my nose into his side, sniffing at his pocket.

"Hey!" he cried out, but he was laughing as he did it. "Do you smell what I baked for you? I stuffed a couple in my pocket."

Aiden baked for me? He pulled out a cookie in the shape of a dog biscuit.

Baked for me, Fluffy corrected.

I just sighed internally. Insufferable mutt.

Aiden held out the cookie, and I leaned my head forward and gently took it between my teeth. When Aiden moved his hand away, I chomped on it.

Yum.

It was delicious. Not too sweet, yet satisfying. Crunchy, peanut buttery, with a nice texture. Best of all, Aiden had made it just for us.

More, Fluffy grumbled, and then I was nosing at Aiden's pocket again. I knew he had at least one more cookie in there. Maybe even two.

"Hey, hey!" he laughed, gently trying to twist away, but I was rather determined to get my nose into his pocket. Damn pocket wasn't that big. Aiden was giggling, though, so I didn't stop sniffing at his pocket. Then he was laughing even harder, and somehow he ended up on his butt on the ground.

I knew he wasn't hurt, because he was still giggling wildly. "I guess the recipe came out tasty for dogs."

I almost had my nose in his pocket—one more wiggle and a chomp of my teeth and I'd have the cookie. Only Aiden grabbed my head and pulled it out of his pocket, drawing my face up to his.

So pretty, Fluffy murmured.

His eyes were lit with laughter, and I didn't think I'd seen him so carefree before. We had done that for him.

"Sit," he ordered, and I plopped my own butt onto the ground, staying close and still looking at his face.

He started rubbing my head, and I grumbled a bit in contentment, making Aiden laugh again.

"You want another cookie? Here you go," he said, taking it out of his pocket and handing it over. I crunched away on it, pleased with both the flavor explosion and the calming feeling of Aiden's fingers running through my fur.

Ours, Fluffy insisted.

Yes. Aiden was ours.

We walked for a bit after that, and Aiden told me about baking a new recipe and Cass giving him a raise. I listened and walked beside him, and his hand found its way into my fur again and again. It was soothing, and I was sad when we turned back. I knew it was a therapy night for Aiden, though, so he'd be heading off for that appointment.

He took out his phone when we were almost back and sent a text, and then he veered off toward Jude's house.

Ah, he was going to have Jude drive him to therapy. That worked. Maybe I would go growl at Liam a bit for the awkward situation he'd put Aiden in. Although Quinton hadn't seemed to recognize me, and perhaps that was for the best. Growling at Liam might need to wait.

"I'll see you later, Fluffy," Aiden said before we got to the edge of the woods. I usually trotted off and watched him from afar as he got wherever he was going, but he seemed a bit cautious as we got to the house, so I sat down and watched him.

He gave a little laugh. "Gonna watch to make sure I get inside ok? You really are a good guard dog."

With that he walked up to the back porch of the house Jude and Corbin used, knocked on the door, and went inside when Jude yelled out for him to come in.

I continued to wait, and before long I heard Jude and Aiden head out toward the car in front. Car doors slammed, music started up—the Beatles, of course—and then Jude was driving Aiden to therapy.

Go with Aiden, Fluffy grumbled, but I knew Jude would wait for him outside in the car, so I didn't need to follow them there. Plus it might be awkward if a stray "dog" was wandering around outside his therapist's office.

Still, I did wonder if Corbin knew his therapist. I could hear him and his crow puttering around inside, so I walked up to the back door. I had been exceptionally quiet, but Corbin was there to open it anyway. I was never sure what Corbin knew from his witch background and what the crows told him.

I walked in, and the crow perched on Corbin's shoulder flew down and landed on my back.

Crow pack, Fluffy rumbled, recognizing the bird. This crow and I had played before, and he was fun and friendly, so I swished my tail at him while he playfully tried to bite at it.

Corbin sat down at the table, looking at us fondly like we were his two kids goofing off. Eventually we got tired of playing, and Crow flew back onto Corbin's shoulder and started preening his hair.

Corbin stared at me, and I stared back.

Eventually he said, "You know, you're going to have to go human if you want to talk to me. I haven't perfected the art of mind reading yet."

I sighed, and then I turned human. Corbin motioned to the basket by the back door with his chin. Yes, they kept sweatpants there. I didn't understand why everyone felt the need to walk around with pants on when it was just us, but I walked over and pulled a pair on anyway.

Stupid human rules.

I sat at the table across from Corbin, asking, "Do you know Aiden's therapist?"

"Ahh," he said, like my question somehow gave him insight into the universe.

Corbin knows things, Fluffy said, and maybe my question did give him some insight. He was a knowing person. He was close to his hellhound and his crows, and we respected him.

Corbin tilted his head, looking crow-like himself for a moment. I simply waited.

"Why would I know his therapist?" he finally asked.

"Haven't you taken him there?" I asked.

"No. It's been mostly Jude or Cassius, and sometimes Liam and Quinton." He shrugged his shoulders, and Crow stared at me. He would fly off right now to check on things if Corbin needed him to.

"Cassius would know. Jude and Liam, maybe not. They don't listen to their hellhounds enough," I said.

Corbin looked less relaxed then, sitting up straighter, his crow cawing gently at me.

"Atlas, what don't they know about Aiden's therapist?" Corbin asked slowly, kind of like he was speaking to a child.

I huffed. I was surprised he didn't know. After all, I could smell her on Aiden after his sessions.

"She isn't human."

CHAPTER 4

AIDEN

"And how is that going?" Helene asked.

I sometimes did telehealth, but she wanted to see me in person at least twice a month. It wasn't that I didn't like going out, because I did, but I didn't really like to go out alone, and I felt bad making Cass, Kushiel, Q, or one of the guys wait for me in the outer office or the car while I did therapy.

Probably something else I should talk about *in* therapy.

"Um, it's going ok," I answered.

She tilted her head, staring at me. Damn, she was good. She had glasses and curly brown hair in a top bun, and she somehow looked both young and mature at the same time. She was sweet and kind, and yet she also had this take-no-shit attitude. She was sitting in one of the comfy chairs a few feet away from me, and I had my legs tucked up underneath me in another comfy chair.

I liked that no matter what I said, I never seemed to shock her. Like, ever.

I bet she had a great face for playing poker.

I sighed. "Ok, so it isn't going ok giving Liam and Q their space. I had a nightmare last night, and then I couldn't sleep, but I promised I wouldn't disturb them, so I got up and baked and then went for a walk this morning before work. It helped. I'm just... tired."

"Who did you promise?" she asked.

"Huh?" I asked, fidgeting in my seat.

"Did you promise Liam and Q that you wouldn't disturb them?"

"Um, no..."

She pushed her glasses up her nose. "So you made a promise to yourself that you wouldn't 'disturb' them. Have they given any indication that you sleeping in the same room is disturbing to them?"

I huffed. "I don't just sleep in the same room. I sleep in the same bed. I cuddle with them, for goodness sake. I'm a grown man and it's like I need a nightlight and a freaking security blanket, only Q is my security blanket. And I leave the hallway lights on."

"Aiden, you went through something very traumatic. You had a year with nothing but fake kindness and almost no human interaction. It's natural that you're touch starved and want human contact, and Q has given no indication whatsoever that he minds. In fact, he seems to embrace it, from everything you've said. He's had his own trauma, so perhaps it's also helpful to him. Have you considered that?" she asked.

"Uh... no, I guess I didn't."

"Because you lived for a year, and maybe longer than that, based on what you've said about your family, with people who treated you like a commodity, not a person.

"Q values you as a person—you've told me this. He values your interactions. You're used to seeing the world as being made of people who give and people who take, and you have always been the giver, so it feels awkward that you think you're 'taking' from Q. But Aiden, good relationships are both a give and a take. Both parties get something important from each other."

I nodded my head. I knew what she was saying was true. "But I still feel like a stupid little kid—"

Helene cut me off. "Aiden, I'm going to stop you right there for a moment. What do I always tell you?"

I sighed. "You tell me to be kind to myself and to give myself grace."

"Yes, meet yourself with kindness. It is *amazing* that you get up and go to work each morning. It is *amazing* that you are making friends and working at something you are passionate about. You have made incredible strides, and I will not let you beat yourself up because you have certain needs, even if you think they're unconventional.

"And let me just add that cuddling with another human being is *not* unconventional. If you knew some of the things I've heard about in sessions..."

I laughed, just like she meant for me to. I guessed she was right, too.

"What's really bothering you, Aiden?" she asked gently.

"I don't know. I guess I just feel like everyone around me is moving on, especially Q, and sometimes I feel like I'm still stuck in that room, you know? Like yeah, I get up and work and bake, but sometimes I feel like I'm just *existing*, just waiting for the next bad thing to happen. Because that's what being in that room was like most of the time. Being alone and just waiting for him to come back, for better or worse." I shrugged.

"But you aren't alone, Aiden, and this is why you not going in to see Q and Liam when you have a nightmare concerns me. Is it possible that you're putting yourself back into that room without even meaning to?" she asked gently.

Fuck. I got tears in my eyes, although I didn't really know why.

"Maybe," I finally answered. "Maybe I have been sort of isolating myself without even realizing it."

"And why do you think you're doing that now? Has someone pushed your boundaries, or are you uncomfortable with someone?"

"No," I shook my head. "I really like Liam. I'm not uncomfortable around him at all. Toby, Dexter, Jude, and Corbin have been super nice, and they haven't made me uncomfortable either. Toby definitely wants to be friends, and sometimes that's kind of weird, but he's really respectful and doesn't push me at all."

"So maybe you think you're getting too close to people? Could that be why you're starting to isolate yourself? What are you afraid will happen if you get close to people?" she asked.

Fuck. She just went for all my weak points. I knew why I didn't want to get too close to people, but I didn't want to talk about it. Not now. I just shook my head at her, and then I pointed to my wrist. Our time was up anyway.

"I don't like to end our session with you feeling badly, Aiden. I can make more time if you want to talk about it."

"I don't want to talk about it. Not today. I think today has been enough for me," I answered.

"Ok, Aiden. That's ok. I want you to know that you're doing great and amazing, even if it doesn't always feel that way. I want you to be kind to yourself, and I really want you to make a conscious effort to not shut people out this week. Do you think you can do that?"

I nodded at her, then I added, "Yeah, I can do that."

"Maybe you can talk to Liam or Q about disturbing them, and see what they say. Do you think you could do that, as well?"

I nodded again. "Yeah. Thanks, Helene."

She smiled, and we confirmed our next session, then I headed out of her office and down to the car. Jude was waiting right out front, and I breathed out another sigh and rubbed at my eyes as I got in the car. Jude just started silently driving. He was good about giving me a little space after therapy.

Sometimes therapy really sucked. It helped, sure, but sometimes I guess you had to feel a little worse before you could feel better. And yeah, lately I had felt like I was back in that room.

Being someone's captive for a year wasn't what I expected.

Yeah, it was terrifying in the beginning, but I felt like that time was a hazy dream. Eventually, it was just... mundane.

It was the same every day. I was alone all day and overnight, but I had basic television streaming and books, and in the evenings he came in to see me for our "dates." It got to where it was... I don't know. I don't want to say it was nice, but sometimes I could pretend, just like he did. I could pretend he was my boyfriend, and for a little while, I wasn't so alone.

Yeah, I knew all about how "normal" that was, and Helene had said that I could feel like I loved my captor and also like I hated him, and it was ok to feel both those things. But I never loved him. He was just, I don't know, a distraction. He was a way to not be so alone.

I hated that room. I could still close my eyes and see it vividly—the curtains and the bedspread and the television and the bookshelf bolted to the wall. I could see the scratches in the bookcase, the smudge on the tv screen that you could only see when it was shut off. I could see the crack in the wood floor.

Sometimes I felt like I was still stuck in that room, all alone. Like I was sitting on the bed just waiting for him to come in, and all of this was a daydream.

That thought was shattered by the sound of sirens. I looked in the rearview mirror, and sure enough, there was a cop car behind us. I looked over at Jude, who had definitely started speeding, only I hadn't really noticed because I was caught in my own thoughts.

He was grinning like a loon, both hands on the steering wheel.

"What are you doing?" I asked.

He looked over at me a little sheepishly then. "Shit. Do you have issues with cops? I can totally outrun him if that's better for your mental well-being."

"Um, no, I do not think running from the cops would be better for my mental well-being, Jude." I couldn't help a little snark in my response—I guess Q was rubbing off on me.

"Ok, great!" he said, pulling over to the side of the road.

He was smiling like a kid in a candy story as he watched in the rearview mirror as the officer got out of the car.

The guy was probably mid-forties, and he was scruffy in a sexy way. He had that dad-bod thing going on, where you could tell he was strong and fit, but he wasn't muscle-bound. He was also scowling, and it suddenly hit me.

"Jude, is this the sheriff you were talking about the other day?" I asked.

"Yup!" Jude answered gleefully.

I just slid down in my seat. I didn't know what the hell Jude's fascination with the sheriff was, but he thought the guy was cute and sexy and all that, and apparently he really liked to annoy him. And the sheriff looked annoyed as soon as he saw Jude.

Jude slid the window down. "Ah, here comes the sun! Good afternoon, Paul."

Paul looked even more grumpy. "It's Officer—"

"Of course it is," Jude said, cutting him off to hand over his license and registration. "You know you're my favorite Beatle," he added, winking.

The sheriff was just staring at him and didn't bother looking at the documents. He looked at me, raising his eyebrows. "And you are..."

He was looking at me, waiting for an answer, and I froze. Panic flooded through my system, and I didn't even know why. I had legal documents. My name would check out, yet somehow I couldn't seem to open my mouth. This sheriff seemed too smart. It was like I could sense the predator in him, even if I thought he was a *good* kind of predator. My family was looking for me, and I couldn't trust anyone.

"This is Aiden," Jude cut in, drawing the attention back to himself. "He works at Cass's coffee shop. Surely you've seen him there?"

I breathed. Yes, I had a job. I'd been in town awhile. Nothing to see here.

Only the sheriff looked back at me, and his stance shifted ever so slightly as his eyes glanced back toward Jude in an assessing manner. His entire demeanor changed from annoyed but relaxed to alert.

It was a stance that promised violence if things weren't what they seemed. I knew that look, and I realized the problem. Here I was looking panicked in Jude's car and not speaking. It was probably rather suspicious, and I did not need Jude getting taken in for questioning because I looked like I was kidnapped or something.

I unclasped my lips, saying, "Yes. I work in the back, baking. I don't really like people."

Jude looked over and smiled at me. "Hey, it's ok. You bake really good shit." He looked back at the sheriff then, and I caught a hard edge to his look. "Aiden isn't a people person, and there's nothing wrong with that."

Jude's defense of me seemed to set the sheriff at ease. "Of course not." He looked at me then. "Your cookies are amazing. I stop in pretty frequently for them."

I smiled at him before looking away. Praise made me feel weird, and I didn't quite know what to say. That was ok, because Jude took over.

"So, what's up, Mister City Policeman?" Jude asked. I kind of thought that was a lyric, and based on the sheriff's grimace I guessed he recognized it.

"You were speeding, Jude Smith," the sheriff answered.

"You gonna give me a ticket? Maybe then I can go to court to negotiate it," Jude said, and he sounded almost like he was suggesting something obscene.

I looked over, and he was smirking at the sheriff. Then he actually winked. My god, we were gonna get thrown in jail.

The sheriff looked aggravated and flustered at the same time. "Just... slow down."

"Okey-dokey, Mister City Policeman," Jude answered.

The sheriff huffed and handed Jude's documents back through

the window, only I noticed that Jude made sure their hands touched.

The sheriff pulled back, looking flustered and grumpy as hell, and then he turned and stormed back to his car.

Jude started the car and began whistling as he pulled out onto the road. He had a mischievous look on his face.

"Jude, I swear, you better not do anything stupid so he pulls us over. Again," I said.

"Aww, that's no fun, Aiden. He's so cute. And such a good person. And he's so easy to rile up. One day I'm gonna make him really flip out, and that's gonna be such fun." Jude laughed happily.

I just stared at him. "You and I have very different definitions of fun."

"Ah, that we do, Aiden. That we do. But I have a feeling the sheriff might be more interested in my kind of fun than he knows."

With that cryptic comment, I leaned my head back and closed my eyes for the rest of the ride. Whatever Jude and the sheriff had going on, I had enough to worry about. I just hoped I hadn't pinged his radar. My name was solid, and he could look into that and not come up with anything. I'd changed my looks, and my year in captivity had changed me even more, so even if my family was circulating pictures, I'm not sure people would know it was me.

Still, I couldn't help but worry. Maybe I needed to talk to Liam about my family. Maybe it was time to come up with a plan, or at least see what they were doing. Helene was right—maybe I needed to let myself out of that room and face the world.

I was tired of being scared all the time.

CHAPTER 5

ATLAS/FLUFFY

"I've checked out her background thoroughly. I find no indication that she's anything other than human," Liam said, typing away and staring at his computer. "Her background and family checks out, and there are no strange blips in her history. I've seen her, and her soul looks perfectly fine, plus I know you wouldn't allow Aiden to be around someone with a darkened soul. Are you sure she isn't human?" he asked, looking over at me.

I just yawned, showing my teeth.

"This would be so much easier if you would answer questions, you uncultured mutt," he grumbled, turning back to his computer. "I'm not even sure what I'm supposed to tell Quinton when he gets out of the shower."

It didn't seem hard. Quinton had already met Fluffy. What was the big deal?

It was all a lot of worry over nothing. I regretted saying anything to Corbin about the therapist, but I assumed he knew. He hadn't, and he'd called Liam, who had demanded I go to Quinton's so we could "figure it out." I wasn't going to show up at Aiden and Quinton's place in human form, so he had opened the door to Fluffy.

He hadn't seemed pleased.

I didn't care. I was now in the house, and it was up to Liam to explain how I got there. I'd get to see Aiden as soon as he got home without waiting for a walk. I wasn't planning on hanging around or anything, but it would be nice to see and sniff Aiden for myself. Sometimes he was sad after therapy.

Liam huffed again, continuing to type away on his computer. He got so worked up over things. I definitely wasn't going to mention that one of Toby's friends also wasn't human, or at least not totally human.

Fluffy sniffed in my head. *They should already know.*

Eh, we were a little closer to our instincts than most, so I didn't really blame them. Corbin probably would have known if he'd seen the therapist, because he was witchy like that. I'd known the minute I'd smelled Corbin that he was something else too, but that was so long ago that I barely even thought about it.

I heard the shower shut off, and Liam looked up. I was guessing he was also cranky that he hadn't gotten to sneak in there with Quinton, who was apparently showering off "the stench of coffee and baked shit."

I had waited until he was in the shower to come in, and Liam had commenced with his complaining and researching.

I heard a car coming up the driveway, and I perked up.

Aiden, my hellhound growled happily, my tail thumping in happiness.

Liam looked over at me, smirking. "Oh, you've got it bad, Fluffy."

I just bared my teeth at him. Quinton was still shuffling around in the bathroom when I heard Jude walk Aiden up to the door.

"You're not getting any baked goods after that stunt," Aiden was grumbling.

Jude just laughed. "He's so cute, though, isn't he?"

Aiden just mumbled, "Bye, Jude," before opening the door and coming in.

Sad, sad, sad, Fluffy huffed. Aiden did smell sad, but it wasn't extreme distress.

Once the door was shut, Jude sauntered off, whistling. Aiden spotted Liam first, and then he looked over and saw me sitting in the living room.

His entire face lit up, and he dropped his bag and rushed over. "Fluffy!"

We fix, Fluffy growled, pleased.

Because Aiden did smell happy as he rushed over, knelt down, and wrapped his arms around me to hug me.

I stared at Liam, grinning. He just raised his eyebrows at me. Quinton came out at that moment, paused for a moment, stared at us, and then just kept walking into the kitchen like a huge hound in his living room was perfectly normal.

"You keeping him as a service dog now? Because I am not vacuuming up the fur—that totally falls on you," Quinton grumbled.

"Aww, you'd make a great service dog, wouldn't you, Fluffy? You're so sweet," Aiden cooed.

Liam started choking at the table, and I just glared at him. Asshole.

"He could stay here sometimes, couldn't he?" Aiden asked, turning to look at Liam. "I'm not sure where you guys usually keep him, but I don't mind if he stays here sometimes."

He sounded hopeful, and since he was looking at Liam and Quinton was messing around in the kitchen, I bared my teeth at Liam in warning.

"Um, yeah, sure... Whatever Fluffy wants," he answered, managing to just mildly cough a bit when he said the name Fluffy.

Total asshole.

Aiden didn't notice, though, and he plopped down on the floor next to me, leaning his back against the loveseat.

Cuddles! Fluffy grumbled, and we promptly laid across his legs, being careful not to put too much weight on him. He rested his arms on my back and began petting me, and I could smell the nervous energy come back.

"I guess it's good Fluffy is here, because I may need an emotional support animal for this," Aiden said.

Quinton came in and sat down on the couch across from us, and Liam followed, bringing his computer.

"Everything ok? What can we help with?" Quinton asked.

I liked Liam's human, and I gave him a grin. It was good that Aiden had such good packmates to care for him.

Our mate, Fluffy grumbled. *We take care of him.*

I tilted my head a bit. *Aiden needs lots of support. Packmates help.*

Fluffy grumbled in agreement, so at least that wouldn't be an issue. As for the mate comment... It didn't surprise me that Fluffy knew that. I suppose we had known for a while.

Humans are weird, Fluffy answered, and I sensed a world of judgment behind that.

My hellhound had known that Aiden was our mate, but my other half didn't always process instinctual things. I wasn't sure when it had happened, or if the bond was there from the start. Fluffy just huffed at that question, though, and he was right—it didn't matter. Aiden was ours. That's all that mattered.

Aiden took a deep breath, and I rumbled softly against him. His hands squeezed in my fur before he loosened them, so I reached my head up and gave his face a lick. He smiled at me and pulled me against him. I didn't mind. We would do whatever he needed to get him through what he was about to talk about.

"So... I think it's time I talked about my family. And it's probably also time that I found out exactly what they've been up to, since I'm assuming you've probably kept tabs on them, Liam," he said.

Liam nodded his head. "Yes, I have. Would you like to know that first?"

Aiden shook his head. "No, I think I'd rather get the story out first. Then you guys will have context, I guess."

Quinton cut in, saying, "You don't have to talk about it if you don't want to, Aiden. We'll do whatever we need to, and you don't have to explain."

Good packmate, Fluffy rumbled, and I agreed.

"No, it's ok. It's better if you guys understand what we're dealing with," Aiden commented. He hunkered down, and I leaned my weight gently against his torso while still sprawled across his legs.

"My family isn't evil. At least, I don't think they are. They're just... very rich. I know it sounds stupid, but morals are different when money can take care of so much. My family is old money, involved in government and academics and basically everything. We're talking top one percent here. Do they do illegal stuff? I'm sure they do. Everyone does illegal stuff, even if it's speeding. The rich version is just much bigger than speeding.

"Growing up was fine. I had tutors and hobbies, and I knew my parents cared for me. I went to the best boarding school, but I liked it there, and I wanted to go. If I hadn't, my parents would have moved me. I made and lost friends, fell in and out of love, got good grades and bad grades—despite being crazy rich I think it was almost normal. I was never in the spotlight, and I knew I had a privileged life.

"I was going to college for business—the best college, of course. I didn't really like business, but I did what was expected of me. I read books and baked in my spare time, and I don't know, I guess I had the privilege of youth. I didn't think about my future all that much. I didn't worry about it."

Aiden breathed out and stroked my fur. I could tell we were coming to the difficult part.

"One evening we were at a family dinner. I have an older brother. He's twelve years older, so we were never close. It was my parents and him, and they started talking about me getting married. My brother was already married with two kids. They were talking about these different women as options, and the time of year for a wedding, and how many kids I should have, and I just... I saw the future, and I couldn't do it."

Quinton gasped. "You told them you were gay and they disowned you?"

Aiden shook his head. "Nope. I told them I was gay, and they all just stared at me for a minute. And I will never forget it. My mother looked over at my father, and she said, 'Isn't Robert's nephew gay?' Then my father looked down at his plate, cut into his steak, and said, 'Yes, but they have no real political influence. I believe Dwight's boy is bisexual. I think the Carmichaels and the Rothchilds also have a few options.' And the conversation just carried on like it didn't even matter."

Aiden was gripping my fur now, and I could tell that Liam was a bit confused. "It's good that they didn't care if you were gay, isn't it?" he asked, looking unsure.

Aiden shrugged. "I guess so. It was more that it didn't even matter. I was a commodity. They didn't care that I was gay. Of course, I didn't want them mad or kicking me out or anything horrible, but... They didn't care."

Quinton made a humming noise. "I get it, Aiden. It was like they didn't care about you as a person at all."

"Yes. They were talking about my life and my future like it was a business plan. I guess it was. My mother knew I was upset, and she came up later and talked to me." Aiden blew out a breath. "She said she had married into this family, and there was no getting out of it. That sometimes sacrifices had to be made for the family, and as long as I was a member of the family, my life would follow a certain course. I still remember it—she was sort of fiddling with stuff on my dresser, and she wasn't looking at me.

"And then she said, 'If I ever wanted to leave and be free from the obligations of this family, I would have to disappear. I couldn't tell anyone where I was going. Not anyone. Not even my children. I used to dream of being a painter, you know. I used to think about how I would just be gone one day. I could find people to make fake documents, and then have someone make fake documents based on those fake documents. I'd have so many layers to my identity that I'd be impossible to find. I would go get a little house by the water and paint.'

"She looked at me then, and I could see she was a little teary. 'Of course, I would never do that. I love my boys, and I chose to marry into this family. I knew what I was getting into. I know you didn't, sweetheart. I'm sorry you have so few options.' And then she came and kissed me on the head and left."

Aiden paused, and we all absorbed his story.

"So, your mom basically told you to go disappear and follow your dreams?" Quinton asked. "Why couldn't she just fight for you to be a baker and date and stuff like normal? I don't get it."

Aiden sighed. "It's a different world. I don't even know how to explain it. She could've fought, but I wouldn't have been free no matter what. My grandfather and my father are hard men, and you just don't cross them. They're used to getting what they want, and eventually everyone falls in line with that. I was being groomed to take a part in the business, and I didn't have it in me to fight my family. I think my mom knew that.

"Money comes with danger, too. I had a bodyguard for a roommate at college even though I was registered under a pseudonym. It wasn't just random threats, either. I wasn't stupid. I knew we had enemies. Money like that... a family like mine... there are a lot of strings."

I rumbled against Aiden. He was brave, and he had done what he needed to do in order to be free. It was almost like he read my thoughts, because he chuckled dryly.

"In the long run, I ended up getting kidnapped anyway, just not for ransom."

"Aiden!" Quinton gasped. "You had no idea you would be kidnapped by a psycho!"

Aiden just shrugged again, and he leaned down and rested his head against me.

Liam was poking around on his computer now, and he spoke up. "You did an excellent job covering your tracks, and I've added some layers of protection to that. It was a photo and my intuition that made me realize who you were. I don't think most would be able to figure it out based on your new identity. Would you like to know what's going on with your family?"

"I guess so. I mean, it's been almost two years. For a long time I thought they'd turn up at any moment, but they never did. I kind of thought maybe they were just letting me go. I left a note and asked them to, so they knew I wasn't kidnapped or something." He laughed harshly, sitting up again. "Little did I know what the future held."

I grumbled against him, and he squeezed my fur. I didn't want Aiden feeling like any of this was his fault. I reached up and licked his face again, and he leaned down and hugged me.

Liam watched with an eyebrow raised, then he went back to his computer. "Your family did indeed seem to leave you alone for quite some time. There was talk of you being off doing business abroad, and you even sent a memo or two through work." He raised his eyebrows at that, mumbling, "They were quite well done and stylistically similar to other emails you'd sent."

"So they were covering for him, but not looking for him?" Quinton asked.

"Not at first," Liam confirmed. "But about seven months ago, your grandfather passed away."

Aiden made a funny little noise in his throat.

Quinton smacked Liam on the arm. "Geez! Give a guy a little warning!" He turned to Aiden, "I'm so sorry, Aiden."

Liam just looked confused, and I gave a head tilt in response. I wasn't sure what he'd done wrong either. Obviously Aiden's grandfather wasn't pack if he hadn't even looked for his grandson. I had the slightest bit of tolerance for his mother, because she had thought of him and looked out for him in the same way some of the hellhounds had been given to Wilder by their parents. If you couldn't take care of someone who should be pack, you made sure someone could.

"It's ok. We weren't close. Grandfather was the head of most of our businesses, though," Aiden admitted.

"Yes, well, your brother has stepped into that role," Liam said.

"My brother? Not my father?" Aiden asked, sounding confused.

"Your brother. There doesn't seem to be any infighting about it, either, and he's been looking for you, quietly but determinedly, since the death of your grandfather. A portion of the inheritance is yours, but it isn't a larger share than his, and it doesn't affect the daily runnings of the many enterprises your family is in charge of. I honestly have no idea why he would be searching for you. You continue to send the occasional memo to the company, and it all looks very normal. It doesn't appear that most people even know you're missing."

We all sat in silence, contemplating things. It was all rather odd for me to understand. Aiden's family wasn't evil, according to him, but they didn't care that much about him. He had run off rather than live a life not of his own choosing. My hellhound and I both respected that. It seemed rather silly that disappearing was the only solution, and it seemed even more odd that suddenly he was wanted back.

What was the brother like? Could he be an evil soul?

"I was never close to Caleb, so I couldn't really say too much about his character," Aiden admitted, almost like he could hear my question.

Mate, Fluffy just grumbled. I didn't think that included mind reading, and Fluffy huffed at the thought. *Don't need to read minds. Read feelings.*

"Most of your family is morally gray at the very least, but that isn't uncommon for a lot of humans. I can't get a sense of your brother, however," Liam said. "His presence online is almost nonexistent as of a few years ago. He puts very little in writing, even email or texts. It's almost suspicious how absent he is from having an online footprint. Anything digital seems to come through secretaries and underlings."

Aiden's hand stopped rubbing my back, and he stared at Liam. "Years ago? So before I left?" he asked.

Liam nodded.

"I don't know why that would be," Aiden admitted. "Nothing happened, as far as I know. It's been more than a few years since he graduated and started working. Again, we were never close. There was a big age gap. It was almost like he was an uncle or something. He was away at school and then off living on his own by the time I was old enough to get to know him. He was nice to me and fun, but we just weren't close."

Liam was typing away, and I could sense Aiden getting sad. I stood up and stretched, leaning against him lightly. He laughed, gripping my fur with his hands.

"Must be time for a walk," Aiden said. "I'm gonna go throw some warmer clothes on."

He got up and headed into his bedroom.

Quinton turned to Liam. "I don't like this. A brother you can't trace or get a feel for? Aiden was apparently never in the family business. How shady are they, really?"

Liam shrugged. "They're not clean. No family that has that much money ever is. We're talking old money, prestige, and influence. We aren't talking mob or drug running or human trafficking, but the rules do not apply to people like that. Or at least they think they don't."

"You make the rules apply to everyone, though, my sexy stalker," Quinton murmured, leaning up and kissing him.

I yawned loudly before they could get too carried away. Quinton looked over and laughed, then he looked back at Liam.

"I'm just gonna make sure Aiden's ok before his walk. I don't even know if he ate dinner," he said, and he got off the couch and headed toward the bedroom.

Liam looked at me. "A brother with no online footprint searching for him, a wealthy and at least somewhat corrupt family, and a therapist who isn't human. I don't like any of this."

I bared my teeth in agreement. I didn't think the therapist was anything to worry about. The brother, though?

We'll protect our mate, Fluffy rumbled.

Yes. Yes, we would.

CHAPTER 6

It was a cold evening, but somehow it seemed like Fluffy was giving off enough heat to keep me warm as we walked. Granted, he was a big freaking dog, and he was... Well, he was pretty fluffy, hence the name. He probably loved the cold weather. I bet he'd love it if it snowed. I could picture him running through the snow, me throwing snowballs for him to chase.

I'd never had a dog. I'd wanted one, but with traveling and going away to school, I knew it wasn't practical. I'd read so many stories as a kid about a boy and his dog, and it just seemed so magical. But then 'normal' life had always seemed magical to me. Most kids dreamed about being rich. I dreamed about being middle class and playing with the kids on my street and getting into kid adventures.

Money was a cage. It was a locked room with bars on the window. Sure, the room was so huge that most people never noticed you couldn't get out, but I had noticed. I had wanted something different.

After my mother's talk, I had planned, saved money, and covered my tracks, but for the first few months I still waited for my family to walk into my job and laugh at my silly little adventure and take me home.

Only they never had.

I wasn't sure if I was happy or sad about that. Helene would say I could be both things at once. I desperately wanted them to look for me, but I also wanted them to let me go.

Maybe I had been kidnapped because I'd been looking for someone who needed me desperately. Someone who wouldn't just let me go like my family had.

I knew Helene would say that type of thinking was toxic, but I couldn't help blaming myself sometimes. I feel like I had to have sensed that there was something off about him. Helene said hindsight was 20/20, and I'm sure she was right, but I still wondered. Deep down, had I known? Had I liked that he seemed like someone who wouldn't let me go? Had I flirted with him even though he was a huge red flag? Or had I really thought he was just a nice guy?

Fluffy bumped into my leg and growled a bit. I laughed. "Yeah, yeah, I know. I was thinking, and they probably weren't productive or useful thoughts."

Fluffy growled a little again, but it wasn't really a growl. It was a sort of huffy, grumbly sound.

"I don't know why Caleb would be looking for me. If I had known that a month after I left, maybe I would've been happy. I don't know. But I don't want to see my family. I'm not the same person I was when I left them, and I can never be that person again. Maybe I could have settled into the life they had planned for me and been ok with it, but after everything I've been through... I can't go back there. I can't be that person. I don't want to be that person."

Fluffy bumped playfully into my legs again, and I veered a little to the side, laughing. "Helene would be really proud to hear me say this, but I guess I like my life right now. I get scared, and I know I'll always have issues, but I have real friends, and a job I love, and a connection to people and a place. And I even have a dog."

Fluffy nipped at my jacket and pulled, and I laughed again. "Ok, so maybe the dog should have come first. Are you gonna come back to the house with me? I bet I can sneak you in. You probably wouldn't want to sleep in my bedroom, but it might be nice having a guard dog inside."

Fluffy just smiled his doggy smile up at me, and I pulled out the granola bar Q had shoved into my hand before we left. I hadn't eaten dinner, and I should probably head back and do that. I had also never asked about the delivery from earlier, and I was curious what that was all about. Therapy and my mission to share my past had sort of taken over my thoughts.

"I guess we should head back," I sighed. "This granola bar isn't very appetizing."

Fluffy gave a light bark in agreement, turning with me to walk back to the house.

"Hopefully we can be done talking about my family. I just want to pretend the evening is normal. There's been enough excitement for one day," I murmured.

I looked down at Fluffy, who was staring at me and wagging his tail. I ran my hand along his back, which I could do without bending down since he was so freaking tall. It probably wasn't appropriate that I'd grown so attached to the guard dog. I wondered if that made him less effective in guarding everyone? I didn't know, and I couldn't bring myself to ask the guys. I didn't want to give up Fluffy.

When we made it to the back door, I smelled food. I couldn't imagine Q or Liam cooking, and when I walked in and saw the take-out containers, things made sense. Fluffy followed me in, and I barely had time to wonder about feeding Fluffy before Q was ushering me over to the table.

"Spaghetti and sausage from your favorite place! Don't ask how it got here so fast," he remarked.

Yeah, I probably didn't want to know. Liam and the guys were... different. It was best if I didn't try to wrap my head too much around those differences. They had saved me, they watched out for us, and I trusted them. I was comfortable leaving it at that.

I sat at the table as Q handed me a plate piled with spaghetti, and before I could even take a bite, Liam was putting a take-out container on the floor for Fluffy.

"Can he—" I started to ask, but Fluffy started chowing down, so I figured whatever human food was in there must be ok for him. Liam would know.

Liam and Q sat at the table, plates in hand, and we all started eating.

I waited until we'd all had a few bites before I asked, "So, what's up with the new bed? It looked huge."

Q looked at Liam. "Yeah, Sexy Stalker, you never did quite explain that. I mean, I know we have some adventurous bedroom lives, but do we really need that much space?"

"Ewww!" I cried. "I *do not* want to picture you guys having sex in that bed. Oh my god, I sleep in that bed sometimes!"

"Aww, don't worry Aiden, we make sure to never leave a wet spot on your side," Q joked.

I threw my napkin at Q, and he caught it, laughing. I was joking around, but also... ewww. I really didn't want to think about that. We were totally platonic cuddlers. Of course, I knew they had sex, but it was some abstract thing that didn't affect me. They were really respectful like that.

"Well, you haven't been coming in as much to cuddle, and since needing more space was an issue, I figured a bigger bed would work," Liam said, taking another bite and chewing.

Q looked at me. "You felt squished? You should have told us! I could have scooched over."

Ok, first of all, warm fuzzies, because they clearly cared about my comfort. But...

"Liam, what do you mean about space?" I asked, starting to get suspicious. I had told Helene that. But I'd also mentioned it while rambling to Fluffy in the woods. So either my therapist's office or the woods were bugged. Maybe both.

Liam looked at me. "You weren't coming in to cuddle in order to give us space."

Q looked at Liam, then looked at me. "You thought we wanted space?"

Liam nodded like the question had been addressed to him. "So I bought a bigger bed. Now the problem is solved, and Aiden will come in to cuddle whenever he wants to," he said, looking really proud of himself for his problem-solving skills.

Q and I had a moment to stare at one another in exasperation, because Liam was being Liam, which was generally sort of clueless at normal behavior.

"You're an idiot, but I love you," Q said to Liam.

Liam looked at Fluffy in confusion, like he would know the answer as to why Liam was an idiot. Fluffy had his head tilted like he was confused, too, and I couldn't help the laugh that escaped. It made sense, since Liam had about as much sense as a dog.

Q turned to me then. "Why on earth would you think we need space? Have we *ever* said we needed space? Have we *ever* implied we didn't want you coming in for cuddles? Hmm? Here I was, thinking you were all moving on and healing, and I was all sad that you didn't come in for so many cuddles, but of course I couldn't say anything, because good for you and your healing journey, but I fucking miss you when you don't come in for cuddles!"

Q was genuinely pissed, but I couldn't help the laugh that burst out of me.

He pointed his fork at me. "Don't you laugh, asshole. And we now have a huge ass motherfucking bed so you better be in tonight for some damn cuddles. Fuck, bring Fluffy if you want. We could probably fit Corbin and Jude in that bed too."

Fluffy's tail was thumping, but Liam looked appalled. "We are not inviting the whole pack into bed."

I ignored his wording. Helene would say it was denial to ignore when Liam called us humans or made weird comments like that, but that was fine. I could only deal with so much. Instead I said, "And that brings me to my question, Mr. Creepy Stalker. How did you know I was giving you guys some space?"

Liam looked at Fluffy, like the guard dog would rescue him from answering. Well, that probably answered my question.

"Are the woods all under camera and audio surveillance?" I asked.

Liam sort of half nodded. Ok, so most of the woods then, probably. Q just rolled his eyes, and I really couldn't be too mad. I mean, it was their property. They probably kept track of Fluffy that way too. Plus, I knew Liam was a little over the top about security, and it did keep us safe.

Was I rationalizing? Of course I was. Most people would probably see all this as a giant red flag, but ever since Liam had threatened to 'hunt me down in a very nice way and bring me back willingly' if I ran away because 'consent was important,' I'd had a hard time being really threatened by him. It was sort of sweet, in a creepy stalker way. And apparently there were good creepy stalker ways and bad creepy stalker ways.

Who knew?

I just nodded my head, though, and went back to eating. Q was grumbling under his breath about Liam and spying and unplanned deliveries, and Liam was smiling like he was enjoying Q's grumpy mood. He probably was. They were weird like that.

And I was only a tiny bit jealous. Not of either of them, but that they had that with one another. I loved them both, and they accepted me totally and completely, but I didn't think I'd ever had what they had. I was probably too broken for that.

As if sensing my mood, Fluffy came over and rested his head on my thigh. I pet him, taking comfort in his soft fur. He always felt so soft and clean, and just running my hands through his hair calmed me down.

I *was* happy. I had friends. A job I loved. I *was* healing. It was all good. Which reminded me… "Q, I looked into that yoga studio you sent me, and I'll go if you're sure you don't mind coming with me."

"I asked you to go and sent you the information," Q answered. "I mean, I don't have yoga stuff, but the place says they have some there to borrow."

"I really appreciate it," I answered. I couldn't picture Q doing yoga, but he was insistent that he wanted to go with me to a class, and maybe it would help him too. I did love yoga, and I'd missed it.

We finished eating, making small talk about our day, and then we watched some of *The Great British Baking Show*. Liam fiddled on his computer, I sat on the floor and cuddled with Fluffy, and Q complained about cookies being called biscuits (he really couldn't seem to get over that).

When it got late and Liam started making the security rounds, I went to the bathroom to wash up and brush my teeth, then headed into my room to get ready for bed. Fluffy followed me without me calling him, which I was glad of. Liam didn't seem to mind that I'd totally adopted the guard dog, but I didn't want to push it, either.

I changed into pajamas while Fluffy sat in front of the door, and then I stood there, undecided. He tilted his head at me.

"Do I go in there now? Or do I sleep in my bed?" I mumbled to Fluffy. "Now I feel like I have to go in for cuddles, at least tonight, and I don't know what I'm supposed to do. Unless they want, like, alone time or whatever, and then ewww, I do not want to interrupt that."

Fluffy huffed at me, turned around, and scratched at the door.

I sighed. Fluffy was probably ready to head back to wherever he spent his nights, maybe with Jude or Corbin. I opened the door, but rather than making his way toward the back door, he headed for Liam and Q's room. I followed, and he nosed the door open and went in. Ok then.

"Get your ass in here, Aiden," Q rumbled from the bed.

The covers were flipped over on my side of the bed already, and man, the bed really was freaking huge. Fluffy was sitting by my side, and I walked over and crawled in. And continued crawling, because did I mention the bed was *huge*?

"Where did you find this bed?" I mumbled, finally making it over to Q.

"Alaska!" Liam announced proudly. "It didn't actually ship from there or anything, but it's an Alaskan bed. I don't know why they need such big beds in Alaska. One would think a smaller bed would be better to conserve body heat when it's so cold."

Q snorted at Liam, and Fluffy seemed to take that as his cue, because he jumped up on the bed and laid down next to me, scooching his body close to mine.

Liam picked his head up, looked over, and mumbled, "Seriously? You better not get any hair on my blankets, you uncultured mutt."

He gave an oomph then, so I guessed Q had elbowed him, and I tried not to laugh at them. Q flipped the covers over me and wrapped his arm around me, and Fluffy scooched in closer to my other side. I was wrapped in a cocoon of warmth, and I dozed off listening to everyone's breathing.

I slept all night, and I didn't have any nightmares.

Chapter 7

Atlas/Fluffy

I had ear plugs in, because I wasn't really a fan of the screaming, so although I didn't hear Liam come down the stairs, I smelled his presence.

Our kill, Fluffy rumbled.

Yeah, he's probably just coming to talk, I assured my hellhound.

Fluffy huffed, and I agreed. Talking was overrated. I sighed and took out the ear plugs.

At least the guy wasn't screaming anymore. I mean, he didn't have a tongue now, and his vocal cords were pretty damaged. The grunting when he saw Liam was still kind of annoying, though.

"He's not going to save you. If you're really unlucky, he might join in," I told the guy.

"Nice job on him. What did this one do?" Liam asked, sitting on the stairs.

"Kids," I said, because that was all I needed to say.

Liam nodded. Everyone knew I went a little nuts when children were harmed or neglected in any way. Even if that wasn't a person's primary sin, I made sure they paid for the children who were collateral damage in their fucked up lives.

I was probably working out my own childhood trauma of

being abandoned or some shit like that. Whatever the case, the world would be rid of one more black soul, and I saved pups along the way.

I picked up a hammer off the table nearby, and I was about to start with a few well-aimed blows when I heard Liam sigh.

No fun, Fluffy grumbled.

I agreed. I turned around, raising my eyebrows and grunting at Liam. Obviously whatever he was down here for couldn't wait.

"So, you and Aiden…" he started, and then he trailed off, like I was supposed to know what the fuck he was getting at.

I just stared at Liam. The guy behind me whimpered, and I turned around and shushed him before turning back.

Liam sighed again.

I continued to stare. I could wait. I had all the patience in the world, and I wasn't going to ask. He was the one who had come down to bother me. I had nothing to talk about. If he had something to bring up, he could damn well bring it up.

"You can't pretend to be a dog forever," Liam finally said.

"I'm not pretending. It's not my fault none of you ever mastered another form aside from your hellhound," I answered.

Liam sighed again. He was so dramatic.

"You know what I mean. Aiden thinks you're a dog. You've been cuddled up in bed with us or just Aiden for weeks. You take walks with him every day. He talks to you—I've heard him," Liam said.

"So?" I asked. I failed to see what he was getting at. It was nice that Aiden talked to me. I enjoyed listening to him, and he clearly enjoyed my company. I didn't see what the problem was.

"So don't you think Aiden might be a little upset when he finds out you lied to him?" Liam asked, clearly exasperated.

"I never lied to him," I answered, turning back to the hellbound soul.

Only Liam sighed dramatically again. "Fine. You left some

important details out. Quinton is going to be mad as hell, too, and he's gonna wanna know why I didn't tell him."

I turned back, smirking. "It's not my fault your mate can't tell who's pack. He should know it's me." Liam didn't seem satisfied, so I added, "He probably does know it's me on some level. Aiden knows deep down, too. They have good instincts. They'll come to terms with it when they're ready. There's no need to rush."

Liam stared at me, and eventually he nodded. I was about to get back to work when he spoke again. "How's the cabin coming along?"

"It's done. We hooked up water and electricity last week. I spend my spare time there when Aiden is at work. I think he'll like it."

Liam looked vaguely alarmed at that. "What do you mean, you think he'll like it?"

"Well, at some point we might want separate residences," I explained. "Of course we'll still enjoy a puppy pile for cuddling, but Aiden and Quinton don't need that every night."

"Atlas," Liam said slowly, like he was talking to a pup, "you cannot kidnap Aiden and bring him to your cabin."

I sighed this time. "Of course not. I would never harm my mate."

Liam's eyebrows shot up in surprise. "Your mate?"

Fluffy huffed in my mind, but I didn't bother replying. I just gave him a look.

"Do not look at me like I'm an idiot. How was I supposed to know?" Liam defended.

No instincts, Fluffy rumbled.

Well, Liam had *some* instincts, especially when it came to his technology stuff, but maybe not so much when it came to dealing with hellhound stuff. I didn't bother answering him. I turned back around and got to work.

Kneecaps were so breakable. Really, so many human bones were easy to break, especially with a hammer. I even turned around and offered Liam a turn, because he was here, after all, but he just shook his head. He was probably right—this one was pretty much done. He was barely conscious.

Fun's done, Fluffy grumbled, and I agreed.

I placed my hand on the hellbound soul and let my fire consume him, letting it lick over my own skin when I was done in order to get rid of the blood. It burned up the sweatpants I had been wearing as well. Liam rolled his eyes at me when I was standing naked in front of him. I smirked, then turned into my other form. He didn't have to look at me naked, and I didn't have to talk to him. It was a win all around.

Unfortunately, it didn't stop him from talking.

"Toby is having some friends over this evening, and Quinton thinks it would be nice if Aiden went, too. Aiden has apparently reluctantly agreed. He's gotten comfortable with Toby, and Sebbie and Josh are good souls that wouldn't harm him," Liam explained.

I trusted his judgement, but I'd still be close by just in case Aiden needed me.

I knew Dexter and Liam would be nearby for protection, but I assumed Corbin wouldn't be. How no one realized he was never here when Toby's friends came over, I didn't know. I was betting there was some type of connection between Corbin and one of Toby's friends, but I wasn't sure whether Corbin even knew that yet, or if he was just following the dictates of his witchy instincts.

Corbin understood that there was a time for everything. He wouldn't be down here lecturing me about telling Aiden I was a hellhound.

At any rate, it wasn't Aiden's protection I was worried about. It was his mental well-being. If he needed a walk break during the gathering, Fluffy would be there.

"Aiden's brother is still poking about, and he's hired a handful of people to look for Aiden, too. I've covered Aiden's tracks every-where I can, but it's still best to be on guard."

I growled in response. I was always on guard.

"I heard from Wilder," Liam added. "I think he'll be coming soon. I kind of wonder if he'll have a new packmate for us."

Good. Pack is happy, Fluffy grumbled, and I agreed. Our pack was getting bigger, hellhounds were finding mates, and the ties between us were stronger and more solid because of it. It was good.

I thumped my tail in response. It would be good to have Wilder back. He was the head of our pack, and things never quite felt complete until he was with us.

Liam sighed again—such a drama queen—and he finally got up and headed out of the basement. I followed, ready to go wait for Aiden to be done with work. It was time for our afternoon walk together.

⌘

I was lying near a side window at Toby's, where I could hear the conversations inside and also see if anyone came up to the front of the house. Aiden and Quinton had walked over more than an hour ago, and Josh and Sebbie were already here.

Not human, my hellhound said, not for the first time.

Yeah, yeah, I knew. Sebbie was definitely not human. We weren't quite sure what he was—he didn't smell like Helene, so they were something different. He was a pure soul, though, so I didn't worry about him with Aiden. He seemed like a cheerful little thing from the conversations they were having inside.

Josh came out onto the front porch at that moment. I could see him typing away on his phone.

Hurt, Fluffy rumbled.

Yes, he smelled hurt. Something wasn't right with him. It wasn't sickness, but maybe physical injury? Maybe just sadness. Humans got sad sometimes.

Needs cuddles to feel better, Fluffy said.

Yeah, no. We can't go cuddling random humans. Some people don't want cuddles, I answered.

I saw Josh rub at his eyes, and before he could go back in, Aiden came out. Josh was looking out into the front yard, and I thought he was trying not to cry. Aiden just stood next to him, not saying anything for a while.

Finally, Aiden said softly, "It isn't your fault."

I didn't know what that meant, but Josh started crying then. His sobs were silent, but I could see him shaking and hear his breaths. Aiden just stood closer until their arms were pressed together and looked out into the yard with him.

Just needs a packmate, Fluffy rumbled, and I agreed. Sometimes you just needed a packmate there with you.

Eventually Josh settled down and stopped crying, and he nodded his head a few times before he said, "Sorry. Thanks. I'm ok."

Aiden looked at Josh's phone and said, "May I?"

Josh nodded his head, and Aiden took the phone and typed something into it. "I'm under Amanda - Work in your contacts. Call me if you ever want to talk, ok? I know... I know what it's like, you know?"

"It isn't..." Josh started, but Aiden just gave him a look, and he stopped whatever he was going to say. Josh just nodded instead, and then they went back inside.

Josh needs pack, Fluffy rumbled again.

I agreed. Something was going on there, but Aiden was apparently in tune with it, and he'd let me know if I needed to do anything. Toby would let Dexter know, too.

I heard Aiden make his excuses inside, and I realized that he was done with people for today. I slunk around to the backyard, ready to watch him walk home.

He came out the back door, and he seemed to be searching the darkness.

Aiden wants walkies, my hellhound growled happily.

I mentally rolled my eyes. Walkies? Seriously? Could we not come up with a better name than 'walkies'?

Fluffy huffed, and I walked out of the woods so that Aiden could see me. He looked relieved when he did, and he walked down the back steps and out toward the woods until he was next to me.

I was a bit surprised when he leaned down to hug me, and he smelled a little sad, too. He rubbed his face against my side, and eventually he got up and started walking. Rather than going towards home, though, he headed in the opposite direction. Our land didn't extend too far in this direction—it mostly went back into the protected woods—but there was still a fair amount of forest before he'd happen upon the main road. Plus, we were with him for safety.

"There's a trail this way, according to Toby, so I thought we'd try that. I could use a longer walk this evening," Aiden said, as if he could sense my thoughts.

We happened upon it after a few minutes. It was a wide, well-used trail, and Fluffy grumbled—the smell of other people was annoying. It was evening and it was dark out already, but the day had been relatively mild, and this path had seen a lot of traffic in the recent past.

My hackles were raised a bit, and I wasn't sure why. I bumped against Aiden's leg, and he reached down to pat me. I wanted to turn back, but I had no idea why, and I couldn't very well tell Aiden we should turn around.

We were probably two miles down the trail when I smelled it. Human. Not rotten, but questionable. I growled low in my throat, and Aiden stopped walking. I wanted to tug him back towards home, only I didn't want to call attention to us either.

The human came around a bend in the path ahead of us and stopped short on seeing us. I bared my teeth and growled.

"Woah, that's quite the dog you have there. Isn't there a leash law around here?" the guy asked, and he definitely sounded nervous.

Maybe he was just out for an evening walk, like Aiden. I didn't trust him though.

"Uh, sorry. He's trained. He won't attack you or anything," Aiden said, holding onto the fur on my neck.

I didn't think it was to hold me back, though. This man made Aiden nervous, too. He took a couple steps closer, and I growled again.

"Wow. What kind of dog is that? He's really huge!" the guy commented, stepping forward again.

Predator, Fluffy growled, and I agreed.

Aiden took a step back, and I stepped in front of him, growling more loudly.

"Alden Astor?" the man asked.

Aiden gasped beside me, even though the guy had said Alden and not Aiden. I could see the man reaching for something, but there wasn't time to do more than make sure Aiden was protected.

It wasn't Aiden he aimed at, though. It was me.

Stupid human, Fluffy growled as fifty thousand volts of electricity flowed through my body. I let out a howl, calling to my brothers, as my hellhound form burst out at the charge of electricity. I lunged at the man before he could do anything stupid, like try to tase Aiden.

He wasn't a hellbound soul, but I wasn't sure I could hold back from killing him if he hurt my Aiden.

CHAPTER 8

AIDEN

One minute we're having a nice walk through the woods, and the next thing you know, some random guy tases Fluffy.

Only Fluffy isn't fluffy anymore. He's all... fiery.

He's standing over the guy, who's pressed to the ground, and he's growling, and he's freaking huge, and he's literally got flames licking along his back.

I'm just standing there like an idiot trying to process what the hell just happened. Fire Fluffy turns around to look at me, stops growling, smiles at me with a doggy smile, and wags his tail. In the next breath he's looking back at the guy and growling again.

Ok, then. Fire Fluffy is friendly. At least to me.

I probably should have been scared of Fire Fluffy, because, you know... fire. And growling. And *really big* teeth. Aside from the split second where I was worried about Fluffy because he'd been tased, I really wasn't scared. Which was kind of amazing.

Now what the hell was I supposed to do about Fire Fluffy and random taser guy? It occurred to me then that I had my phone. I pulled it out, and I dialed Liam. I don't know why I dialed him and not Q, but I did.

"Jude's on his way," Liam said without even waiting for a hello. "Are you ok?"

"He turned into Fire Fluffy," I said stupidly. Because, yeah, I was feeling a little shell-shocked.

"Are you hurt?" Liam asked.

"No. Some guy tased Fluffy, and he turned into Fire Fluffy," I said again.

I swear Liam muttered "Lucky" under his breath, then he said, "Yeah, that'll do it."

I heard footsteps then, and I turned around to see Jude running towards me. Only it hadn't been long enough for Jude to get here. At least I didn't think so. Maybe I was in shock?

"Jude's here too fast," I said, and then I hung up the phone before Liam could even answer.

Jude wasn't even panting or out of breath. He stopped in front of me and looked me over, totally ignoring the growling fire dog on top of the strange guy.

"You ok?" he asked me.

"He turned into Fire Fluffy," I said again, because somehow my brain just wasn't wrapping around that fact.

"Yeah, he does that," Jude said, like it was perfectly normal.

He walked over to the pair, and Fire Fluffy stepped off the guy. Then he was just Fluffy again, sitting there and wagging his tail.

Jude did something to taser guy—I couldn't see what—and I knew he was unconscious by the way his body went lax.

"I don't suppose you'll change and fill me in on what the fuck happened?" Jude said to Fluffy.

Fluffy shook his head. Like, the dog shook his head no.

Jude huffed, and Fluffy trotted over to me, leaning against my leg. I automatically reached down to rest my hand on his fur, and Jude just looked at us and huffed again.

"I guess that means I get to drag this asshole back, then. Lovely," he grumbled.

Then Jude slung the guy over his shoulder and started walking back down the path, like this was all perfectly normal. Fluffy gave a grumble, and I followed Jude, because what the heck else was I supposed to do?

Jude walked fast, always a few feet in front of me. He kept turning to check on me and smiling, though, and I had the sense that he was purposely not walking next to me.

Probably so I couldn't ask why Fluffy had turned into Fire Fluffy. Because that wasn't normal.

"You turned into Fire Fluffy," I said to Fluffy. He looked up at me, and I swear he grinned. "I didn't know you could turn into Fire Fluffy."

He just bumped gently into my leg, and we continued walking. We were back at the house really quickly, and I didn't know if it was because I was trying to keep pace with Jude's speed-walking or if I was just too lost in being shocked to gauge time correctly.

"Oh, this is gonna be fun," Jude said, delighted.

I had no idea what he meant until we turned toward the front of the house and I saw the police cruiser in the driveway.

Oh. Oh, no. This could not be good. Because taser guy was still hanging over Jude's shoulder, and although Fire Fluffy wasn't currently fiery, I had no idea if he would get fiery again.

Josh, Sebbie, Q, Toby, Dexter, and Liam were all gathered on the front porch talking to the sheriff. Because of course it was the sheriff.

"Hey, Walrus!" Jude called out.

Everyone on the porch turned to us, and Q actually face-palmed himself when he saw Jude carrying a guy over his shoulder.

"Jude, what the fuck?" Toby asked, looking slightly panicked.

The sheriff just raised his eyebrows as we walked up to the porch, though.

"What've you got there, Jude," the sheriff asked, surprisingly calm for someone looking at a guy carrying an unconscious man.

"Oh, this is just some random guy who tried to kidnap Aiden, so we're gonna bring him down to the torture basement to find out what he knows," Jude answered, smiling.

The faces of everyone behind the sheriff were actually comical—everyone looked horrified and shocked.

The sheriff was looking at us, though, and he just sighed.

"You wanna come down to the torture basement and help? We won't kill this one, because he's not a bad sort. We'll just carry out a little light torture for information," Jude said, smacking the guy's ass.

He actually smacked the unconscious guy's ass. I was sure I looked horrified, too, because the sheriff turned to me.

"I don't know how you put up with this prankster," he said to me, and then he walked down the steps toward his cruiser while we all stared.

"You sure you wanna leave, Walrus? We could have fun! It would be a great first date!" Jude called out.

The sheriff ignored him, waved a hand at everyone, and got in his car. He started to pull out, then rolled down his window to call out, "Stop calling me Walrus!"

"Coo Coo Kachoo!" Jude shouted back, and the sheriff pulled out, probably a little more quickly than necessary.

I had gone insane.

That was the only explanation. I was still trapped in my kidnapper's room and had created an alternate universe in order to distract myself from my boring existence. Or maybe I was in the bakery and I had fallen and hit my head, and this was all some kind of fever dream.

"What. The. Fuck. Jude!" Toby cried out.

Jude just smiled, walking up the steps with the unconscious guy. "Isn't he cute? All gruff and grumpy. Why was he here?"

Josh turned red at that and mumbled, "I better go."

"Do you really think your dickhead boyfriend called the cops because you were out?" Toby asked, looking outraged.

Josh just shrugged. "I don't know, but you guys have no neighbors, so who would have called in a noise complaint? He's really pissed. We had a pretty big fight. I probably shouldn't have gone out."

"Still, that's fucking petty," Q said.

"Eh, it could've been this guy," Jude said, jostling the guy on his shoulder.

Sebbie rolled his eyes. "That's right. Your next murder victim." He obviously didn't take Jude seriously, either, because he turned to Q and Liam. "The offer still stand to drive us home?"

"Of course," Liam answered.

They walked down the steps toward one of the cars, and Jude called out, "Just light torture!"

Josh and Sebbie just waved, getting in the back seat while Q and Liam got in the front.

And off they drove, leaving Jude, me, Toby, and Dexter.

"What the hell happened?" Dexter asked, looking at the guy on Jude's shoulder.

I thought that taser guy should probably be getting heavy, but Jude acted like carrying him around was like having a sweater draped over his shoulder. Then everyone was looking at me, because yeah, I was the only one who actually did know what happened.

"He was looking for me," I said, because he had asked for Alden Astor. I hadn't heard that name in a long time.

"Ahh. We'll get the details out of him," Dexter said, looking slightly gleeful. "You gonna help, Atlas?"

Atlas? I turned to look behind me, but there was no one there. I'd heard about their reclusive brother, only I'd never met him. Then I realized that Dexter was staring at Fluffy, who was baring his teeth at Dexter.

Jude looked at me, then at Fluffy, then at Dexter. Then he gave a fake laugh. "Ha ha. You mean Fluffy."

Toby looked confused. "Atlas can turn into a dog and not just a hellhound?" he asked. Then he started mumbling to himself and walked into the house.

"He's plotting, so I better... yeah..." Dexter said, pointing over his shoulder and following Toby inside.

Jude turned toward me, and I swear he gave Fluffy a sympathetic look. "Yeah, I'll just leave you two to... talk... or whatever." Then he bounded up the stairs and into the house behind Dexter and Toby.

It was just me and Fluffy left outside, and I wandered toward my house, not looking at Fluffy, who bumped occasionally into my leg.

Fluffy. Fire Fluffy.

Atlas?

I unlocked the door and stepped inside, and Fluffy came in. I shut and locked the door and went and sat on the couch, and Fluffy came and sat in front of me.

"You're not a dog, are you?" I asked. "I mean, I guess you're a dog, but you're not just a dog."

Fluffy panted at me. I took that as a yes.

"Will you change?" I asked.

Fluffy took a step back, and then he was Fire Fluffy again. He was bigger, and there were flames on his back, and he was beautiful in a sort of scary way, even though I wasn't afraid of him.

Then he was Fluffy again. Only...

"Your name isn't Fluffy," I said.

He growled at me, not showing teeth or anything, but I knew he was disagreeing with me.

"It isn't. It's Atlas. You're Atlas. Dexter called you Atlas," I insisted, like saying the name so many times would make it real.

Fluffy—Atlas—growled at me, then panted, then growled again.

What the fuck did that mean?

"You turn into a person," I said.

Fluffy, or Atlas, came over and rested his head on my knee and whined, looking up at me.

"Are you using sad puppy dog eyes on me right now?" I asked.

Because he totally was. He was staring up into my eyes, head resting on my leg, and he looked fucking sad. I put my hand on his head and couldn't help sliding my fingers through his fur.

We sat like that for a few minutes, and I felt some of the panic start to fade. I hadn't even realized how upset I'd been. Because that guy had said my name—my old name—which meant I'd been found.

Then there was the whole Fire Fluffy-Atlas thing. The guard dog wasn't a guard dog. He was a person. Or... I don't know what he was. Not human, obviously. I thought about all our interactions, and I realized I should have known something was weird. He had always seemed to know what I was saying. He was never on a leash, and no one seemed concerned about him or claimed him as their dog. He had been there whenever I needed a walk, and I trusted him.

Maybe that was why I didn't want to think about him not being normal? On some level I must have known—I had wondered if he was a hallucination, after all.

I'm not sure if this was better or worse than a hallucination.

I didn't hear the car come back, but I heard Q giving Liam hell well before they reached the house. I almost grinned. Why be outraged when Q could do it far better than I could?

He slammed the front door open, stalked in, and pointed at Fluffy.

"You!" he yelled.

Liam followed him in, shutting the door and giving Fluffy a dirty look.

"You have been *sleeping in my bed* and you didn't tell me you were Atlas? What the fuck? What the fuck is that bullshit? And why the fuck do you look like a dog?" Q ranted. He turned to Liam then, pointing at him. "Can you turn into a dog? Did you not tell me you could turn into a dog?"

Liam put his hands up and looked almost afraid of his boyfriend, which was kind of funny.

"No! I just have my hellhound form. Atlas was raised by wolves, so he adopted a new form as a pup in order to have a pack," Liam answered.

Q and I both stared at him.

"Are you fucking serious?" Q asked, staring at Liam.

"We all tried to have other forms, too, when we first met Atlas, but even he doesn't know how he did it. A survival mechanism, I guess. I swear I don't turn into anything else," Liam answered.

"Not about that. Oh my god," Q muttered, turning and looking at Fluffy.

I looked down, and Fluffy was totally giving Q sad puppy dog eyes now. I smacked his side. "Stop that," I insisted.

He looked at me and grinned.

"You were seriously fucking raised by wolves?" Q asked.

Fluffy panted.

"That means yes," I said.

"Well, fuck. I can't really yell at him now, then," he said.

"Plus, I told you when Aiden first mentioned a dog that we didn't have one and it was probably Atlas," Liam added.

Q looked mad again then, turning and pointing a finger at Liam. "I thought you were fucking with me! Because when I saw Fluffy, he sure as fuck didn't look like a hellhound. You neglected to mention he had another form."

Liam started to open his mouth, but Q cut him. "And you also didn't say anything when Fluffy came over. You called him Fluffy!"

"Well, he is Fluffy," Liam said, like that made perfect sense.

"No, he's not! He's fucking Atlas!" Q cried out.

"Well he couldn't be fucking Atlas, because he *is* Atlas," Liam reasoned.

"That's what I *just said*!" Q shouted.

Dear god, it was like a comedy of errors. Q was pissed, Liam looked confused as hell, and Fluffy was just resting his head on my lap like this was all perfectly normal. Liam looked over at him and raised his eyebrows.

"Care to help me out, Fluffy?" he asked.

Fluffy bared his teeth at Liam. I took that as a no.

Apparently Liam did, too, because he sighed. Then he said, "Atlas is... a little feral. He likes to stay in his other form a lot of the time. His other form liked the name Fluffy, and he adopted it. His hellhound is Fluffy, but his person is Atlas." Liam shrugged then, like that was perfectly normal.

Q just stared at him. Then he grinned a total evil villain grin, and I couldn't wait to see what was coming. "Does that mean I get to name your hellhound? How about it, Pookie? Snookums? Buttercup?"

Liam looked a little more appalled with each nickname, and I couldn't help the laugh that escaped.

It seemed to break the tension. Q sighed, and Liam went over and pulled him into a hug. "I'm sorry, my little hellcat. Fluffy didn't want me to say anything, and I thought you would realize."

Q grumbled a bit, but he hugged Liam back. They broke apart, and he looked back at me and Fluffy. "Why doesn't he change into a person now, though?" he asked.

"Because Aiden isn't ready for him to," Liam answered, like it was the most normal answer in the entire world.

Q's mouth opened in surprise, and I'm sure my face matched his. I looked down at Fluffy, but he wasn't giving me sad puppy dog eyes. He just looked knowingly at me.

Maybe he was right. I wasn't sure I actually was ready to meet Atlas yet.

Fluffy was my friend and companion, and people... Well, people weren't always safe.

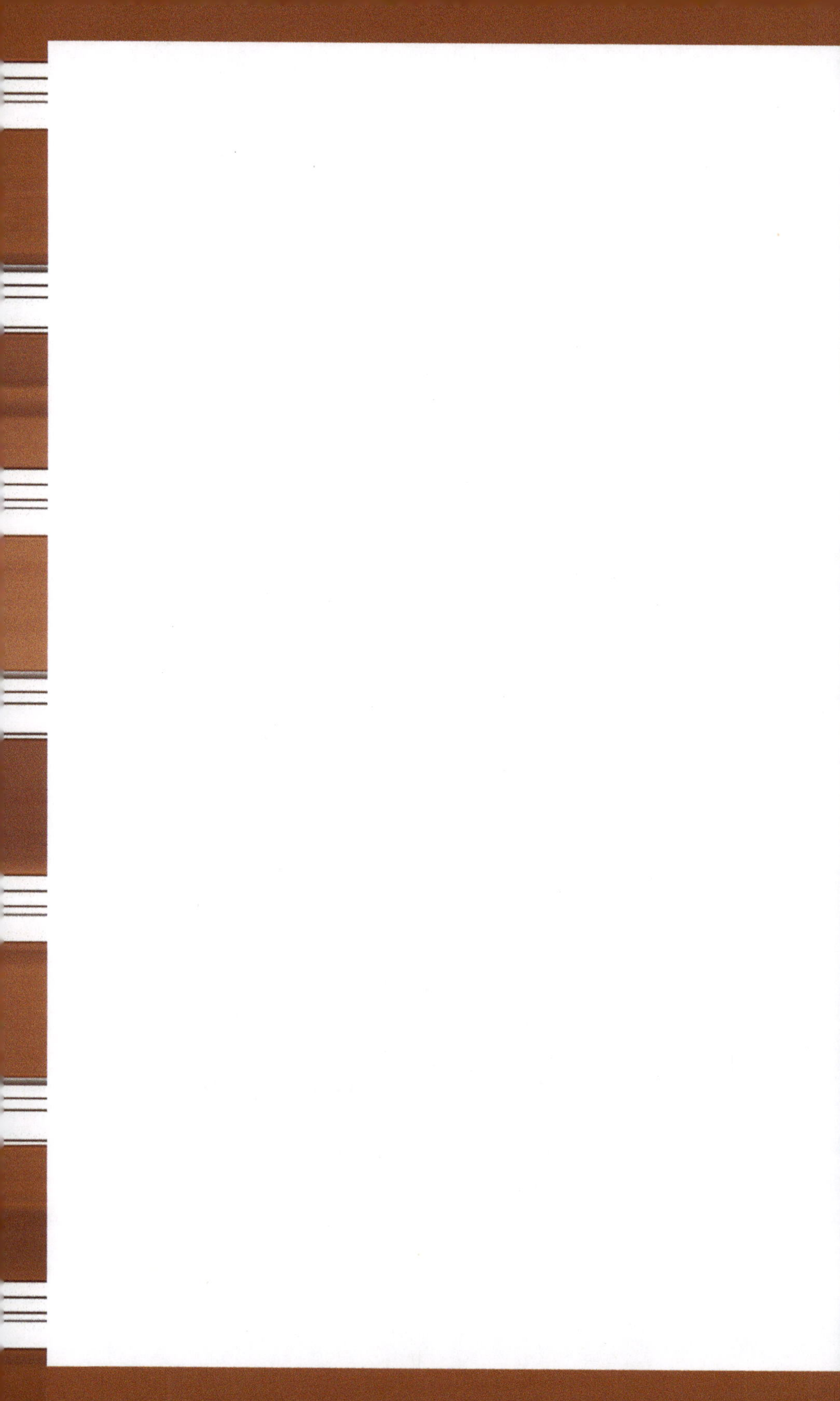

Chapter 9

Atlas/Fluffy

Aiden got some snacks together even though they'd eaten at Toby's. It seemed to soothe him to fiddle around in the kitchen. Liam poked away at his computer, frowning and muttering occasionally. I figured he was digging into the guy in the basement.

Jude knocked on the door before long, and when Q let him in, he said, "Oh, do I smell cookies?"

Aiden frowned at him. "You literally told the sheriff you have a torture basement. Why do you deserve cookies?" Then he stopped frowning, adding, "Wait, do you *actually* have a torture basement?"

Jude made his way over to the kitchen island and snagged a cookie. "We're hellhounds. We send evil souls to hell. We may have a little fun doing it, but trust me, these are really, really awful people who deserve to suffer."

Aiden glared at him. "You didn't answer the question."

Jude just smiled, taking another bite of the cookie.

"We're all gonna end up in jail," Quinton muttered.

"Nah. He likes me. He just doesn't know it yet," Jude said, smiling. "He's so cute, isn't he?"

"My god, you're like a teenager with a crush," Quinton snarked.

"Well, he is dreamy. I'd totally put a poster of him up on my bedroom wall," Jude answered.

Stupid talk, Fluffy grumbled, and I agreed. We had more important things to worry about. I growled low in my throat, and Jude and Liam both looked at me.

"Right. Why don't you two head over to see what our guy knows, and I'll hang out with these two and eat cookies," Jude said.

"We don't need a babysitter," Quinton muttered.

Liam just walked over and kissed him. "It would make me feel better. I know it's a trial putting up with this asshole, but we shouldn't be long."

I walked over and stood next to Aiden. Liam and Quinton were still murmuring to each other and kissing, and Aiden looked over at them then at me. "I'm not kissing you goodbye. I'm mad at you."

I gave a little whine, and he pet my head, sighing. I leaned against his legs for a moment, and then I walked off toward the door, Liam following behind me.

I changed into human form inside Dexter's old place, snagging a pair of sweatpants from a basket by the door. If the sheriff did decide to check, Toby's house didn't actually have a torture basement—that was in Dexter's old house, which I guessed was Jude and Corbin's place now, and in the third house, which had been Liam's. Only Liam now stayed with Quinton, so that house was basically empty most of the time, aside from when Liam was working.

Their living arrangements were confusing, and I had no idea where Wilder would stay when he got here, but I wasn't concerned. I had my cabin out in the woods, and I'd been getting it ready for Aiden. Maybe I'd take him to visit it soon. He could add his own touches to it and make it a comfortable space for himself.

Not that I expected him to come live there right away. He

could live with Quinton for as long as he needed to. We had eternity together, so I wasn't worried.

Need to claim him, Fluffy grumbled. Yeah, we'd get to that too. I didn't want to rush Aiden.

We headed down to the basement, and the guy was tied up in a chair. He smelled scared, but he was staring defiantly at us.

"This is kidnapping," he said.

Liam took another chair and turned it around, straddling it and staring at the guy. I leaned against the wall, arms folded.

"Michael Frey, thirty-six years old, former military who was injured in the line of duty, became a private investigator and bounty hunter. You sometimes bend the rules a bit, but you generally do that when it's for the greater good. You're not evil, so don't worry, we won't kill you," Liam said.

The guy—Michael—looked a little surprised at all of the information that Liam had.

"How do you know all that?" he asked.

"Oh, I know more than that. I know about your family—your parents in that nice retirement village, your sister and her kids, your girlfriend—you really ought to propose soon, since I know you ordered a ring," Liam said.

The guy got paler with each mention of his family members, but he kept his lips tightly closed.

Liam continued, "I know that Caleb Astor's secretary transferred funds into your account approximately three months ago. Quite a sum, and I'm assuming you'd get more for handing over his brother. I also know that you're working alone on this case, and I don't believe that you updated Mr. Astor about your current whereabouts. Your last update has all nearby locations checked, but not this area. You aren't the only person on this case, by the way—he's got people all over the country on it. You just happen to be the unlucky one hired in our backyard, so to speak."

"Leave my family out of this," Michael said.

"You were told his brother was missing and had been coerced

by an abusive ex that he was now on the run from. You were told that he would be resistant to help because he would think it was his ex looking for him, but his brother only wanted to get him home safely where he could be protected. You were told to do whatever was necessary, as long as Alden wasn't permanently harmed," Liam finished.

The guy just stared at him. Liam stared back.

Boring, Fluffy grunted. Yeah, it was. But Liam was good at getting information, and this guy wasn't hellbound, so torture really wasn't on the menu. They stared at each other for a while, and eventually I shifted my stance, and the guy looked over at me. He paled a bit. I probably did look slightly more menacing than Liam.

"His dog turned into..." Michael started.

"Yeah," Liam answered. "Not that anyone will believe that. Hallucination, probably. Maybe you got a little shock from using that taser."

"What do you want?" Michael finally asked. He looked resigned.

"How did you find Alden?" Liam asked. "I can't find a trail you followed. I know you looked into the coffee shop and found out where Alden lived, but what set you onto the shop?"

Michael looked like he was mulling over what to share. Finally he said, "Luck. I was showing his picture around, and some guy mentioned that it looked kinda like the baker at this little coffee shop he'd been to when he was passing through Paradise Falls. I didn't actually know if it was Alden, but I came to check it out. I had no other leads to follow, so I chased this one down. I managed to see him at the shop, but he looks different from the picture. I figured I'd check it out anyway. I was just hoping to get a look at the property. It was stupid luck that he was walking that path when I was on it."

I grunted, and the guy looked at me again.

Liam sighed. "The problem, Michael, is what we're going to do with you. We don't really know why his brother is looking for him, but I don't have a good feeling about it. There is no abusive ex. He's on the run from his family, and they mostly left him alone until recently. You really aren't a bad person, so we can't kill you. But we also can't have you giving up Alden's location to his brother."

Michael hesitated, and then he gave us more information. "I never spoke to Caleb Astor, only the secretary. She was... Well, let's just say she made it clear that Mr. Astor didn't mind if there was collateral damage. It rubbed the wrong way. I'll bend the law and do what I need to, but I'm not out to hurt random people. The story about the ex changed a little bit when I met her in person. It seemed fishy, but it was one brother looking for another. I figured it wasn't my business as to why, and he clearly didn't want his brother hurt." Michael shrugged.

I heard footsteps, and Corbin appeared, crow on shoulder.

"Who the hell are you guys?" Michael asked, staring at Corbin.

"Alden's protection," Liam said.

Corbin walked over and placed his hand on Michael's shoulder. The crow hopped down onto it, too, cawing in his ear. The guy moved his head away and grimaced, but he didn't struggle.

"What do we do with him?" Liam asked Corbin.

Corbin thought for a moment, his crow cawed, and then he nodded. "I'll take care of it," he answered.

I shrugged and turned to go upstairs, and Liam got up to follow me.

"Hold on. Wait a minute," Michael said, sounding a little frantic. "Why are you guys leaving me with him?"

"Don't worry. He won't kill you. He'll just do some witchy shit. I'm sure you'll be fine," Liam answered, and then we walked upstairs.

The guy was still calling out, but there was a caw and he fell silent. Corbin was good with witchy shit. My hellhound trusted that he'd protect Aiden. He knew Aiden was pack.

When we got to the door, Liam put a hand on my arm, stopping me. I turned to stare. I was anxious to get back to Aiden, and I didn't really want to talk.

"Atlas," Liam started, and then he trailed off.

I just continued to stare. He eventually let my arm go, and I pushed down my sweatpants and turned back into Fluffy. Liam sighed, but he opened the door, and we went to the back house where Aiden and Quinton were. Jude heard us approaching and met us outside. Liam started to fill him in, but I had no patience for more talk. I walked in.

Quinton was in the bathroom, and I could smell Aiden in his room. The door wasn't shut, so it was easy enough to walk over and push it open. I leaned my body against it until it was partly shut, but I didn't latch it. Aiden didn't like closed doors.

He was already laying in bed, his back to me. The nightlight illuminated his side of the room, but I was in relative darkness. I hopped up onto the bed, laying down next to him. His breathing was even, but I knew he wasn't sleeping.

He didn't turn around when he spoke. "Will you change to talk to me?" he asked. "I don't want you to change if you don't want to change, but I kind of want to talk to you."

I was human in a moment, laying naked next to him. He was under the covers, though, and I was over them. I tugged a blanket at the foot of the bed up and over myself. I wasn't sure how he'd react if he turned over.

"I'm not sure if I'm ready to meet you yet. I know that's really stupid, since I know you already, but... You were a dog. Even if you weren't a dog, I thought you were a dog," Aiden said.

I grunted.

"Yeah, ok, maybe I knew there was something more to you. Maybe I should've asked questions, but I sort of made it my policy to not ask the guys too many questions. Then you turned into Fire Fluffy. Or Fire Atlas," he said.

"My hellhound's name is Fluffy," I answered.

He shifted, but he didn't roll over. "Liam's hellhound doesn't have a name. I got the impression that they weren't, like, separate?"

"My hellhound was the only company I had for awhile. He talks to me. I don't think anyone else is like that," I said.

Aiden made another noise, but he still didn't turn over.

"Why didn't you tell me?" he finally asked.

"You weren't ready," I answered. "That's ok. I like being with you in any form."

Aiden was quiet for a while, and I wondered if I should change back or stay in human form. I didn't mind either way. I just wanted Aiden to be comfortable.

Finally, he spoke. "I might still want cuddles. I don't know…"

"That's fine," I said. "We like cuddles."

I didn't know if he wanted me to change, but Fluffy didn't have arms to wrap around him, so I scooched closer and snuggled him close. The sheet and comforter were between us. He was stiff at first, but I sniffed along his neck and breathed in his scent, and he relaxed at the familiar routine—Fluffy liked to breathe his scent in, too. It was warm and comforting. Eventually he put a hand on my arm, gently rubbing along it, like he was learning what I looked like from touch.

I thought Aiden was almost off to sleep when he spoke softly again. "I can't believe your hellhound lets me call him Fluffy. I definitely can't believe he likes it."

"It's the first time anyone has ever given us a name. Of course we love it," I answered, and I snuggled him closer, breathing in his scent again. He felt relaxed and warm, and I let myself drift off, thinking I'd change back to my other form before Aiden woke in the morning.

CHAPTER 10

AIDEN

Warmth pressed against my back, and there was an arm around me. I thought of burrowing into the warmth and falling back asleep, but I was awake, and my mind was already racing.

Fluffy was a person.

I still wasn't sure that had totally sunk in. His arm was muscular and huge. His breathing was deep and even next to me.

I kind of wanted to see him.

I didn't want him awake, though, as weird as that may have been. I gently, slowly shifted away from him. He didn't pull me tighter or anything, and eventually I managed to roll over enough so that his arm was off me.

I sat up in bed quietly, turning to look at him.

His hair was dark and shaggy, and he had stubble and a goatee. I studied his features. His face was relaxed and looked calm, and I thought of Fluffy, always so calm. His eyelashes were long and beautiful, and I kinda wondered what his eyes looked like. One arm had tattoos on it, but the rest of his body was a dark, golden color. The blanket was pulled up to his waist, and his chest was muscular, his nipples dark little points.

He was built like a fucking tank.

I felt a slight stirring in my dick, because he was beautiful and attractive and I *knew* him, and my stomach swooped nervously at the feeling of arousal.

Nope. Not thinking about that. Nope, nope, nope.

Fuck.

I breathed my way through my mini-crisis. The entire time, Atlas lay there, not moving an inch, his breathing not changing in the slightest. He didn't even twitch, and I'm not sure how I knew, but I thought he was awake and maybe had been this whole time.

"You aren't asleep, are you," I whispered.

He opened his eyes and looked at me, but he didn't move a muscle. His eyes were striking and intense, and yet they were warmly regarding me at the same time. It was like looking into Fluffy's eyes, which was slightly disconcerting. I felt that swoop in my stomach again, because I thought I saw affection in those eyes, and my nerves took hold again.

I looked away, taking a deep breath. There was a man in my bed. Only there had been men in my bed before. Quinton and Liam, and apparently Fluffy, although he had been a dog at the time.

I told myself that having a man in my bed was ok. I was ok. Nothing had to happen.

I looked back up at Atlas, and he was just patiently staring at me, not moving at all, and I felt a jittery feeling in my body like I'd had too much caffeine.

"I'm scared," I whispered. I thought he would have questions, only Atlas just slowly blinked, then he lifted his arm up, like he was waiting for me to climb back in to snuggle, even though he was the reason I was scared.

Only I defied logic and did exactly that. I turned away from him and slid down under the covers, and his arm wrapped around me, but not so tightly that I couldn't wiggle away if I wanted to. He sniffed at my neck again, which made little goosebumps rise

86

along my skin. It was nice, and it was also familiar, and I could almost pretend it was just Fluffy behind me. Almost.

When he was done sniffing me, he took deep, even breaths, and I found myself matching his breathing. In and out, in and out. My heart rate slowed, and some of the nerves faded. He was so fucking warm, like an inferno at my back, and his deep, even breaths were calming. He smelled nice, too.

"You're a person," I finally said.

He grunted in response, and really, what was there to say?

He didn't ask me anything. I knew he would answer anything I asked, but I really didn't even know what to ask or say.

Eventually my stomach growled, and Atlas loosened his arm like he knew it was time to get up. I rolled out of bed and headed out into the house to go to the bathroom, and I didn't look at Atlas.

Cowardly? Yup.

I peed, brushed my teeth, and splashed cold water on my face. I stared at my reflection in the mirror. Eventually, I opened the door, ready to go figure out what the fuck I was gonna do.

Only Fluffy was standing by the back door, tail wagging, just like every morning. So I went into the bedroom and threw on some warm clothes. I grabbed a muffin from the kitchen and took a bite, then I grabbed some biscuits for Fluffy, who was sitting and patiently waiting by the back door.

We walked out, and I ate my muffin and fed him the biscuits. He took them gently from my hand. We walked in silence for a bit, and then I spoke.

"You're a person. I'm not sure I can wrap my head around that. I feel like I should tell you that you can be a person when we walk, but..."

Fluffy grumbled—not quite a growl but close to it.

I looked at him, and I swear he was giving me a look.

"You don't mind being a... wolf, or hellhound, or whatever?" I asked.

He wagged his tail, gave a doggy grin, and then started walking, looking back and giving me the "Are you coming?" stare.

I caught up to him and kept walking. He was clearly leading the way this morning, and I followed him in a direction we didn't usually take. It wasn't long before I could see a structure up ahead. I knew we were still on the land the guys owned, because Liam's cameras were all over.

Fluffy was wagging his tail, and he bounded ahead and then bounded back, obviously excited. I couldn't help but laugh—he wasn't usually exuberant, and the fact that he was the silent, grunting guy in my bed this morning made the whole thing even more comical.

I walked faster, and... Wow.

"It's gorgeous," I said, taking in the cabin.

Fluffy went inside somehow (I wasn't going to ask how a dog opened a door), so I followed him. Everything looked brand new inside, although it was unfurnished. I wandered around, admiring the woodwork and the large open rooms. There wasn't even a door on the bedroom yet.

"Did you build this?" I finally asked. Fluffy was sitting in the middle of the living area, and he panted in reply.

"Wow. This is where you're gonna live?" I asked again. "Or where you already live?" I corrected, because he had been staying somewhere before he started sleeping at my place.

He panted at me again.

"It's beautiful," I said, turning in a circle. It was so open and airy. There were tons of windows, and it felt spacious inside for a cabin.

My phone rang at that moment, and I looked at it. It was Helene, my therapist.

"Hello?" I answered.

"Hi, Aiden. I know we're scheduled to meet later in the week, but I had a cancellation, and I wondered if you wanted to come in this afternoon?" she asked.

"Oh. Actually, yeah, I think that might be good," I said, staring at Fluffy. He just wagged his tail.

"Ok. I'll see you at our usual time. Bye, Aiden."

"Bye," I murmured, and then she was gone.

"I have therapy tonight," I told Fluffy. Then I took one last look around. "I also need to get ready to head to work. This is a really beautiful place, Atlas. I hope..." I trailed off, blushing. "I hope you'll still visit."

He looked at me, tilted his head, panted, then grumbled. I wasn't sure what that meant, but I figured I wasn't rid of him, which made me glad despite my panic this morning.

We headed back to my place, Fluffy walking along beside me. I didn't talk much, but I reached down and ran my hands through his fur now and then. I knew he was a person, but I really didn't want to lose out on this time with him. It was ok to still pretend a bit, wasn't it? I guess I could ask Helene later. Somehow or other. I grinned at the thought of telling her the truth.

Fluffy licked my hand, and I laughed. I had felt weird this morning, unsettled, but I felt better now after our walk. I could almost convince myself that nothing had changed.

⁓ ⁓

Everything had changed. Of course everything had changed. I was rinsing off my baking equipment from the day, stuck in a whirlwind of thoughts.

You'd think I was an ostrich burying my head in the sand. If they were even the ones who buried their heads in the sand. Some kind of animal did it, anyway, and I was apparently the same. Because, yeah, my dog turned into a guy. A very attractive guy. A guy I had... my stomach swooped again, but I had to face it.

I had a physical response to Atlas. I thought he was beautiful. I had felt the stirrings of interest, and I hadn't felt that since...

Yeah, so panic mode was back. It was good that Jude was

already here, waiting to drive me to therapy. Not that I could explain any of this to my therapist. What would I say? *Hey, Helene. It turns out my super sweet and loving dog is actually a really attractive guy, which sends me into a spiral of panic because I was held hostage and assaulted for a year, and I haven't really had any thoughts about people being attractive since then.*

Yeah, I didn't think that would work. I mean, maybe the last part would work. Maybe I could just say it was like a friend of a friend or something and not even mention the dog part.

Cass poked his head into the kitchen area. "Aiden, I think everything is as clean as it's going to get. You alright?"

I looked at him, startled. Yeah, I'd been washing dishes for a really long time, and I needed to go if I wasn't gonna be late.

"Um, yeah. Ok. I'm ok. Yeah," I muttered unconvincingly.

I walked out, and he carefully rested a hand on my arm, giving me plenty of time to duck away.

He looked thoughtful for a moment, then he said, "You know, everything will work out, and you'll be ok. You'll be ready to move on when you're ready to move on, but you *will* move on."

I nodded at him and kept walking, my throat thick. Jude called out a greeting, and I just nodded back. I was keyed up and I knew it, and Jude didn't say anything as we walked out to the car. When we got there...

"Fluffy!" I said, smiling.

He was sitting in the back seat, panting out the window, and I climbed in next to him. He settled half laying on my lap, and I ran my hands through his fur, feeling calmer just because he was here.

And wasn't that kind of fucked up? Atlas made me nervous and anxious and scared, but I was comforted that Fluffy was here. I knew they were the same person, but my brain just equated humans with bad things.

Jude just started driving, and I leaned my head back. We got to the therapist pretty quickly, and I was glad I wasn't riding in the front to see the speedometer. If Jude was trying to get caught speeding again... I mentally rolled my eyes at his antics with the sheriff.

I got out of the car, and to my surprise, Fluffy followed me, trailing behind me as I walked up to the building.

"Um, I don't know if dogs are allowed," I said softly.

He just panted at me and followed me into the building when I opened the door.

Ok then. We made our way to Helene's office, and I didn't even have time to sit down in the waiting room before she called me into the office.

I walked in, and Fluffy followed. He nosed the door shut behind him, and Helene looked up. I was standing there all awkward, and Fluffy was sniffing the air. Helene stared at him, then she sighed.

"Nope, you can't stay. I don't think he can talk about you in front of you," she said, walking over to the door. She opened it and stared at Fluffy, saying, "You can wait out there, but if I hear a peep from you, you're out of the building, got it?"

Fluffy trotted out, and she shut the door behind him, going back behind her desk and motioning me toward a chair.

What. The. Hell.

"Umm..." I murmured, then I trailed off, because what was I supposed to say? And why did Helene talk to Fluffy like he was a person who understood her?

Helene just stared at me patiently, but I couldn't even think of where to begin.

"Aiden, I'm sure you have some unpacking of emotions to do, and I can guarantee you that anything you say will be absolutely fine, no matter how crazy it may seem," Helene said calmly.

I stared at her, confused and unsure.

"I'm your therapist, Aiden," she said gently. "I have only ever kept your best interests in mind and tried to help you heal, and I will continue to serve in that role. Anything you tell me, no matter how crazy you think it sounds, is totally fine. This is a no judgement zone, remember?"

She had helped me in so many ways, and I did trust her. Then there was Fluffy—he'd left me alone with her, and I trusted his judgement, probably more than my own. Which was ironic, because I was also panicked because of him.

I guess it was time to "unpack" my feelings, as she called it. How she acted toward Fluffy wasn't important. Head in the sand? Maybe, but I had enough to worry about without wondering if my therapist knew Fluffy was really a person.

Chapter 11

Atlas/Fluffy

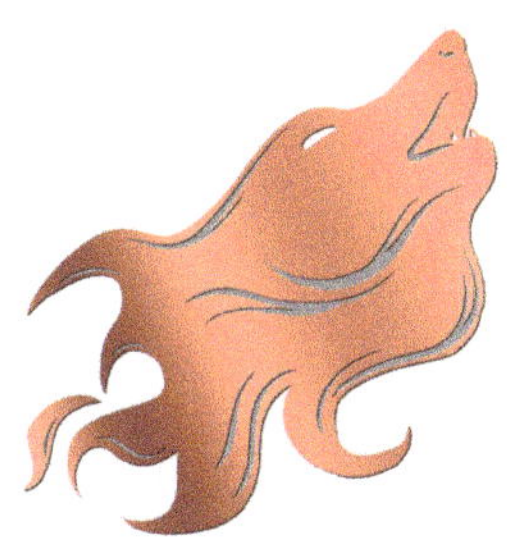

I resisted the urge to growl. I was relegated to the office, but I could still hear everything, which I'm sure Aiden's therapist knew.

She was definitely not human.

She was also a pure, shining soul, so I knew she didn't pose a threat to Aiden. Still, I wanted to be in there to help Aiden deal with his anxiety.

I did also understand that some of that anxiety was because of me, and his therapist was probably right that he wouldn't talk about me in front of me.

I heard her reassure him as I sniffed around the waiting room, and they got the small talk bullshit out of the way.

Huh. There was a pair of black sweatpants and a black t-shirt sitting on a chair in the corner. Was I supposed to change into a human or something? They looked to be my size, which I briefly wondered about. Helene was something with foresight or knowledge or some kind of witchy mojo.

I mentally shrugged. Didn't matter as long as she helped Aiden heal.

I sat down by the door again, focusing back on their conversation. Aiden was struggling over what to say, continuously starting and then stopping, obviously unsure.

Helene finally said, "Just let it out, Aiden. Just blurt out whatever is on your mind and stop worrying about finding the right words."

I heard a deep breath in, and then Aiden blurted out everything in one long train of thought. "My friend turned into something unexpected, and I love my friend but now he's not what he was before, and I don't know what to do about the fact that an attractive half-naked man was in my bed this morning, and I felt something and I got scared."

"Ok, then. Let's start with the man in bed," Helene said calmly. "You know him and are familiar with him, right?"

"Sort of," Aiden answered. "I know him, but I don't know him like that."

I knew Aiden had been nervous and scared this morning, but I didn't exactly know why. I had just done my best not to spook him.

"I haven't... Since what happened..." Aiden started, but he just trailed off.

"Aiden, we've discussed a lot of aspects of your kidnapping. We've talked about how you had very conflicting feelings toward him, where you both dreaded his coming to visit but also looked forward to it because it was a break from the monotony of your confinement, and how any emotions you have are ok." Helene paused, and then she said gently, "We have never discussed what happened sexually between you and your captor. Perhaps it's time to lance that wound so it can begin to heal."

I almost growled, but I remembered what Helene said about me making a noise, and I had no idea how good her hearing was. I was not getting kicked out. What if Aiden needed me? Still, I didn't like the idea of him dealing with that trauma if he wasn't ready to.

Helene spoke again. "I can tell this makes you nervous and upset, Aiden. If you aren't ready to tackle this, that's ok. If you do want to tackle this, is there anything I can do to help get you through it?"

"I just..." he said, trailing off.

I wasn't sure what motion he made or what expression he had, but I heard Helene get up and come over to open the door.

"Fluffy, would you mind joining us in order to provide some emotional support for Aiden?" she said.

I walked into the room without having to be asked twice, walked straight over to Aiden, and stood by him. He was sitting in a chair, but he slid out of it and onto the floor, his legs straight out, and I gently laid my upper half on his lap. He immediately put his hands in my fur, nervously rubbing and fidgeting.

I didn't mind. He could pull my fur out if he needed to in order to get through this.

Helene sat back down, and Aiden took a deep breath. I rumbled softly against him, leaning into him a little more and letting him know I was here for him.

"He really pretended we were boyfriends. I know I've talked a lot about the beginning and how it was all sort of a blur of panic and being sedated. It seems so long ago, that part of things. The time when I still thought maybe I could get away or I would get rescued," Aiden said.

Helene nodded. "Yes, we have, and we've talked about how strong you were to face each day even when you realized you couldn't escape."

"It wasn't sexual right away. He bathed me and fed me when I was drugged, and we had 'a fight,' as he called it, if I tried to escape or didn't do what he wanted. Eventually he started to kiss me good-bye, and then it turned into more than just a kiss goodbye. It was kind of awful, but I had kissed him before. We'd made out a little once at the bar, and I just tried to tell myself this wasn't that differ-ent." Aiden laughed wetly. "He wasn't even a good kisser, but hey, I could pretend. It seemed a small price to pay to make him happy."

"Then what happened?" Helene asked gently.

"Then he wanted more. He talked about it. How long we had been dating, how attractive I was, how he was turned on by me. I knew he wanted more from me. He tried groping me while we made out, and I just couldn't… I couldn't get turned on, no matter how much he touched me. He said it was ok, because he knew I'd gone through 'health issues,' and that was why he'd had to take care of me when I first arrived. It was like he was living in this fantasy world.

"Then he took my hand and had me touch him. I'd seen him get angry, and I didn't want to deal with the repercussions of us 'fighting.' It seemed like such a small thing, to jerk him off. So I did it."

I was tense and angry, and Helene gave me a look. I tried to relax my body. I didn't want Aiden to think I was judging him. I was angry, but not at him. I wished his captor were still alive so I could torture and kill the hellbound mortal all over again.

"You were fighting for survival and making sure food, water, and general comforts weren't withheld, Aiden. There is no shame in what you did," Helene assured him.

I grumbled low in my throat and licked his arm, assuring him that Helene was right. My Aiden was a survivor. He had lived through this, and I could control myself to hear about it. Helene gave a slight nod in my direction, like she understood what I was thinking. Maybe she did.

"He was happy with that for a while, and it got… I don't know. It was like doing the dishes or something, you know? It was kind of boring and monotonous, but I moaned and said how sexy he was because I just wanted him to finish more quickly. All the while I was daydreaming, or, if I'd gotten us positioned correctly, I would watch tv while I did it if he wasn't looking at me. I tried to position us that way a lot." Aiden laughed wetly again, wiping his eyes.

"It's ok, Aiden. That's all perfectly normal. Anything you felt or experienced is ok," Helene reminded him.

"Then one day it wasn't enough. He had been hinting, and when he got up after our 'dinner date,' I put my hands on him. We weren't kissing anymore then, at least, and I knew I could get it done pretty fast. Only he pushed me down, and he said maybe it was time to 'move our relationship along.'

"So I took him in my mouth. I thought, I've given blow jobs. I wasn't that experienced, because I hadn't been away from my family for that long to explore my sexuality, but I liked giving blow jobs. I thought to myself that I could do this. I could just pretend it was someone else, and I could do it. He held my head and guided me, but he wasn't rough. He moaned and called me pet names, and he told me to swallow him, and when he was done, he kissed the top of my head and left the room."

Aiden was breathing heavily, and tears were leaking from his eyes. His hand was fisted in my fur, and I welcomed the little tug of pain. It kept me grounded. Kept me from howling in anger. I licked his arm again, and his hand loosened.

"I threw up. When he left, I threw up," Aiden admitted. "And then that became the new norm, and I didn't throw up anymore after the first few times."

"It's ok, Aiden," Helene said softly.

"He tried to have sex with me once. I couldn't stop crying. I was bent over the bed, my pants around my ankles, and I couldn't stop crying. He couldn't stay hard. I think the fact that I couldn't pretend... he didn't like that. He was angry. He hurt me, and then he left. He didn't come back or feed me for days, and I kind of wondered if he'd ever come back or if I was going to die of starvation. By that point it had been months in that room, and I was thinking maybe that wouldn't be so bad.

"But he did come back. He apologized for our 'fight' and waited for me to apologize too. He made me give him a blowjob, and then he left. He brought up sex again a week or two later and asked me if I ever enjoyed penetrative sex with anyone. I told him no. I couldn't imagine... I just couldn't. He seemed disappointed, but he told me that was ok."

Aiden sniffed. "He was distant after that, and sometimes I thought... I thought about it, you know? I thought about trying to approach him for sex. Trying to treat it like a hook up and just go for it. I'd never gotten that far, but surely I could just pretend and watch tv. Treat it like a root canal or something, you know? But I couldn't bring myself to do it."

I was rumbling softly against Aiden pretty steadily now. I was fighting off anger and the urge to turn into my hellhound, but I focused instead on caring for my mate. He didn't need anger right now. He needed me to just be here and be calm. It was hard as fuck, but I could do it.

Helene nodded at me, got up and handed Aiden some tissues, then sat down and spoke. "That's ok, Aiden. Sometimes we can do a lot of things to survive, but we have to survive mentally, too. If there was something you couldn't bring yourself to do, that's ok. Any reaction in such an extreme situation is ok."

"He decided we should 'break up' not too long after that. He told me he had found someone else, and that we could still be friends and I could live with him until his new boyfriend was ready to move in."

Helene hummed and nodded.

"I felt relieved," Aiden admitted. "I didn't have to be his 'boyfriend' anymore, and I didn't have to do the things that went along with that. I knew he was probably going to kill me, and I... I don't know, I kind of accepted it.

"But I also felt guilty, because I didn't want him to kidnap someone else. I thought a lot about escaping, but he was more cautious than ever before, and he came to see me very little and didn't stay long, just dropped off supplies. I was alone a lot at the end," Aiden said. "I know that's why I crave human touch and companionship so much."

"And we have talked about how that is perfectly ok," Helene reassured him.

Aiden took a moment to blow his nose, and then he said angrily, "I feel like I shouldn't be this damaged. He never *really* raped me, you know?"

Helene cut him off. "What he did was rape, Aiden. He forcibly, against your will, violated and penetrated you, and it doesn't matter that it wasn't done anally. He held you hostage, abused you, tried to brainwash you, and repeatedly raped you," Helene said. "Do not underestimate what you survived. Do not minimize your trauma because something didn't happen."

She paused, taking a moment to collect herself, because I could tell it all made her angry, too. More softly, she added, "That also doesn't mean that your trauma will control your future. You went through something horrific, and you came out the other side of it. Aiden, I am so proud of you for that. I am in awe of your strength every day."

Aiden was quietly crying, but he nodded his head. She gave him a moment to collect himself, and he rubbed my fur as he calmed down.

Helene gave him time, then she continued, "It's ok to be scared of sex and to be scared of men. Being scared and distrustful is a natural defense mechanism, but it is something you can work through. If you're ready, let's circle back to what you were upset about when you came in today."

Aiden cleared his throat awkwardly, and his hands released my fur.

Helene looked at me and said, "Perhaps it's time for your emotional support dog to head back into the waiting room."

I grumbled a bit as I got up. Helene got up and opened the door, and I slowly walked toward it, looking back to give Aiden a bit of a pleading look. I would much rather stay with him. Helene just laughed at me and said, "Scoot out, Fluffy. He'll be done soon." As I walked by, she whispered, "Good job in there," and then the door was shutting behind me.

I paced, finally letting the anger out. I may have taken on my hellhound form for a few moments, but I was careful not to set anything on fire. I wasn't an out of control pup, after all.

My Aiden was so brave. He had survived horrors, and I know he had downplayed the physical and mental abuse because that wasn't the focus of this session. He didn't even understand the depths of his bravery.

I was finally calm enough to pay attention again to their conversation inside, and I sat down, going back to my dog form just in case the next patient walked in.

"So you've explained that you know and trust this man, and all the reasons why you trust him, but this morning you felt panic in his presence? What was different about this morning?" Helene asked.

"Well," Aiden started, pausing. "Well, before this morning, he was a dog. Then this morning when I woke up, he was a half-naked attractive guy."

"I see," Helene said. "So you didn't see him in a sexual manner before this, but this morning he stopped being a 'dog' and became an attractive man."

I could practically hear the air quotes around the word dog, and I rolled my eyes. Helene knew perfectly well that Aiden was talking about me, I was sure of it, but if she wanted to play along, that was fine.

"Yes, exactly," Aiden answered, and I could hear the relief in his voice at her explanation. "He was half naked and in my bed, and I... it literally made me feel a little sick."

"I see," said Helene.

"And now I feel like he's not safe, and I can't look at him like that," Aiden said mournfully, and I growled a little at the thought, but Helene coughed loudly, and I stopped. Oops.

"Is he the same as he was before? Aside from your perception of him, of course," Helene asked.

"Umm, well, I guess so," Aiden admitted.

"Does he exhibit the same traits, does he act the same way, and does he treat you the same?" she asked.

"Well, yeah," Aiden admitted.

"So you see him in a new light, but the fact is, he hasn't actually changed at all. You just see something different you haven't seen before," she told him.

"I mean, I guess so," Aiden admitted.

"So he hasn't changed, Aiden. Not really. Your perception and your feelings changed. What do you feel toward him?" she asked.

Aiden paused, breathing deeply. "He's kind, and he's patient, and he's always been there for me, and he's now an attractive man, and I haven't thought about anyone in that way since before everything happened. They've all been like brothers to me."

"But this man doesn't feel like a brother?" Helene asked.

Aiden blew out a breath. "Nope. Definitely not a brother."

"Did he make advances toward you, Aiden?" she asked.

"No! He wouldn't... he knows..." Aiden started.

"I see. So you trust him enough to trust that he wouldn't make you uncomfortable. So it's yourself that you don't trust?" she asked.

Ouch. She went for the soft spots.

Aiden grumbled. He obviously agreed.

"If he won't push you, and you don't think he'll ask you to do anything, why are you afraid of your feelings? What are you afraid will happen?" she asked.

"I don't..." Aiden started, but she cut him off.

"I know it's hard, but really think about it. If things went in a relationship direction, what would scare you about that?" she asked.

"I don't think I can sexually satisfy anyone, ever. I think I'm too messed up, and I'll be too in my head during sex, and I can't imagine someone even trying to have sex of any type with me," Aiden said softly.

"Would you like to have sex again?" Helene asked.

"Yes," Aiden answered immediately. "I mean, someday, yes, I would. I used to really enjoy doing things with partners. I don't want to lose that forever. I just can't imagine anyone dealing with me. I can't imagine dealing with myself. I'm a mess. I felt nauseous because I wanted to touch a naked guy. I'll probably throw up after sex."

I growled again, and I heard another cough in warning. Still, I couldn't help the low rumble that was coming out of me. If Aiden *never* wanted to have sex, that was perfectly fine. If all he ever wanted to do was cuddle like last night, I would be happy.

He was my mate. I would take care of him. I would protect him, even from myself. I wanted to barge through the door and reassure him that he *never* needed to do anything he didn't want to.

"Aiden," Helene said softly, "give yourself some grace. Maybe spending more time with him as an attractive man as opposed to just a friend will help you?"

"I don't know," Aiden admitted. "Maybe."

Helene continued. "Yes, it may be hard, and it may be a process, but all these feelings do not mean you cannot have a sexually fulfilling life."

"I know that," Aiden admitted. "I still... I can't lose him, Helene. I can't. He's a part of my routine. He makes me feel safe. He's important to me, and I can't lose him because I'm a fucking mess."

"Has he indicated that you would lose him?" she asked.

Aiden just scoffed, and I could sense his frustration. He said, "We're out of time."

Helene sighed. "Please give yourself grace, and maybe spend more time with this attractive man, ok?"

She cleared her throat meaningfully, and I had the idea that she was talking to me somehow. But what was I supposed to do?

"Perhaps I'll even meet him in my office someday," she added.

Ahhh. Was I supposed to be the attractive man now? I wasn't sure how that would work being naked and all, because people usually cared about that stuff. Then I remembered the clothes on the back chair. I quickly changed forms and pulled on the pants and t-shirt. No shoes, but barefoot was better anyway.

Helene was making small talk about their next appointment, and I stood well away from the door so I wasn't too close for when it opened, because I could hear their voices just on the other side of it now.

When she did open the door, she winked at me before ushering Aiden out, closing the door behind him. He looked at the shut door in confusion for a moment, and then he turned and saw me, and he flushed a pretty pink color.

"Ah. Hi," he mumbled.

I grunted in response, then turned toward the door, then turned back to look at him, tilting my head. Was he coming with me or what?

I'm not sure what I did, but he breathed out a laugh, and he gestured me forward.

"Lead the way, Fluffy," he said.

Always Fluffy for our Aiden, my hellhound rumbled, and I agreed. He had given me that name, and no matter what form I was in, I would always be his Fluffy.

CHAPTER 12

AIDEN

Seeing Atlas in his human form had thrown me off, but then she'd grunted and tilted his head just like Fluffy, and it was kinda funny in a slightly hysterical way. He didn't seem to mind it when I'd called him Fluffy, either.

He didn't seem to mind much, in his human or dog form.

We walked out to the car, and Jude looked momentarily surprised to see a human instead of a dog, but he didn't say a word. Atlas slid into the back seat, and I followed him. I felt jittery and nervous. Part of it was the guy next to me, but a lot of it was also just going through all that history with Helene. I felt a bit like I'd run a marathon or something—worn out and exhausted but also amped up with adrenaline.

It was like Atlas knew, because he looked at me, raised an eyebrow, and lifted his arm up slightly. I could practically hear him asking for cuddles. I hesitated, and then I looked at his eyes. He was totally making Fluffy puppy dog eyes at me.

I almost laughed, but I figured it would come out hysterical. Instead, I leaned into him, and he pulled me gently closer, resting my head against him and petting my hair. It helped soothe me. I could see Jude in the rearview mirror continuously looking back at us.

"If you speed so we get pulled over, I'm gonna smack you," I said, because I felt like I needed to say something.

Jude grinned. "Nah, I don't hear the police car at his usual spot."

"You don't hear the police car?" I asked, confused.

"Yeah, they're gonna need to fix that exhaust system on the cruiser he always takes," Jude answered. "It sounds different from other cars."

I sat for a moment, cuddled into Atlas, and then a thought struck me. If Jude could hear a police car up the road and tell it apart from other cars...

"Jude, how good is your hearing?" I asked.

"Ah, well..." Jude mumbled, looking in the rearview mirror again.

"Could you hear a conversation in another room?" I asked.

"I mean, yeah, that's not hard. Maybe even in another house. But don't worry—I listen to music in the car, and I never listen in on your therapy sessions," he reassured me.

Like that was what I was worried about. I didn't even know I *should* be worried about that.

Atlas had heard everything, then, not just the part he'd been in the room for. That was probably why he'd changed into a human. Helene had suggested I spend more time with him that way.

I looked up at Atlas, but he just blinked down at me, tilting his head. I saw no guilt for eavesdropping, but he also didn't look... lustful, or pitying, or like anything at all had changed. He looked like Fluffy, comforting and kind.

Because he was Fluffy.

I looked away. Too much for my brain to handle right now. Atlas was warm, and his grip was gentle around me, and he smelled nice. Familiar. I felt the jitters fade from my body, and a deep wave of exhaustion rolled through me.

I woke up on the couch in my house, my head on Atlas's lap, a blanket tucked around my body. Atlas's thigh was a freaking tree trunk, but somehow it still made a comfortable pillow. His arm was resting on me, surrounding me in warmth.

I had a vague, fuzzy recollection of being carried in the house like a little kid and being gently shushed by Atlas when I tried to protest. I also sort of remembered Jude spreading the blanket over me as I nestled down and laid in Atlas's lap.

It was kind of embarrassing.

I sat up, and Atlas's hand flexed against me, almost like he didn't want to let go, but he did it anyway. I clutched the blanket around me and looked at him. He stared back.

"How long was I sleeping?" I asked.

Atlas shrugged. "Hour?" he guessed.

I stared at him some more, and he tilted his head the tiniest bit, like he was listening.

"Do you want us to change?" he asked.

It took a moment, but I remembered what he'd said about his hellhound being his companion when he was little.

"Were you seriously raised by wolves?" I asked. Then I felt my face heat in embarrassment. "Oh my god, ignore that I just asked that."

A small grin spread across his mouth, and if I thought he was attractive before... holy shit. Atlas smiling was otherworldly. He was beautiful.

"It's ok. You can ask anything," he reassured me. "Yes, I was abandoned as a pup. My hellhound is... sort of separate. It's all me, but it's two sides of me. It's like talking to myself in my head." He frowned then grunted, obviously frustrated that he couldn't seem to explain it.

"It's ok," I said, reaching out and patting his arm. "I was really lonely in that room for a long time. I'd make up these fantastical stories in my head, like the books I read. I would sit and just daydream sometimes, imagining there were people there with me. Sometimes it seemed more real than the room did."

I felt weird admitting that, but Atlas just nodded like he understood exactly what I meant.

"Did you hear everything I told Helene?" I asked.

He tilted his head again. I must have been pretty proficient at reading Fluffy body language, because I could practically hear him say, *Yeah, so what?* He was so like his other form sometimes, and it reminded me again that he *was* Fluffy.

"You heard that I think... Well, that I saw you as... you know," I said, but Atlas still just stared. "Although maybe you don't see me like that, you know, so it doesn't matter how I see you like... you know," I finished.

Could I be any less clear if I tried? Had I ever been so freaking awkward?

Atlas seemed to be having an inner debate with himself. I could practically see him having a conversation with Fluffy.

"Just tell me," I finally said. It was better to know whatever it was, whether it was that he wasn't interested in me at all, or that he was interested in me in that way. Both were sort of equally terrifying, if I were honest.

"You're my mate," Atlas finally said, and then he stared at me, like he hadn't just dropped a freaking bombshell on me.

Liam called Quinton his mate. Dexter called Toby his mate. They were two madly in love couples. They had sex. They were practically married.

"But..." I sputtered. I couldn't be Atlas's mate. I was a freaking mess. We hadn't even kissed. I hadn't even known he was a person until recently. "I can't be your mate."

Atlas just nodded his head calmly, and it kind of pissed me off.

"You can't just tell some guy that he's your mate, you know. Because that isn't ok. I've seen mates, and they're madly in love and would kill for each other, and they have sex and live together and are perfectly normal couples," I burst out. I stood up, starting to pace.

"I would kill anyone who harmed you," Atlas said calmly, like that was perfectly normal. He added, "And we live together."

"We do not!" I yelled. I had no idea why I was yelling, but I was.

"We haven't slept apart in weeks," Atlas stated.

"Because you were a dog!" I shouted, throwing my hands up.

Atlas just tilted his head, as if that made no difference in the world.

"You don't love me," I said, staring at his face.

"Of course I do," he answered, like that wasn't another fucking bombshell. "And you love Fluffy," he added.

"Like a friend, yeah, but not like..." I trailed off, not sure what to even say to that. I started pacing again, then I stopped, pointing at him. "We haven't had sex. We haven't even kissed! And you licking my face does not count!"

"No, we haven't," he agreed.

"Do you want to have sex?" I asked, suddenly worried that maybe he didn't even mean he loved me like that. Maybe he just meant that he loved me as a companion, because yeah, I did love Fluffy like a companion, but I felt like I hardly knew Atlas, and this whole thing was freaking crazy.

Atlas tilted his head again. "If you want to. If you are never comfortable with that, then that's ok, although I would love to give you pleasure someday if you'll let me."

"This is... this is insane! I don't even know you!" I cried out.

"Of course you do. You tell me everything. You cuddle with me every night. You cry on me and share all your burdens. I watch over and protect you, and I find comfort in being with you. Every moment I spend with you is a blessing."

I didn't think I'd ever heard Atlas say so much at one time, and... Shit. I sat down, putting my head in my hands.

He wasn't wrong. He was my closest confidante and my

favorite companion. We'd spent months together, walking the woods every day, then sharing a bed. He just hadn't ever said a word, because he'd been a dog.

"We can't be mates," I said one more time in desperation.

"Why not?" he asked.

"Because I'd be a shitty mate! I get to pour my heart out, and cry on you, and get cuddles. But I don't know if I'll be able to kiss you or have sex with you, and I really don't think I'll ever again be able to give another blowjob, even though I used to like it, because the very thought makes me nauseous. You never got to pour your heart out to me or tell me your problems. I'm broken and traumatized, and I take and take, and what the hell do you get out of it?" I asked, looking at him across the couch.

"I get you," he said simply.

Like I was enough. I felt my face scrunch up as I tried not to cry.

He scooched over slowly, like he didn't want to startle me, and he wrapped me in his huge arms, pulling me close against him.

"You are everything, and I have gotten comfort and joy from being with you. I like hearing you talk. I will take whatever you give me, and I will be thankful for it," he whispered against my ear. "You are my pack. You are my mate."

I cried a little against his chest, but I felt rung out, like I didn't have that many tears left in me. He was gently rocking me, and his chest was rumbling against me, and he was super warm and smelled so good.

This felt too fast. Insanely fast, although I had known Fluffy for months. I depended on him. I needed him in my life. I loved him, but obviously not like that, because he'd been a dog, even if deep down I knew he was more than a dog.

Then he'd turned into a human, and he'd cuddled me, and he'd been attractive, and it was like I didn't know him at all. I guess I didn't know him in that way, but he was still the same inside. He still made me feel safe and warm and protected.

He also now sort of made me feel horny, which I tried very hard not to think about. But trying hard not to think about something never worked, because then I was thinking about his big strong arms surrounding me, and his warmth, and his earthy, forest-like smell, and his really long eyelashes, and his full lips.

Shit. My stomach swooped, but Atlas just made a louder rumble against me, holding me tighter, almost like he knew I was panicking. He took deep breaths in and out, and I tried to match his breathing.

"I survived because of my hellhound. But when Wilder took me in, I had to learn that sometimes my hellhound didn't understand human things. I had to remind him about human rules. Sometimes I still do. He listens when I do, but sometimes I need to reason with him," Atlas said.

I breathed against his chest, unsure what he was trying to tell me.

"It's like you have a hellhound, too," Atlas said. "It got you through your time in that room, and maybe it helped with your family before that. It's hard to reason with your hellhound, because it wants action, but sometimes you have to tell that half of yourself that you're safe now. That you don't have to be afraid or fight or run away. That people can be trusted and won't hurt you."

I was quietly crying again, clutching Atlas, because he wasn't wrong. I had run on instinct for so long. I'd thought I had a happy childhood, but I'd always been following the unspoken rules, walking on a tightrope, making sure to not disappoint anyone. It had been a lifetime of pleasing others, of doing what was expected of me.

Atlas rumbled softly under me, and he rubbed my back until my tears slowed.

"You're safe with me," Atlas finally murmured. "I will never do anything you don't want to. I will always let you decide. You're safe."

I took a breath and pulled away, wiping my eyes. I needed a

minute, so I got up and went to the bathroom to blow my nose and process everything. It had been a lot. Talking with Helene, then Atlas's bombshell. I still couldn't even process that. How could I be anyone's mate?

I heard the door open then and voices in the living room—Liam and Q were home. I took a few deep breaths and splashed some cold water on my face.

I walked out to see them unpacking takeout food from a bag. I bet Jude had told them I had a rough therapy session, and they decided to get dinner. All the guys were really nice about stuff like that. I knew I was lucky to have them.

Q came over and hugged me. I'm sure he could tell I'd been crying.

"You ok?" he whispered in my ear.

I nodded, hugging him back. We separated after a minute, and I looked over at Liam, who had opened up his computer at the kitchen island. He opened his mouth to say something, and I heard a low growl coming from Atlas, who was still sitting on the couch.

"Don't you get all growly with us, you asshole," Q snapped, pointing his finger. "I'm still mad at you."

Atlas didn't look the least bit fazed by that. He actually yawned, which of course just pissed off Q even more. I could sense a Q snarkfest coming on, and I'm sure Liam could too, because he perked up when Q started marching toward Atlas.

I knew Atlas wouldn't actually do anything to Q, but Liam got up and intercepted him, grabbing him around the waist.

"Now, my little hellcat," Liam grumbled.

Q was staring at Atlas, and he looked like the claws were about to come out. "He's *my* roommate, and you don't get—" he started.

Atlas cut him off. "He's my mate."

Liam and Q just stood there, staring at him, then, in unison, they turned and stared at me.

"He says I am," I shrugged, then a slightly hysterical giggle broke out of me. I covered my mouth and tried not to get teary again.

Q's mouth was actually open. Then, like something out of a horror movie, his head rotated around to stare at Atlas. I could tell he was seething.

"You're his *what*?" Q asked hoarsely.

"His mate," Atlas said, like he was commenting on the weather.

"And how long have you known that?" Q asked.

Liam was rubbing Q's arms and sort of rumbling against him, probably trying to calm him down. Q looked ready to explode.

Atlas shrugged. Q looked back at me.

"He just told me. I said I couldn't possibly be his mate, because you guys are mates or whatever and Dexter and Toby are mates, and we aren't like you guys are, but he just said I'm his mate, so… yeah," I finished, shrugging uselessly again.

Q turned back to Atlas.

"You can't just tell him that!" he yelled, and I saw Liam's grip on him tighten, although Liam's face looked confused.

Atlas tilted his head, reminding me again of Fluffy.

"Why not?" he asked simply.

"You can't… You just…" Q looked at Liam for backup, but he looked just as perplexed as Atlas. Q shrugged out of his grip with a mutter about "damn hellhounds."

He looked at me. "They're just fucking clueless sometimes. The whole lot of them," he muttered. He turned back to Atlas, and I could feel a rant coming on.

I just didn't have the energy. I was done with the day. Done with feelings and trauma and big news.

"I'm hungry," I said, and everyone stopped and looked at me. There must have been something in my face, because Q sort of deflated. Atlas came over to me. He didn't put his arm around me, but he sort of leaned against me, just like Fluffy always did.

"I'm done for today. I just need food, a shower, and bed," I said, and then I turned toward the takeout.

Everything else could wait until tomorrow.

Chapter 13

Atlas/Fluffy

My Aiden was exhausted. I knew that Liam had news for him—I could tell by his hyper focus when he'd set up the computer, but I also knew now wasn't the time. I wasn't sure why Quinton was all fiery, either, but I was glad he realized Aiden was done for the day.

We ate without any more drama, then Aiden went in for a shower. Liam shot me a meaningful glance, and I nodded my head. I'd listen to whatever info he had.

Quinton looked back and forth at us, sighed dramatically, and said, "I'm bringing Aiden in to cuddle with me. You guys can go do your hacking and murdering while we're in bed."

Liam kissed him, which turned into a bit of a make-out session.

I wondered if Aiden would want to kiss me at some point? I certainly wouldn't rush him, but I thought I would enjoy it. I didn't have much experience with sex. I'd had an encounter or two in bars and clubs, but nothing stood out. Survival had taken up my younger years, and sex had just never seemed important. I took care of myself when my needs arose, and I was fine with continuing that.

I had meant what I'd told Aiden, though. The thought of giving him pleasure was... exciting to me. I felt myself harden a bit at the thought. I wanted to sniff him and lick him and kiss him all over. If he didn't want to touch me, that was fine. I knew how to take care of my own pleasure. I would like to be responsible for his pleasure, though. It didn't seem like his captor had touched his body much, so I wondered if being pleasured with no expectations would be ok with him.

I also wondered if Aiden would ever want to have anal sex. He had seemed to express some interest in the idea of it. Maybe I needed to find out more about giving pleasure to others. Surely humans had how-to manuals for things like that. I'd have to ask Liam.

The bathroom door opened, and Aiden came out. Quinton walked over and dragged him off to his bedroom, insisting he needed cuddles after a long day. Aiden shot me a look, and I nodded my head at him. We'd join him later. He seemed to understand, because he let Quinton lead him the rest of the way, and they pulled the door partly closed, but not all the way.

My Aiden didn't like closed doors. It was why the bedroom in the cabin didn't have a door at all. I never wanted him to feel trapped anywhere.

Liam walked over and sat on the couch next to me, his computer in his lap.

"I think they were upset over something," Liam commented.

I gave him a look—it didn't take a genius to know they were upset.

Liam sighed. "I knew the whole you being a human thing was still bothering my little hellcat, but he seemed upset about the mate thing. I don't understand why that would upset him. Aiden is pack now. He should be pleased."

I shrugged. I didn't get it. Honestly, I had no idea why no one else had realized we were mates. It was obvious, or at least it should have been to hellhounds. Humans were sometimes weirdly clueless about things.

That was ok, though. They were pack, and we would take care of them.

"So, your man has a bit of a problem…" Liam started, turning the computer toward me.

What followed was a mind-bending conversation about dark spiderwebs and onions inside networks (which didn't seem physically possible to me), and I let Liam drone on about his weird computer shit, nodding when it seemed appropriate. He eventually got to the point—Aiden's brother had upped the stakes and hired a hitman to kidnap Aiden. The hitman was, from everything Liam could tell, a hellbound soul.

"I'm not sure why it took all that explaining. You could've just said we get to go kill someone," I replied.

Liam huffed, leaned down, and smacked his head against the top of his computer, which looked a little awkward.

Such a drama queen.

"It's important because obviously something has changed. The contract isn't for Aiden's death, but hiring a hitman to retrieve him is a big step up from private investigators. The brother clearly doesn't care about killing people. He wants Aiden alive for some reason—that's very clear in the negotiations—but anyone else is disposable," Liam commented.

Details, details. "We can torture the information we need out of the hitman," I said. "You *do* know where we can find him, don't you?" I asked.

Hopefully all Liam's computer shit had proven somewhat useful.

Liam sighed. "Of course I do. That's also part of the problem. He's closer than I would like, and we need to know how he traced Aiden this far. I've covered Aiden's digital tracks very well, but we can't go kill anyone who helped him initially."

I tilted my head at him. Was he *sure* we couldn't just kill them?

"I checked—they're not bad people. We can't kill them, Atlas," he repeated, because I'm sure he could tell exactly what I was thinking.

I sighed that time. Liam was never any fun. Not that I would really kill innocent people, but scaring them a bit for information wouldn't cause any harm. Then again, torturing the actual hitman would be far more fun.

"Someone needs to stay here," I commented. I wasn't leaving Aiden and Quinton alone.

Liam nodded, typing a message in his phone. It buzzed a second later, and he nodded again. We waited for a moment, and I heard footsteps and a caw outside the door. Corbin was here, then. I hoped his bird wouldn't wake the guys.

Liam and I went out, and he and Liam made some small talk, but Corbin knew the drill. He would protect our mates, and I had no patience for talking.

Liam drove, and he was right—our hitman was a little close for comfort. He was holed up in a house in the woods less than two hours away from Paradise Falls. He shouldn't have been that close.

It was actually a pretty cabin, and I admired the woodwork as we strode up the steps. I could smell only one soul inside, so I kicked the door down. Liam walked in first, the idiot, and he got shot for his troubles. I heard him grunt, and then I was tackling the guy with the gun. He was fast, but I was faster, and I had no desire to deal with a gunshot wound. They were annoying.

"Fuck!" Liam shouted as I wrenched the gun from the guy's hands.

The guy was strong, built like someone who took their job seriously, but he was no match for a hellhound. I had his wrists held in my hands and forced him to his knees in front of me, facing Liam.

"Do you have *any* idea how much it fucking *hurts* to get shot?" he yelled at the guy, who was still trying to struggle.

Stupid human. He still thought he had hope. I almost laughed.

Liam stuck his fingers through the hole in his shirt, which had some blood spatter around it, dug around a bit, grunted, and pulled out a bullet.

How theatrical. I almost rolled my eyes.

"What the fu—" the guy started, but Liam cut him off with a knee to the face.

I let the guy's dead weight drop to the ground.

"That fucking hurt!" Liam said again, staring at me.

I shrugged. "You went first. Didn't you smell the gun?"

"*Didn't you smell the gun?*" Liam imitated, rubbing at his chest. So dramatic.

I shrugged again. Not my fault Liam's instincts lay more in technology than in the real world. We all had our uses.

He just sighed and mumbled, going to grab his murder bag from the front porch where he'd dropped it.

I looked around. It really was a pretty cabin, and I kind of doubted that the hellbound hitman was the owner—it had decorations and shit. Men like that didn't decorate.

Liam came back in and taped up the guy's arms and legs, then he walked over to grab a kitchen chair. I made a sound of protest, and he looked at me.

"It's a nice cabin," I said.

Liam sighed again, rolled his eyes, and motioned to the guy. Fine, I'd carry him since I didn't want to burn the cabin down or get blood all over. Blood really soaked into wood, and it made cleanup a bitch.

I threw him over my shoulder and trudged out to the woods, Liam behind me. There was plenty of cleared space in the back, and I dumped him on the ground, sniffing the air.

"No one around to hear him scream," I confirmed.

Liam nodded, trusting my judgement.

Liam pulled out a knife, and I grunted. Liam always hated getting messy, and I was always happy to exercise my muscles. He looked at me, raised his eyebrows, and I cracked my knuckles. He made a go-for-it gesture, and I stepped forward. Liam could ask the questions, and I'd do the torture.

This was going to be fun.

<hr>

"Fuck, you make such a mess," Liam complained.

I looked down at myself. Eh, so I was a little covered in blood. I shrugged. I could burn it off. The clothes were a lost cause, but I could ride home in my other form.

The man, or what was left of him, whined pathetically behind us.

"Aww, look—he's trying to crawl away. Isn't that cute. Like he could get away from us," Liam said.

I turned around, and sure enough, he was trying to drag himself forward by his elbows. His hands may not have been entirely intact. Nor his legs, for that matter.

He had killed children. I didn't like it when children were involved. I got angry.

"Are you done playing?" Liam asked. "It's been hours, and I would like to get back to have a little cuddle with our men."

Puppy pile! Fluffy cried.

I cracked my knuckles and twisted my head, cracking my neck. The man whimpered louder, trying to drag himself more quickly.

You done with this one? I asked my hellhound. We had been a bit feral when we'd learned what he'd done.

Puppy pile, Fluffy stated again.

I took that as an affirmative, and nodded to Liam. He could take care of disposal. I'd done all the torture, after all. Wasn't that a thing—like whoever did all the work didn't have to do the clean-up? I thought it might apply to cooking, but surely it carried over to torture as well.

Liam nodded back, and then gave me another once over. "You can't get in the car like that," he said.

Duh. I changed into my hellhound, getting rid of the clothes and blood and everything else. Liam grunted, then he dealt with the hitman. I almost felt bad I hadn't given him a turn. He'd done all the talking, though, and he'd even gotten the man to piss himself. He had really upped his psychological torture game.

I think it was probably Quinton's influence. His mate was bloodthirsty for a human.

We got back in the car and had a quiet drive back to Paradise Falls. We hadn't found out much from the hitman. He'd been in the vicinity because Caleb Astor had told him the general area to look around. The brother had also tracked down the first two aliases that Aiden had used.

Liam had said those were the easiest to track, and then Aiden had gotten better at things, so he wasn't particularly concerned about that. The brother still had quite a few more aliases to go through, and Liam was confident that the last few were untraceable. I wasn't sure how, unless he'd killed at least one of the people who had forged the documents. If one of the later forgers was hellbound, that was probable.

The brother knowing the area where Aiden would be was a bit more troubling, though. I wondered if witches could figure that out? Corbin would have protected us all somehow, and maybe that's why the brother couldn't pin Aiden down completely. I'd have to ask Corbin some witchy questions.

Our hitman had met the brother, and he had described him as a "creepy fucker." He had seemed a little afraid of Caleb Astor, which was interesting. It also confirmed that he wasn't looking for Aiden out of the goodness of his heart. Someone who could scare a hardened hitman was not someone who did things for altruistic purposes.

We made it back in excellent time, and I was guessing Liam hadn't paid much attention to human speed limits. Then again, it wasn't like he wouldn't hear another car coming.

We made our way inside, and Corbin was sitting at the table

feeding his crow some nuts. Neither of them bothered to look up at us. I changed back into my human form, and Liam huffed before he went and grabbed me a pair of sweatpants, muttering about me being an uncultured mutt.

I grabbed them from him and put the sweatpants on before sitting down. For some reason Liam got all weird about bare asses on the furniture. He sat at another chair at the table, and Corbin finally looked up, raising his eyebrows.

"Could a witch track Aiden's location?" I asked.

His crow ruffled their feathers out, and Corbin looked pensive.

"Our hitman knew the general vicinity from Caleb Astor, but there's no reason he should have been able to track that," Liam stated. "I did a wipe of all facial recognition software that pinged for Aiden's features."

Corbin shrugged. "I have protections in place, but a strong witch or an afterlifer could more than likely find a general area. If nothing else, they could trace to where the trail disappeared and see the blackout area. Aiden did a lot of traveling, and I couldn't destroy all traces of his energy anywhere he's ever been."

Liam sighed. "Great. Not just mortals, then."

Corbin looked thoughtful. "There are witches in existence who could do it, and not everyone with extra gifts chooses to use them in the proper way. It would darken their soul to misuse those gifts, but some don't care about such things."

"What about afterlifers?" Liam asked.

"Afterlifers tend to stick to their job descriptions, but a contracted demon or guardian angel could do such things. I'm not sure why they would—they generally exert no harm on those that are not hellbound. It's a whole free will thing. Wilder would know more about that, though," Corbin said.

I perked up. Wilder was coming? I couldn't wait for him to meet my mate. That would be fun. Plus, he was a first generation hellhound, so he'd know more about the workings of the afterlifers.

Corbin's crow cawed and hopped onto his shoulder. He got up and took his leave, giving us both head nods. With that, I stood and headed into the bedroom. Liam followed. Our men were sleeping in the middle of the bed, and they barely even stirred when Liam climbed in next to Quinton and I climbed in next to Aiden. We'd probably only get an hour or so of sleep, but any cuddle time was good cuddle time.

CHAPTER 14

AIDEN

I couldn't focus. How many eggs had I added? Fuck. I stared into the mixer, mad at myself.

It was all Fluffy's fault.

It had been over a week since he and Liam apparently took care of an evil guy who was hired to find me. I didn't ask too many questions. They assured me I was safe for now and they were on top of things.

It was mildly disturbing, and I'd talked to Helene about it at my most recent session. I'd been rather vague about how they took care of it, since I hadn't asked questions, and she didn't seem inclined to get details about that part of things.

She'd then asked how things were going with the man I was interested in.

That was the distracting part. Atlas had told me I was his mate, and that he would like to have sex with me—at least I think he'd said he'd like to have sex with me? It was all a little hazy, because I'd been upset at the time, but he seemed to mean we weren't just friends.

I think.

And then... nothing. Atlas spent more time with me in human

form. He didn't talk much, but I was kind of used to that. We still took our daily walks, and he was usually Fluffy for those, which I kind of liked. I found it easier to talk to him in that form. Then every night, he cuddled me as a human, whether it was in Liam and Q's big-ass bed or in my bed.

And that was it.

No more talk of mates. No more talk of sex or kissing or... anything like that.

Then last night we stayed in my bed, and when I woke up Atlas had been all warm and cozy, his strong arms wrapped around me, and I could feel his hard dick against me. He climbed out of bed when he realized I was awake, and I couldn't help looking at the tent in his sweatpants.

He hadn't done a thing, though. Hadn't made a thing of me looking, hadn't said a word—he just headed into the shower.

So then I was thinking about him naked in the shower, and I was getting turned on. Before I could get in my head about it, he was done and standing there in a towel. A drop of water rolled down his chest, and I'd hightailed it into the shower myself.

Where I'd thought about Atlas. I'd found myself stroking my dick as I thought about his smell and his warmth and that droplet of water running down his bare chest.

I jerked off in the shower.

I didn't do that often. I knew I was all messed up from my time being held captive, and arousal gave me a sort of... icky feeling. I could ignore it sometimes and find pleasure, but sometimes I got caught up in my head, and then it was useless to try and get myself off.

I had enjoyed my orgasm, yes, but I was expecting the usual icky feeling to hit me afterwards. Only there had been some kind of ruckus going on in the kitchen. I'd stuck my head out to see Fluffy headbutting Q every time he went to take a sip of coffee, while Q threatened his life in rather creative ways and Liam insulted his doghood.

It had been kind of hysterical, and it wasn't until I was at work that I realized there had been no icky feeling. No weird guilt or sadness after my orgasm. No stomach roiling because things just felt *wrong* somehow.

Which was great. Really. Totally great. Wonderful.

But then I got stuck in my head again. Did I want to try something with Atlas? Did Atlas want to try something with me? He had said… I think he'd said that he would? But also that we didn't have to.

Did I want to? That was the question. I knew there were some things I couldn't do. Not for a long time. Maybe not ever. But other things… I would like to touch Atlas. I think I would like it if Atlas touched me. But what if I touched Atlas or he touched me, and then that icky, wrong feeling came, and I freaked out and started crying or threw up or something?

I didn't think throwing up during or after intimacy would go over well.

I turned off the mixer. I hated to waste the dough, but I had no idea what I'd added or forgotten. I was too distracted today to try new recipes.

The kitchen door flew open, and Q stalked in. He stared at me and sighed dramatically. I might worry, except that was pretty typical Q.

"So, Toby wants to talk to you," he said.

"Okay," I responded, wiping my hands on a towel. "Should I go out there?"

"No, Cass said he can come back here, but I wanted to warn you," Q said.

Warn me? Warn me of what? Toby was nice enough. We'd hung out. He'd stopped by before.

"He's going to proposition you. I already know this because he asked me. It's just hanging out, and it's not a sex thing, although he might make it sound like a sex thing, because he's awkward as fuck.

I'll go if you want to go, but if you don't, that's fine, too," Q added.

Umm, ok. We had hung out with Toby and his friends once before, so I wasn't sure what the big deal was. Q seemed to be making it a little dramatic.

He gave me one final look, then stormed out of the kitchen, and a minute later Toby walked in. He looked weirdly serious.

"Hey, Aiden," he said, giving a little half wave, even though he was like three feet away.

"Hi, Toby," I answered.

"So, I think you're a really great guy, and you're fun, and we had fun that time you came over, right?" he asked.

I nodded.

"We'd really like you to be a part of the regular group. We started with Q, because, you know, he's prickly but he definitely needed some companionship, and now he really enjoys it, I think, even though he scowls a lot and doesn't always participate. Sometimes he just sits and watches. And you can just sit and watch, too, and not participate much, but it would be awesome if you came, and we promise we won't do anything you don't want to do," Toby said.

He was nervously wringing his hands, and he looked cute in a puppy kind of way, and I could totally understand why Q had warned me that it wasn't a sex thing. Toby totally made it sound like a sex thing.

"You mean to hang out with you and your friends?" I asked.

"Oh, yeah, just you, me, Q, Josh, and Sebbie. Some of the pack stops in sometimes, but they don't get too involved," Toby answered.

"Is it dinner? Drinks? Board games? Charades?" I asked. Q had said it wasn't a sex thing, but I still wanted to know what hanging out entailed. The last time, I'd only stayed a short amount of time, and I had a feeling I wouldn't get away with that this time. This invitation was a little too formal. And yes, I ignored the "pack" comment.

"Oh, charades?" Toby said wonderingly. "I never thought of playing charades! That would be fun, don't you think?"

I smiled. "I don't think Q would be into charades."

Toby frowned. "Probably not Josh either. He's very straightlaced."

I thought Josh was strung so tight he was about to snap, and it seemed like his current relationship was pretty fucked up, but I'm sure Toby knew that. I also wasn't sure how involved I should get. I felt awkward that I gave him my number last time, and he certainly hadn't called or texted, but I felt better doing it. There was something hurt about Josh, and it reminded me of myself.

Maybe I was projecting, though. People could be quiet and serious and not have trauma. Maybe he just had a normal asshole boyfriend.

"What time? Should I eat?" I asked, because Toby still hadn't answered what we'd be doing.

"Oh, we'll have tons of snacks, and we'll order food if we're hungry, and we usually have cocktails. Q doesn't usually drink, and it's fine if you don't want to either. It's just nice to hang out and chat," Toby answered. "You can come over right after work."

Suddenly it did seem like a nice idea. How long since I had just hung out and talked with a group of people? I hadn't had any close friends since I'd left my family. Maybe this was an opportunity.

I nodded my head.

Toby smiled broadly. "I'll let Q know you guys are coming!" he said, bounding out of the kitchen.

Yeah, it would be fun. I was sure. I could leave if I wanted to. And if hanging out with Q and Toby and his friends provided a distraction from Atlas, well... no harm in that.

⊷◈⊶

Toby, Sebbie, and Josh were definitely on their way to being drunk. Josh was sprawled in an armchair looking relaxed and happy, and Toby and Sebbie were dancing around the living room to Beatles songs. Jude was apparently our babysitter, but he was mostly staying out back and out of our way. The other guys had apparently gone to do some work, and I figured I was better off not knowing the details.

I had a cocktail, too, although Q hadn't. I wasn't sure I would have drank anything if he did, but I knew he would look out for me. Look out for all of us, really. Not that I didn't trust Toby, Sebbie, and Josh, because I did. They were good people. Nice people.

I hadn't had alcohol in a long time, and I had a pleasant, warm, happy feeling. I wouldn't drink more—getting tipsy wasn't on my agenda—but I was glad I'd come to hang out. No one crowded me or asked me to do anything, and it was all very low pressure and gossipy.

Q looked a little like he was being tortured, but every so often a smirk would cross his face, and I knew he was amused by their antics. Toby occasionally rambled on about his sexy stalker being a hellhound and how they killed people, but only bad people. I had asked what exactly hellhounds were, and Toby had been all too willing to fill me in.

I wondered about him being so forthcoming in front of Sebbie and Josh, but they seemed to think he was just talking about his latest book, which was kind of comical. In the meantime, I got a nice education on everything I might have wanted to know (and maybe some things I didn't, because Toby could get gory).

"And the knots..." Toby murmured dreamily. He looked at Q. "Right, Q?"

Q scowled at him, and I think he might have blushed a bit, which made me really curious about "the knots."

"New dildo?" Josh asked, because somehow he and Sebbie still didn't know that there was weird shit in the world.

"I wish I was having sex," Sebbie muttered, throwing himself on the couch. "If people would just stop dying for a few days, maybe I could get laid."

"Aww, don't worry, Sebbie, I'm sure you'll find your man one of these days. How about Jude? He doesn't mind a little death," Toby answered.

"Don't get your hopes up on Jude," Q muttered.

I kind of agreed. Jude had that weird obsession with the sheriff.

"I haven't had sex in ages," Sebbie grumbled.

"Good sex is hard to find and keep," Josh said, raising his glass in a toast.

I didn't think that comment boded well for his relationship.

Then my mouth was opening, and I was talking without even processing what I was saying. "How do you even know when you want to have sex when you're in a relationship?"

I turned red as soon as I asked, and I regretted the drink I'd had. It had gone more to my head than I'd imagined. What a stupid question. Was I even in a relationship with Atlas? And who didn't know when they were ready to have sex?

Only no one treated it like it was a stupid question.

"Well, they gotta make you horny," Toby answered. "Like, not all the time, but at least some of the time. Dexter totally makes me horny."

"We know," Q snorted.

"You should trust the person," Josh said to me, looking serious. "At least if you're looking for intimacy. If you aren't comfortable with them outside the bedroom, you won't feel comfortable inside the bedroom."

"They shouldn't run away if someone dies around you," Sebbie added.

Everyone stared at him for a moment, and then Josh translated, "Yeah, like if they don't stick by you through tough stuff, then they aren't worth it."

Everyone nodded their heads, including me. It was true.

"I'm never going to find a boyfriend," Sebbie lamented, sprawling out across the couch and almost tipping his drink over in the process.

Josh, who was definitely tipsy himself, still managed to grab it in time, and they both laughed.

"More drinks!" Toby cried, rushing off to get more alcohol.

While they were refilling, Q got up and came over, throwing an arm around me. "You have to be able to talk about it," he said quietly. "I don't think he'll ever bring it up. He'll leave it up to you, you know. But I see the way he looks at you."

I took a deep breath. That was the problem. I didn't particularly want to talk about it. Although maybe I needed to. I didn't know.

"You ready to head out and leave these tipsy fools to their mayhem?" Q asked me.

We both looked to see Toby and Sebbie giggling over something on Toby's phone, while Josh tried to look disapproving. He was such a big brother type. I still felt like something was off, but maybe I was imagining it. Not everyone had trauma, after all.

"It was a fun night," I told Q, still a little surprised at that.

"Yeah, it was. Our men are home, though—Liam texted me. I'm gonna meet him in his office in the main house to do some 'research,'" Q said, smirking and wiggling his eyebrows.

I laughed. I knew that was code for having some wild sex, and that was fine. We said our goodbyes to the guys.

Toby tried to get us to stay, but we managed to escape his good intentions. Josh quietly said "Thanks" to me as we were parting ways, and I couldn't help but think it was about more than just the fun evening.

We made our way back to our little back house, and Liam and Atlas were waiting outside the front door. Liam and Q made noise about 'working' and hustled off, and I just stared at Atlas for a minute. He really was so beautiful, standing there in the moonlight. He was kind and sweet and protective.

I walked forward, and without letting myself think, I kissed Atlas.

His lips were warm and soft, and I pressed mine against his and waited.

And then waited some more.

Then I opened my eyes, our lips still pressed together. His eyes were also open, and there was fire in them, I swear. I leaned in and pressed my lips harder against his, and I felt the bulge in his pants against me. He was definitely turned on.

But he wasn't doing anything.

I pulled back. He was looking at me all serious like, and he reached his hands up to hold lightly onto my arms. I knew with a simple shrug he would let go right away.

"I kissed you," I said, feeling a little stupid.

Atlas nodded. He was staring at my mouth, and he licked his lips. I struggled to focus, because this was... weird.

He was turned on. He seemed very much like a guy who wanted to kiss. Only he didn't seem to know what to do with me. Was it because I'd had trauma? Was he afraid he was going to break me or something if he kissed me back? I felt my heart drop for a moment, because Atlas had *never* treated me like a victim. Why would he start now? But why else would he be so freaking awkward?

And then I had a rather shocking thought.

"Atlas, have you ever kissed anyone before?" I asked.

His eyes moved up to mine, and he gave a grunt and a half shrug.

I just stared at him, because that was not an answer.

He must have realized it, because he said, "Sex never seemed to matter much. I have experience, though."

And I guess that was all I was getting. What did that even mean?

"What do you want to do?" I asked, because maybe that was an easier question. "Um, assuming you want to do anything with me," I added.

I blushed, because what the fuck. Blurting for the win, I guess. I stalked forward and went into the house, and Atlas followed behind me. I wasn't going to have this conversation outside, and it seemed like it was going to be a conversation.

I threw myself onto the couch, maybe a tad bit dramatically—I think Toby and Sebbie rubbed off on me—and I stared at Atlas, waiting for him to answer. He was standing there looking all puppy dog cute, and I could see his pants were tented with his hard on, which was even more confusing, because I was aggravated but also turned on.

"No making Fluffy eyes at me. What do you want? Do you want to have sex with me? I don't want any secrets. I want to know," I declared, feeling braver than normal. Better to know, right?

His eyes burned bright for a moment, and there were definitely flames in them. He knelt down in front of the couch, putting him more even with my line of sight. He placed his hands lightly on my thighs.

"I want to touch you everywhere, rub my hands across your skin, and learn your body like it's my own. I want to taste you all over. I want to lick your skin, every inch of it, and surround myself with your scent until that's all there is. I want to suck on your balls, and lick back to your hole and taste you there. I want to suck your cock into my mouth until I get a taste of your precum. I can see you moaning and writhing in pleasure, and I want you to grab onto my arms so tightly that I'll have marks from your touch."

Fuck.

My dick was hard, and the look in Atlas's eyes... intense didn't even begin to cover it.

"Atlas," I breathed out.

Atlas looked at me, then he leaned up and pressed his lips to mine. I opened my mouth to him, but still he didn't push. I let my tongue lick along his lips, and I groaned at the taste of him. He was intoxicating. It was like my tongue gave him permission, because he was licking along my lips then, too, a low rumbling sound coming from his chest. I tentatively licked into his mouth, and his tongue met mine.

I slid off the couch and onto his lap, my arms wrapping around him, our mouths slanting against each other. When I broke away to breathe, he kissed along my neck, sending goose-bumps shivering along my skin. I was horny, and I was going to have sex.

And with that thought, I was nervous. I told myself it was ok. It was Atlas. I didn't have to do anything I didn't want to. He would let me take the lead. That was fine. I could take the lead. I had taken the lead before with... Taking the lead was fine, and I ignored the weird swoop in my stomach.

I slid my hand down toward his pants, but his hand grabbed mine, stopping me. He leaned his head against my neck, sniffing lightly.

He linked his fingers with mine, and I felt like crying. I had no idea why.

He rumbled against me, taking deep breaths in and out until I was naturally breathing with him. We sat like that for a few minutes, until I felt more even again.

Maybe I couldn't take the lead like that, because it had been a sort of triggering memory. I sighed.

"Cuddles," Atlas murmured.

I nodded. Yes. Cuddles were exactly what I needed. I *wanted* everything else he had said, but maybe tonight wasn't the night for it. I still felt better, though, knowing that Atlas had somehow known and hadn't let me continue. Maybe he had smelled my nervousness, because according to Toby hellhounds could smell all sorts of things.

I pulled back and looked into his eyes. There were still flames in them.

"I want that. I want what you said, and I don't want to wait forever. I won't let what happened ruin things for me," I insisted.

"I know you won't, but we don't need to rush, either," Atlas said, and then he stood up, picking me up with him. "Now tell me about your night."

I may have given a little squawk in surprise, and then a little giggle as he carried me into the bedroom. Then I did what he asked and told him about the guys as we got ready for bed. By the time we were crawling under the covers and Atlas was wrapped around me, any funky feelings were long gone.

Atlas was right. We had time. I could always seduce him tomorrow. With that thought in my head and a smile on my face, I let myself drift off to sleep.

CHAPTER 15

ATLAS/FLUFFY

Aiden was snuggled up in my arms, his head buried in my chest, but he was starting to stir a bit. I had been awake, enjoying the feel of him in my arms, and I wondered if I should get up when he woke. That tended to be our routine, but something had changed last night, and I wasn't sure what it meant.

Liam and Quinton hadn't come back to the house. Liam had let me know they were staying in the main house, because Quinton seemed to think that Aiden and I were going to have sex. I wasn't sure if Aiden had said something or not, but it seemed like that might have been his plan.

He had kissed me, and it had taken everything in me to hold back and not maul him. I wanted to let him lead things, though. But then he'd gotten all sorts of nervous—I could smell it on him —so maybe that wasn't the right course of action.

Talk, Fluffy grumbled.

I breathed a sigh. Yeah, I supposed this probably required some conversation. I didn't want Aiden to get upset, and if I didn't ask what would upset him, then I couldn't avoid doing it. Usually Aiden told me everything that was on his mind, but last night he had smelled off, and yet he had reached down to touch me anyway. He hadn't told me what bothered him.

I didn't want Aiden to do something he felt bad about.

I knew that he had touched his captor, and maybe it had reminded him of that? Or maybe something about the kissing had made him feel bad? The problem was that I had no idea.

I growled a little in frustration, and Aiden lazily patted my chest.

"No growls, Fluffy," he muttered sleepily.

Then his hand went from patting to rubbing, and he pushed his hips into me. I could feel his hard cock, and I was sure he could feel mine. I sniffed at his neck, and he shivered. He smelled aroused and content and happy—no sour note to his scent.

"My mate," I rumbled, because I felt the need to say it.

"Mmm," Aiden said, and he somehow got even closer to me, so we were pressed full body against one another. I growled at the feeling of his shirt against my bare skin, because I wanted skin. He seemed to know, because he scooched back and pulled his shirt over his head, then I felt him pushing his sweats down under the covers. "You too," he said sleepily.

He didn't need to tell me twice. I pushed my sweats down and kicked them off frantically, and Aiden ended up chuckling at the ruckus under the covers. He seemed to want to stay under the blanket, so I wasn't going to disrespect that, but my legs flailing under the sheets to get the sweatpants off probably did look comical.

When we were both naked, he scooched closer to me again, and I grabbed onto him, holding him close. His skin was warm and soft against mine, and I sniffed his neck again, which made him groan. He still smelled aroused, maybe a bit amused, and happy. I held him close, our bodies pressed tightly together, his head pressing into my chest.

If all he wanted was to lay together, skin to skin, I would be happy. Then I felt a tiny lick against my nipple. It was like a butterfly touch, it was so light, yet I rumbled in approval anyway.

That seemed to spur Aiden on, because he did it again, licking my nipple more thoroughly.

I couldn't help pushing my hips forward, and our cocks were perfectly aligned to rub up against each other. I stopped myself from doing it again, but Aiden made a whining, plaintive sound, so I pushed forward.

He smelled so good, like sunshine and warm afternoons in the forest, with a musky tinge that signaled how turned on he was.

I thrust forward again, and he met me, our cocks rubbing together, the heads catching each other and sending tingles through me. It was exquisite, and Aiden met my next thrust, too, making that whining sound again. I sniffed at his neck, and I couldn't help biting down a tiny bit.

He bucked against me, moaning in pleasure, rutting his hips against me faster. I bit harder, and he cried out. I grabbed his ass in my hands to help us grind against one another. Pleasure sparked through me, and Aiden's little sounds and his smell only made everything more intense.

"Atlas!" Aiden cried out, and I could sense a level of frustration in that cry. Our cocks rubbing together felt amazing, but I knew it wouldn't be enough to drive us over the edge. I wanted Aiden to come apart in my arms. I wanted to give him pleasure.

I pulled back from where my head was nestled in Aiden's neck, and I reached down between us to grab both our cocks in my hand. Aiden looked at me, and the smell of his arousal grew stronger. I was sure there were flames in my eyes, and there was no way to make them go away.

"Let me give you pleasure, Aiden. Can I make you come? Can I make you feel good?" I asked.

"Yes!" Aiden cried out, bucking against me again.

I tightened my hand, sliding it up and down our cocks, the heads bumping, the precum we were both dripping making the slide silky and smooth.

"Do you like that, mate? Do you like my hands on you?" I asked.

"Oh god, Atlas. It feels so good," he moaned.

I sped up, squeezing and twisting my hand at the top, frantically pumping. I leaned my forehead down against his.

"I love being so close to you. I love your smell. I want to be covered in your cum. I want to taste you, mate," I murmured. "Would you like that?"

"God, Atlas, yes. Yes," he panted.

His arms gripped onto my shoulders, pressing tightly, and I rumbled in pleasure.

"I want you to mark me. I'm all yours. Anything you want. I'll give you anything you want," I whispered.

"Atlas!" he cried out, and he reached his lips up to kiss me, frantically tasting me and nipping at my mouth as I did the same. His body was thrusting against me, his breath was heaving, and I felt his warm cum coat my hand as he came on a cry, our mouths still pressed together.

It was my undoing. Feeling him release onto me, smelling his cum—I couldn't hold back, and my own orgasm washed over me. I pressed my forehead against his, slowing down to milk the last of our release. When Aiden gave a soft sigh, I stopped moving my hand.

I didn't want to let our dicks go, though. We felt so good together in my hand.

Aiden opened his eyes and looked at me, a small smile on his face.

"Can I clean you up?" I asked him.

"Yeah," he said, still smelling warm and soft and sated.

I ducked down under the covers and licked at our release against Aiden's stomach, despite him giving a funny little yelp of surprise. He didn't smell upset, though, and his dick twitched, valiantly making an effort to rise again. I grumbled happily at his taste, and his hand reached under the covers to grab me. He didn't pull me up, though. He threaded his fingers through my hair and caressed my head.

I licked him clean and grabbed my sweatpants at the bottom of the bed to wipe myself off, then I came out from under the covers, smiling.

"You taste good," I murmured, drawing him into my arms again.

"That wasn't what I expected when you asked to clean me up," Aiden murmured, but he didn't sound upset.

I kissed his forehead, rubbing my hands against his back as he burrowed into my chest.

We laid like that for a few minutes, but I sensed Aiden starting to get restless. I loosened my arms and looked down at him.

"Talk," I said. Probably not the most well phrased, but Aiden seemed to know what I meant.

"So, that was good," he said. "I mean, that was great!" he hurried to add. "Like, really great! I liked that. A lot. And there were no icky feelings."

"There were icky feelings last night," I said, because that must have been the sour note I smelled on him.

Aiden sighed. "Yeah, there were."

"Why?" I asked. "What made the icky feelings? I won't do whatever it was again."

That seemed like an easy question to me, but Aiden sighed again, burrowing into my chest and rubbing against me before he muttered, "It isn't that simple."

"Explain," I said, then remembered to tack on a "Please."

Aiden laughed a bit, then he rolled onto his back. He got comfortable and rested his head on my shoulder. He seemed to be thinking. That was ok. Sometimes words were hard, and I cuddled next to him while he put his thoughts in order.

"Helene is always telling me to give myself grace and be kind to myself, and that healing doesn't magically happen. I liked kissing you last night. I was nervous that kissing might be a trigger for me, but it wasn't. I guess when I didn't know what to do next, that became kind of a trigger. When I was kidnapped... He would hint at what he wanted, and I knew what I was supposed to do, or else I'd get punished, so I did it," Aiden said.

I couldn't help the growling low in my chest, but Aiden just pet me softly.

"So it was like I was taking control, even though I had no control? I don't know if that explains it well. But I think that I was thinking I needed to do something or you'd get mad, even though I know you wouldn't get mad, but that feeling is sort of ingrained in me.

"And I guess this is where giving myself grace comes in. I guess anyone who is going to be with me is going to need to give me grace, too. I won't always know what will trigger me. You stopped right away, because you sensed something was wrong. Maybe that'll always work, or maybe I'll want to talk through it, or maybe I'll just want to switch gears and keep on doing something. I don't want my ick feelings to be an automatic end to an intimate moment, because sometimes I may have them, and sometimes I might want to push past them."

I nodded my head. "I will always give you grace, my mate. You just need to tell me what you need, especially if I'm not giving it to you." I leaned down to kiss his forehead.

"Yeah, that's hard sometimes, but I'll try. I really liked that you sort of asked me about what you were going to do before you did it today. That was nice. Like I knew I could show hesitance or ask to do something else. I liked that we were naked, too. Maybe that's weird, but a lot of times I was fully clothed when... Well, you know, and I think being fully clothed weirdly makes me feel like I'm not important or not powerful or something. I don't know. He was mostly clothed a lot of times, too. Like I just undid his pants and..." Aiden trailed off and sighed.

I squeezed him tightly and kissed his forehead again, not wanting him to get lost in those bad memories. I said, "I love being naked with you. I will always be naked with you if you want."

He laughed at that. "Well, maybe not always, but I feel like it helped. *You* helped, Atlas. And I'm sorry that I may get weird sometimes, but—"

I cut him off. "Don't ever apologize. You are strong and amazing and beautiful, and you give me so much. I wouldn't want anything else in a mate but you. You're perfect for me."

Aiden sniffed at that, but I didn't smell sadness, so we held each other, snuggling and enjoying our skin touching.

⁂

Aiden and Quinton had off today, so we were able to snuggle in bed until Aiden's stomach growled. He and Quinton must have been on the same breakfast schedule, because not a minute later I heard Quinton rather loudly talking as he walked up to the house.

"Hopefully they're ready for company, although I still think we should have texted first," Quinton said.

He was talking to Liam and... Jude, by the smell of it. I heard a caw and realized Corbin was with them too—sometimes he could disguise his scent as well.

Oh, goody. Almost the whole gang. I sighed as the door banged open loudly and Quinton called out a greeting.

Aiden just chuckled, though, getting out of bed and putting sweatpants and a t-shirt on.

Don't want clothes, Fluffy growled, and I sighed in resignation.

People meant clothes. Very annoying.

Aiden was looking at me and smiling, almost like he knew what I was thinking. "Breakfast, then our morning walk?" he asked.

We always took our morning walk with me in Fluffy form, so rather than get dressed, I changed into my hound form.

Aiden grinned at me, so I knew it was ok, and I followed him out of the bedroom, where the pack was waiting in the kitchen area. Jude had already started cooking, and Aiden grumbled about him not messing up his kitchen organization as he went over to help.

Corbin and his crow were sitting at the table, Quinton was putting plates and silverware out, and Liam was, as usual, glued to his computer.

I walked over next to Corbin, sitting down and giving a head nod to his crow. The crow nodded back at me, pushing a peanut over for me. I knew better than to refuse a crow gift, so I took it from the edge of the table with my mouth, much to Corbin's amusement.

"We're going to need to build another cabin, I think," Corbin said quietly to me.

I tilted my head at him.

"And the one we built will need a bedroom door," he added.

I gave a low rumble of disagreement. Aiden didn't like bedroom doors.

"I don't think you and Aiden will be staying there," Corbin said. I could see that Liam was listening intently, despite staring at his computer. Jude was busy chatting with Quinton and Aiden, though, and I knew the humans couldn't hear Corbin's low voice.

"I think Quinton and Liam will eventually take the main house, and Aiden likes this space and is comfortable in it," Corbin said.

I thought that over. He wasn't wrong. Aiden did love this little house, and he was happy here. I had assumed Liam and Quinton would stay here and we'd sometimes want our own space, but last night Quinton and Liam had stayed at the main house. Aiden had liked the cabin and thought it was beautiful, but I hadn't sensed a strong desire for him to make it his home.

If Corbin wanted to stay in the cabin in order to get away from Jude, since they were both sharing Dexter's old house, I could totally understand that. Jude was pack, but he was also annoying as hell. But that still didn't explain why we needed another cabin.

"Someone else will need the cabin," Corbin explained, "and eventually Jude and I will want our own spaces, so I'll need a cabin too. Not too close to the existing structures."

Huh. I wondered vaguely who would need the cabin. Did he mean Wilder? Wilder usually liked to stay with the pack, so I thought he would stay with Jude and Corbin when he got here, but if this town was going to be a more permanent home, perhaps Wilder would need his own space.

With that thought, the guys started bringing over breakfast, and Aiden set a plate of bacon and eggs on a chair so it was at my level. I gave him a doggy grin and dug in as the rest of the pack sat and started eating. Quinton and Aiden were discussing something about a yoga class, Corbin was eating and feeding his crow, Jude was humming under his breath as he ate, and Liam was clicking away on his computer, taking a bite every now and then.

Happy, Fluffy rumbled, and I agreed. We were with our pack, and everyone was content. If we stayed in this house, that was fine with me. I was happy to live anywhere, as long as Aiden was with me. He was my home.

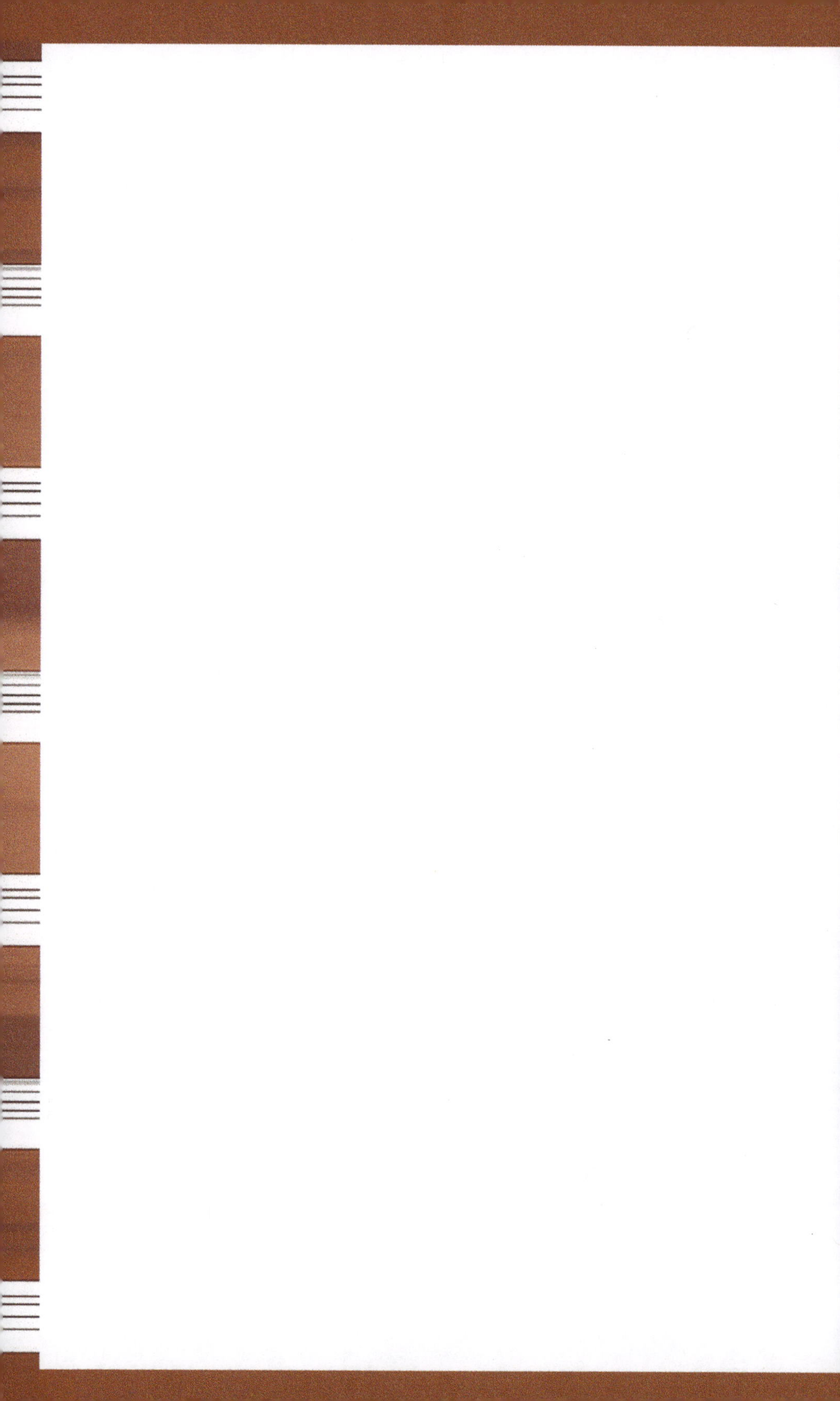

CHAPTER 16

AIDEN

"Are you sure about this?" I asked Q.

"Little late not to be sure," he muttered.

He was probably right, since we were already sitting on yoga mats in the studio. New age music was playing, incense was burning, the lights were dim, and the room was warm but not hot—I didn't think I was ready to jump into hot yoga, and I thought Q might kill me if I made him do that.

The studio was a good size, and we were spaced far apart from everyone else, with Q and I taking positions in the back. It was supposedly a good class for beginners, and since it had been ages since I'd done yoga, and Q had never done it, it seemed like a good fit for us.

It had been a bit of a spur of the moment decision, but since we had off today, Q had said we should take a class. Helene had been telling me to get back into things I enjoyed, and yoga had been one of them. Jude had driven us, because the rest of the guys had gone to work on some construction project.

I thought Atlas's cabin was pretty much done, but maybe not. I hoped he wasn't planning on moving. I really liked him in bed next to me every night. Of course, he might want his own space, which I totally understood. That didn't mean I liked it, but I also didn't need to be codependent. So what if I was already codependent with Q? Ok, I was probably codependent with Fluffy as well. Maybe I needed to try to be more independent? I didn't want to annoy anyone.

My slight spiral was broken by the sound of a singing bowl, and the instructor guided us into Padmasana and began some breathing exercises. It was calming, and I felt the tension slip from my body and the thoughts slip from my mind.

By the time we had done some stretching and breathing and were starting on a flow, I felt loose and limber and relaxed. I breathed deep, enjoying the warmth in my body and the feeling of my muscles working. I looked over at Q, who had good form in the warrior pose. He saw me looking, and made a face. I raised my eyebrows.

"I'm just standing here. Why the fuck does it hurt so much?" he whispered.

I smirked in amusement. The instructor moved us into another position, and I heard Q mutter, "Finally."

He lasted about thirty seconds before he whispered, "Shit. This is worse. My legs are shaking."

I tried not to laugh, although a little chuckle did escape me. Thank goodness the music was loud enough to cover his complaining.

We were both sweating by the time the instructor moved us down to the mats for some work, and Q whispered, "Thank god."

I couldn't help smirking again. I assumed he thought mat work would be easier. By the time we were in boat pose, Q was cursing quietly under his breath again.

"Fuck this breathing into my core. My core is dead. I'm dying," he muttered.

I chuckled, trying to sober my face when the instructor walked by. We ended up in waterfall pose after that, and when the instructor started guiding us into plough pose, I almost started laughing again before Q even said anything. He didn't disappoint me.

"What the fuck? Is this how guys can suck their own dicks? My body does *not* bend that way," he whispered.

I couldn't help the giggle that I tried to cover with a cough. I was smiling as I moved into plough.

"Holy fuck, Aiden—you probably could suck your own dick. Have you tried?" Q whispered. "And how am I supposed to breathe all scrunched up like this?" he asked.

The woman next to him must have heard him, because she looked over and muttered, "Try it with boobs. I feel like they're about to suffocate me."

That was it. I broke position, laughing and coughing to cover it. I took a drink of water to try and get my shit together, but Q and the woman were both grinning mischievously as the instructor looked over at us.

When the instructor told everyone to take a pose that spoke to them in the moment, Q just looked around disbelievingly.

"That person is balancing their whole body on their arms, which are on their knees. And what the fuck is that? Pretzel pose? I don't think the human back is supposed to bend like that," he muttered, looking around.

"That's crow pose, eight-angle pose, and scorpion. Here, try happy baby," I whispered, showing him that one.

"Fuck yeah," he said. "I can do happy baby."

The woman next to us laughed again, and I was still smiling when the instructor led us into Savasana.

"I can definitely be a corpse," Q muttered, making both me and the woman laugh.

I was able to clear my mind and focus on my breathing, and when we did our namaste at the end, I was really thankful for the experience. Everyone was stretching and rolling up their mats.

Q muttered, "A little woo woo at the end there."

The woman next to us came over, chuckling. Q turned a little pink. "Sorry if I was distracting," he apologized.

"Nah, this was probably the most fun I've had in yoga class in awhile," she answered. "I'm Seraphina, but Ser works," she said, putting her hand out. Q shook it and then I did too.

"It was my first yoga class in a while, but I like the studio," I said.

"Yeah, there are some great instructors here. You guys have to tell me when you're coming back—I'll come to class just for your commentary," she said, looking at Q and smiling.

Q groaned. "You mean I have to come back? I don't think I'll be able to walk tomorrow."

Both Ser and I laughed, and we chatted as we finished packing up and headed out. She saw Jude waiting for us outside the car, and she gave a hum of approval.

"He's probably taken. He's slightly obsessed with this one guy," Q said, following her eyes.

Ser sighed. "All the cute men and women are taken. My brothers are both mated to cute guys, and I suppose I've been getting the bug to settle down, too."

I liked that she made it clear she was LGBTQ+ friendly, but I thought her word choice was odd—I didn't think I'd heard anyone but the hellhounds use the word mate before. She walked us over to the car, and Jude gave her a head nod, which was also a little weird. He seemed almost respectful, which was not typical for Jude.

Ser exchanged numbers with us, and we promised to meet up for another yoga class, despite Q's sour face, which just made me and Ser both laugh.

"We're totally going to be friends. I can tell," she announced happily, and then she was off to her own car.

I felt good as I got into the car. I had enjoyed the yoga, I had made a friend, and I had stepped out of my comfort zone and done something new. Yeah, I'd had Q with me, but even if Q didn't want to go again, I felt like I could take a class with Ser.

"Did you know her?" I asked Jude as we were driving.

"Oh, no, not really. She's Nephilim, though, and she's a really good soul," he answered.

"What?" I asked, confused.

"You're fucking kidding me," Q muttered. "You're saying angel offspring are a thing?"

"Well, angel and demon offspring are both Nephilim, but their origins don't determine whether they're good or evil or anything. I'm guessing she's got angelic ancestry, and that group can be really uptight, but she seems pretty awesome. I'm sure you'll be safe hanging out with her. She's a good soul," he repeated.

It was a little too much to wrap my brain around, and I refrained from asking questions the rest of the way home.

When we started up the drive to the houses, Jude said, "All the guys are at Toby and Dexter's having a bite to eat after working on the new cabin. You guys want to head there, or you want to head home?"

I appreciated that he asked, and I looked over at Q. I was ok with more people time, but I wasn't sure if he was.

He just sighed. "Fine, but Toby better not be weird."

Jude laughed, pulling up to Toby's house. "I don't think Toby can *not* be weird."

<hr>

Toby was indeed weird, but it was sort of endearing. He was awkward and super excited we had come over for dinner. Yeah, maybe it was a little odd that he asked about blood splatter while we ate spaghetti (and even flicked some sauce on his shirt to demonstrate —that was gonna be a pain to wash out). I tried to tune out Dexter's enthusiastic answer about blood viscosity and spray patterns.

I didn't want to know how he knew.

Still, it was kind of nice to hang out with everyone. Liam, Dexter, Corbin, Atlas, and Jude were all pretty funny as they teased and harassed each other, and it made me think about just how cold my relationship with my own brother had been.

There hadn't been much joking around or teasing with Caleb, or even the familiarity that the guys had with one another. I always thought it was our age difference, but I realized now how detached he had been. Maybe it was our upbringing and being so focused on appearances, but it solidified that he probably wasn't looking for me out of any sense of love. What these guys had was love; what my brother and I had was... I don't even know. Responsibility? Obligation? I had a few good memories, but there weren't many.

Atlas stuck close to my side and remained silent as usual, and the guys just took it in stride, occasionally teasing him. I thought I might feel weird, since Toby and Q were both mates with hellhounds, but the guys didn't treat me any differently than them. Of course, Atlas had said I was his mate, but I still wasn't sure what to even think about that.

We'd been intimate, and it had been really good. Did I want to be intimate with him again? Yeah, I totally did. Did it hurt in my chest to think of him not being with me? Yeah, it totally did. Was that what it meant to be mates? I didn't know. Maybe I'd ask Q or Toby.

We were cleaning up when the guys all stopped what they were doing and looked toward the door in unison. It was kind of creepy. Liam walked over to his computer, fiddled with it, and sighed. Jude looked over Liam's shoulder, and a wide grin split his face.

"Koo koo kachoo," Jude said gleefully.

I guessed we were about to have a visit from the sheriff. I tried not to tense up. The sheriff was nice. He was a good guy.

Q pointed a wooden spoon he'd been washing at Jude. "Don't you fucking start," he hissed.

"Aww, he likes me!" Jude smiled.

I felt the collective sigh of everyone in the room, and then I heard the doorbell ring. It felt a bit like a bad movie as we all moved toward the door. Because, you know, it didn't look at all suspicious if everyone in the house went to greet the guy. When I turned around to make sure Atlas was with me, I saw Fluffy in his place, and he trotted forward and leaned against me.

Maybe I wasn't the only one who didn't want to deal with talking to the sheriff.

When we got to the door, Toby and Jude were having a bit of a shoving match as to who got to open it. Dexter growled low in his throat, and Jude huffed and let Toby open the door.

"Sheriff!" Toby said, giving a little wave, then putting his hands behind his back. "We were just finishing dinner. Spaghetti!"

He looked down at his shirt, then back up at the sheriff. "Just spaghetti sauce! Haha. We weren't talking about blood pattern stains or anything."

"Although feel free to use your handcuffs on me," Jude murmured.

Dexter smacked him in the back of the head, and the sheriff ignored him completely.

"Writing a murder mystery, Toby?" the sheriff asked.

Toby smiled and nodded. "Yup! Lots of blood splatter in this one!"

"I can't wait to read it," the sheriff said. Then he stood there, looking expectantly at us.

"Oh! Do you wanna come in? We were just gonna have some cookies for dessert," Toby finally asked.

"I'll be happy to provide the milk," Jude muttered, and this time it was Liam who smacked his arm.

I think I saw the sheriff roll his eyes too, but he walked in. Everyone sort of spread out, either lounging on the couch, sitting at the table, or leaning against the kitchen island. I sat on the couch, and Fluffy sat directly in front of me. I noticed that Liam had an arm wrapped around Q, and Dexter was half standing in front of Toby. I thought they trusted the sheriff, but... I didn't know. There was a weird sort of tension in the air now that we were all inside.

I looked back at the sheriff, and he was standing in front of the couch and staring at me. I reached my hand out and rested it against Fluffy's head.

Why was he staring at me? I took a deep breath, trying to relax. Fluffy growled, sensing my tension. Or maybe the sheriff's tension. I didn't even know.

"Quite the guard dog you got there," the sheriff said.

"He's friendly. Unless someone tries to hurt me," I said. I felt like I was making a threat, and it was probably unwise to sort of threaten the sheriff, but something was off about this visit.

"What's going on, Walrus?" Jude asked, and all the joking was gone from his voice, despite the nickname.

The sheriff ignored him and pulled a paper out of his pocket. He unfolded it slowly, and then he reached over and held it out to me.

I didn't want to take it. I didn't know why, but I didn't want to look. The sheriff just stood there, holding it and watching me. I reached my hand out despite my misgivings, and then I looked down.

It was a picture of me. It was old—probably from my last year in boarding school based on the uniform and my age. I felt a little dizzy, and Fluffy licked my face and then looked at the sheriff and growled.

Liam came over and looked over my shoulder, and I heard him mutter a curse under his breath. I wasn't sure if the sheriff heard it or not.

"Where did you get that?" Liam asked.

At his tone, Jude, Dexter, and Corbin all wandered over and looked over the couch to see the picture as well.

"Aww, you guys, we can't kill the sheriff. He's so cute! And he's my Walrus!" Jude whined.

It seemed to break some of the tension, because the sheriff snorted. Only I didn't think Jude was joking.

"Explain," Liam demanded again.

The sheriff sighed. "As far as I can tell, that was emailed to every sheriff and chief of police in the state. It's a supposed kidnapping that is apparently being looked into by the FBI. The email address it comes from is legit, but curiously enough no one else in the FBI seems to know about it."

Liam grunted, going and grabbing his computer.

"Then there's the fact that there's no name with the photo," the sheriff continued, "yet there are identifying features, including a current age and birthday. If they know that, why wouldn't they give the name? The instructions are very specific as well—we are not to engage. We are to inform the FBI agent of the missing person's whereabouts.

"If they know this person is in danger, wouldn't they want them taken into custody immediately? If they're a threat, we would be told to treat them as such. We're just supposed to inform this one particular agent and go about our business."

Liam was frantically typing on his computer. "Yup. Three states total—all sheriffs or police chiefs as well as dispatch got the email."

The sheriff snorted. "Amanda quit last week, so I've been managing the general email account as well."

"Aw, you need some help in the office, Walrus? I'm good at following orders," Jude said, winking.

The sheriff ignored him, saying, "I came to the conclusion that although it bears a striking resemblance to Aiden here, it certainly can't be him, since he obviously isn't a kidnapped person. Still, I thought you guys should know that someone is out there disseminating pictures of someone who bears a resemblance to Aiden."

I was still just holding the picture and staring at it, not really seeing it. The FBI? Three states worth of police agencies looking for me? What the fuck?

Fluffy leaned against me more firmly, and Jude came and took the paper gently out of my hand. I wrapped my arms around Fluffy, burying my head in his fur.

"Hmm, it does look like Aiden," Jude said. "I mean, of course there's an explanation for all this. We're all actually supernatural beings—hellhounds, to be exact—and although Aiden *was* a kidnapped person, we actually rescued him ages ago and killed his psycho stalker. But now his probably psychotic brother is looking for him for reasons unknown. Don't worry, though, because if he's truly evil we'll dispose of him in the torture basement. If he's not evil, which is kind of doubtful at this point if he's bribing FBI agents, then we'll see a happy family reunion."

Everyone was quiet, and I looked up at Jude and the sheriff, my mouth open.

The sheriff was staring at Jude, and he finally muttered, "You're such an asshole."

"Aww, Macca, that's so sweet!" Jude said, actually looking gleeful at the insult.

The sheriff huffed. "My last name is not McCartney, I am not your Walrus, and I don't know how these guys put up with you."

Jude winked at him. "Don't worry, baby—in my life, I love you more."

"Aren't I a rich man," the sheriff muttered, rolling his eyes.

Jude pretended to swoon at that, grabbing his chest and yelling, "He loves me, yeah, yeah, yeah."

Most of the guys chuckled, and the sheriff even cracked a smile. It released the tension, and Toby clapped his hands, asking who wanted cookies.

Everyone started milling about, but I stayed on the couch, arms wrapped around Fluffy. I couldn't stop thinking about the picture.

"Aiden?" the sheriff said softly.

I looked up at him again, holding Fluffy tightly. His eyes were kind, though. They weren't dead or evil eyes. I could see that.

"If you ever need anything..." the sheriff said, trailing off.

"I'm ok. I'm with my family," I replied.

The sheriff looked thoughtful for a moment, then he looked around at all the guys bustling about. They looked busy and were chatting, and yet I knew that all of them had an ear and an eye on our conversation. They would protect me if they needed to.

"I see that," he finally said, nodding at me. "You stay safe, and call if you need me."

With that, he said his goodbyes, despite everyone insisting he have some cookies. Jude made some more flirtatious comments, and the sheriff said something back, but I was too focused on thinking about the damn picture.

What the hell did my brother want? Why was he looking for me?

I was afraid I couldn't hide from him much longer.

CHAPTER 17

ATLAS/FLUFFY

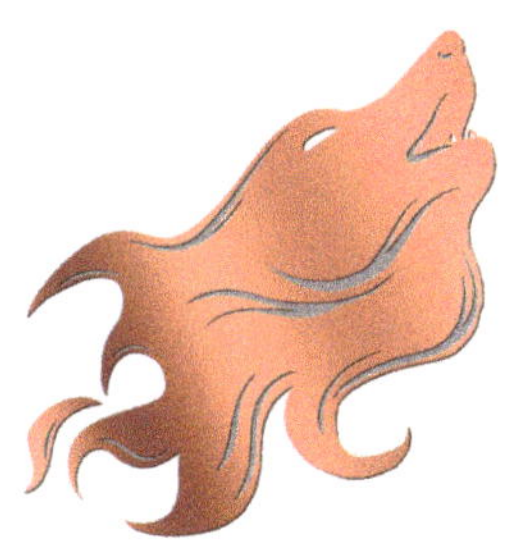

Liam did his best to intercept as many of the FBI emails as possible, and after some research, Corbin went on a little field trip to the FBI office where the agent who sent them was based. I was looking forward to Corbin bringing the man back —that would be a fun diversion.

Still, over the next few days, I could tell that Aiden was bothered. He talked about his brother on our walks, processing his childhood and everything he'd gone through. I think he thought it was a "normal" childhood, but even I could tell it wasn't.

I think the wolves had given me more affection than his parents had given him. Sure, they saw to his needs and provided for his happiness, and they seemed to say the right things, but Aiden had grown up knowing that love was conditional.

Wolves were better than that, and I thought how I was raised was better. The wolves had loved me no matter what.

We were finishing up a walk and heading inside for Aiden to get ready for work when I smelled it. I stopped, sniffing at the air. Smoke, woods, earth—a distinct, comforting scent in the air.

Aiden stopped, looking at me. "Everything ok?"

I sniffed the air again, then wagged my tail. I didn't want him to worry. The smell was close, but it wasn't here yet.

Soon, Fluffy grumbled.

Yes, soon. I bounded into the house, excited, and changed into my human form, grabbing a pair of sweatpants by the door. Aiden's gaze lingered on me, and he blushed when he saw me noticing. I smiled, and he muttered and pointed to his room, rushing off to get ready for work. We hadn't repeated our intimate moment, mostly sleeping in bed with Quinton and Liam for the last few nights, and I knew that was because Aiden had a lot on his mind.

I was looking forward to more intimacy with Aiden, though, in whatever form that took.

I grabbed one of the cookies Aiden made out of the jar on the counter and started snacking on it as Quinton and Liam came out. Quinton stopped dead in his tracks and stared at me. I looked down at myself, but I was wearing sweatpants, so I wasn't sure what the problem was.

"Are you... Is that..." Quinton trailed off, looking at Liam.

Liam looked as perplexed as me, giving a bit of a shrug when Quinton turned back to me.

I took another bite of my cookie. Aiden was such a good baker, and I loved that he made treats just for me.

"Are you seriously eating a fucking dog biscuit right now?" Quinton blurted out.

I looked down at the cookie in my hand. Yes, it was shaped like a dog biscuit, because it was the cookies he made for Fluffy. He was still making the same recipe and continued to bring treats on our walks.

It was tasty. I didn't really see what the problem was, so I just shrugged my shoulders at Quinton and popped the last bite into my mouth.

Quinton rubbed his hands down his face, then huffed and

headed out the door. Liam just shrugged. Yes, humans were so weird sometimes.

Liam yelled out to Aiden that they'd be waiting in the car, and off he went. Aiden came out of his room a minute later. He was still oddly shy about asking for what he needed, so I walked over and gave him a firm hug. He sighed into my shoulder, and I kissed the top of his head.

"Don't get into any trouble while I'm at work," he said.

I gave a chuckle and smiled at him when he pulled back. He blushed, and then he was out the door. Perhaps an intimate moment would come sooner rather than later with all his blushing and his slight smell of arousal. I was looking forward to it.

Once I heard the car pull out of the driveway, I changed back into my hound form and went off into the woods, roaming and smelling the air.

Close, close, close, Fluffy rumbled.

I went full hellhound, running quickly through the woods, following my nose. I was off our land and into the public land when I slowed down, the scent nearby.

I let my own scent fade away as best I could and stalked slowly through the underbrush. I hadn't spotted him yet, but he was so close. I was as quiet as possible, determined to sneak up on him.

This was a game I wasn't planning on losing.

The scent was practically on top of me now, and I hunched even lower, pausing to sniff the air.

Here! Right here! Fluffy insisted.

But I didn't see him. I looked up into the trees—he was tricky like that.

It was then that I was tackled from the side, my body thrown into the underbrush, a large, heavy form on top of me.

I growled and heaved my attacker off.

Cheater, Fluffy grumbled.

Wilder stood up, laughing at me covered in leaves and dirt. I burned them off with my hellfire and showed my teeth, but he just opened his arms up. I jumped up and he caught me in a hug, my fire licking along both of us.

"That's my boy! You *almost* had me. Quite tricky with your scent," he said, hugging me tightly. "I'll always be able to find my boys, though, because you're always with me," he added, letting me go and pressing a fist to his chest over his heart.

I panted at him in happiness, and we started ambling back towards our property.

"It's been too long since we were all together, and my delicate side project could use a bit of a break," he said.

I cocked my head at him, staring intently. Was he adopting another hellhound?

"Maybe," he answered, anticipating my question. "This is truly a unique situation, but I've got some more work to do before I share. Besides, I felt like my boys needed me."

I snorted at that.

Wilder laughed. "Come now, I took a drive through most of the town before sneaking onto the property. This place is like a nexus of afterlifers. I don't think I've sensed so many non-mortals together in an area in centuries. Everyone seems to be very happily coexisting, as well, which is another oddity. You boys chose well."

I gave a light bark at that.

"But some of my boys have found mates," he said, giving me a smirk and a sideways look. "Although perhaps not everyone has told me about it yet. Nevertheless, I had to come and welcome the new pack members."

I wagged my tail and gave a bit of a grumble at the same time. Aiden was my mate, but it wasn't official yet, so I hadn't told Wilder. I wondered if someone had tattled or if he had just sensed it on me. Anything was possible with a pack of brothers and with Wilder being a first generation hellhound.

Wilder talked about some of what he had been up to, filling me in on the last few months since I'd seen him. I trotted along, listening, as we walked toward the house where Jude and Corbin were staying. We paused, though, and he sat down on a tree stump, looking out over the woods and breathing deeply. I leaned against his side, and he pet me, smiling.

Wilder never minded when I didn't answer back. He never minded when I stayed in hellhound or dog form. He seemed to sense the train of my thoughts, because he spoke after a moment.

"Do you remember when I first brought you home as a pup? You didn't change into your human form for at least a year, maybe two, and then there you were, this scrawny-looking kid. I knew you had to be older, but your human form must not have aged as quickly since you spent so many years in your wolf form. You never did tell me how long you were with the wolves, and that was ok. But I worried for you. Always the most out of everyone, I worried for you," he said, gripping my fur as he stared at me.

I licked at his hand. I knew I had worried him. I had been an angry, untrusting pup. Wilder was full of endless patience and love, always there, always giving me what I needed before I even knew I needed it.

"You will always have a pack with your brothers, and I will always be your father and love you."

I licked at his hand again. I knew that.

"I think your hellhound didn't always believe that. You had so many years without a true pack, and it left its mark. But I sense a calmness to you now. A peace that you never had before. I think your mate, whether he's claimed you or not, has made that happen. He's brought you closer to the pack, and he's made your hellhound trust more," Wilder finished.

I changed into my human form, because I supposed I did want to answer Wilder. He lifted an eyebrow slightly, which was as good as shouting in surprise for him. I wanted to tell him how much I loved him, how much he had done for me, and how grateful I was for him.

"Aiden named my hellhound Fluffy," I said instead, not sure why that seemed the most important thing to say.

Wilder only nodded his head, though, looking thoughtful. "I should have thought of that. We waited until you could tell us a name, because I wanted to give you that control. I should have thought that you would want to be given that, though. I'm sorry, Fluffy."

My eyes felt wet, and I blinked at the moisture. Wilder seemed to understand, because he stood up and hugged me tight. In the past, I probably would have broken away first, but Aiden had gotten me used to contact, and I hugged Wilder back tightly.

"I can't wait for you to meet my mate," I finally rumbled, clearing my throat.

Wilder stepped back, smiling. "Me too, son. First, though, let's check in with the rest of the boys. Corbin is almost back."

I heard a caw in response, and I looked up to see crows in the trees. I didn't smell Corbin or the rotten soul he was supposed to bring back, but Wilder's nose and senses were better than even mine.

We walked the rest of the way toward the house, and we barely made it into the backyard before Jude came bounding out like a puppy.

"Wilder!" he shouted, launching himself at the man. Wilder grabbed him, hugging him tight. Liam and Dexter both must have heard or smelled the ruckus, because they came from the direction of their houses. Dexter got there first and got a long hug, and Liam waited patiently for his turn.

"Corbin is gonna be pissed," Liam muttered after he got his hug.

As if on cue, we all heard the car engine and smelled the hellbound soul Corbin was bringing back. We headed to the front of the house, and we all ignored the ruckus in the trunk as Corbin got out of the car to hug Wilder in greeting.

"Pack's all here!" Jude muttered happily. "Well, hellhound pack, at least."

"Yes, my boys have added a few humans to the mix," he smiled. He sniffed the air then, eyes closed. "Oh, you've got quite a bit more than that here, though."

He must've smelled Sebbie. He wasn't human, but I wasn't sure what he was. I wanted to tell Wilder that letting the guys know might not be a great idea—they hadn't reacted well to the news that Aiden's therapist wasn't human.

"Dangerous?" Liam asked, and I swear I saw his fingers twitch, like he was ready to start typing away on a computer.

"No," said Wilder slowly. "Not dangerous. I sensed only harmony as I made my way through Paradise Falls. A lot of afterlifers, though. I haven't known so many angels and demons to reside in one place, nevermind all the other afterlifers and offspring," he said.

Jude cocked his head. "I've met Aiden's therapist, and she didn't smell like Nephilim, although I did see one the other day."

Wilder just laughed. "Oh, my boys, you've got a lot more than Nephilim here. Heaven and hell have had more creatures in them than angels and demons, even if some left for the mortal plane so long ago that most have forgotten of their existence."

We all pondered that, and then there was a particularly loud thump from the trunk.

"Any trouble?" Liam asked.

Corbin shook his head, and his crow cawed at us, ruffling his feathers. So a little bit of trouble, then, but nothing to speak of.

"Family torture session?" Jude asked hopefully, looking at each of us.

"We have a few hours until we have to pick up Quinton and Aiden," Liam answered. "Although the uncultured mutt might want to put on pants."

I looked down at myself and shrugged. I'd grab some sweats in the house.

"Toby is writing, and he can reach me if he needs me," Dexter said.

Corbin nodded, and his crow stretched its wings in delight.

There was nothing like a little torture to make a family reunion complete.

<hr>

The FBI agent was as hellbound as they came. Wilder let us have our fun with him as he proudly looked on. The man was amazingly resilient, and it became quite a bit of fun to see who could break him first and by what means. Psychological torture, threatening loved ones (not that we would ever hurt them), physical torture—he really did withstand a lot. Corbin even tried some witchy shit on him, but Corbin only shook his head after he put both his hands on the man's head.

Liam sighed after a couple hours. "We're gonna need to pick up the guys from work soon," he grumbled.

I sighed too. I wanted to see my Aiden more than anything, but I was hoping to have some news for him.

Wilder strode forward, and we all stepped back. We'd had our fun, and it was time for a first gen hellhound to take over. He leaned in, and he began whispering in the man's ear, flame engulfing them both but not burning them. The man began screaming in panic, but Wilder just kept whispering. He placed his hand on the man's chest, and the screams became high pitched yowls of pain, but we could see no damage to his physical form.

Wilder could do things that none of us could, and he never fully explained it all. I wasn't sure he even remembered everything he could do. He had probably forgotten more in his long existence than we would ever know.

Finally the man began talking, and Wilder backed away to let him speak.

He made no sense, though, and Liam grabbed a computer to

start researching. He talked about "the mark," "the next generation," and the "old man" who he had always worked for. Aiden was needed for something, and it sounded perhaps like some kind of ritual.

"The old man is dead," Liam said, assuming like the rest of us that he was speaking of the grandfather.

The agent just laughed maniacally. "He never dies! He will never die! So what was I supposed to do? I was a new agent, and some... being with powers, who can't die, approached me. All I could do was help him!"

"There are always choices," Corbin stated.

"Death! Death was my only other choice!" the agent cried out. "And now he'll find me, and it'll be worse than death!"

"You should not believe everything you're told. There is nothing worse than what awaits you in hell for all that you've done," Dexter growled. "He chose you because you relish in the agony of others. You always had a choice, and you chose to follow darkness for your own evil satisfaction, for greed, and for power."

The man was crying then, and we left him tied up and trudged upstairs.

"The grandfather isn't dead?" Liam muttered, frantically typing away.

Dexter gave a wave and muttered something about Toby, heading off toward his mate's house. Corbin sat at the kitchen table, where he had somehow acquired peanuts to feed his crow.

Jude stared at Liam, glued to his computer, then at me. He sighed and rolled his eyes. "Come on, I'll take you to pick up the guys. That one is gonna be lost in his computer for a while," he said, pointing his thumb at Liam.

Wilder looked over at us. "I don't like this. Too many afterlifers. The universe is... unbalanced. And yet..." Wilder shook his head, and waved us off while he sat down, losing himself in thought.

I stripped my sweatpants and turned into Fluffy, and Jude and

I headed to the car. I was excited for Aiden to meet Wilder, but I was also concerned. His grandfather faking his death didn't seem like that big of a deal—humans did that sort of thing sometimes—but Wilder seemed troubled.

If a first generation hellhound was troubled, then there was definitely a reason to be concerned.

Chapter 18

Aiden

Work went relatively quickly, even though I couldn't get the image of Atlas standing naked in my kitchen out of my head.

He was beautiful. His dark, golden skin, his muscles, his tattoos standing out against them, his firm stomach, those thick, corded thighs... and yeah, his dick. He was just swinging freely like he didn't have a care in the world. And when I stared at it for long enough, it came to life and started to get hard.

Which was a little scary, and a little flattering. Ok, maybe a lot flattering. He was freaking beautiful, and I was... Well, I knew I wasn't ugly, and I didn't have a negative body image, but I also didn't think my stare alone was enough to get someone hard.

But it was for Atlas. He got hard snuggled up against me, he got hard if he saw me partially clothed, and he got hard if I looked at him. I think he even smelled my arousal sometimes, because the damn sweatpants he wore (without underwear, mind you) would show his interest when he got a whiff of me.

Sweatpants on Atlas should be outlawed. Holy shit. If he wasn't strolling around naked like he didn't have a care in the world, he was strolling around in sweatpants and no shirt.

It seemed like my libido had finally woken up.

I had talked about it with Helene at my session yesterday. I had meant to talk about my brother and the picture and the sheriff, and I did mention some family things, mainly the fact that maybe my childhood was a little worse than I thought it was. Nevertheless, it wasn't long before we were on the subject of Atlas and my feelings for him.

Helene had said she was proud of the fact that I acknowledged my interest, and she had encouraged me to take things at my own pace, whatever that might be. She said it sounded like I had a very supportive partner, and she was sure he would be kind and accepting no matter what happened.

I knew she was right. The idea of initiating anything was scary, though. That's when Helene had suggested that maybe I didn't need to *really* initiate—maybe I just needed to let Atlas know that it was ok if he initiated.

Ugh. Why did everything have to be so complicated?

The kitchen door opened and Q came in. He was frowning. I wasn't surprised—he usually looked pissed off after a few hours of customer service. He was a grumpy fucker, but for some reason the customers seemed to adore him. It was like getting insults along with your coffee just made some people happy. Maybe it was because he was never really hurtful—he didn't say mean things or mock people on sensitive issues (unless you counted a love of pumpkin spice as a sensitive issue). He was just overall grumpy as fuck.

I raised my eyebrows at him, because he was just staring at me expectantly.

"Josh came in. He's sitting at a table drinking coffee, and he looks like someone kicked his puppy. And Cass isn't here," Q announced.

"Ok..." I said, unsure where this was going.

Q rolled his eyes. "Well I sure as fuck can't talk to him to see what's wrong."

"You want me to go talk to Josh?" I asked.

Q threw his arms up in the air. "I don't know! He looks all sad and shit. I certainly can't fix it. You talked to him at Toby's house."

I resisted the urge to laugh. Q really was dramatic sometimes.

I took off my apron and washed my hands, heading out the kitchen door to the shop. Thankfully, it wasn't that crowded, and Stephanie was working the counter. Josh was sitting at a table in the corner looking pretty unhappy. Q made a go-over-there gesture to me, and I heard Stephanie telling him to get his ass in motion and make some coffee. Those two were like peas in a pod—they loved yelling at each other.

I grabbed a plate and a muffin from the bakery case, then I walked over to the table. Josh looked up when I set the muffin down and gave me a smile, but it looked forced.

"Hey, Aiden. Thanks. This looks delicious," he said. He motioned to the seat across from him, and I sat down.

"No problem. You look like you could use a little pick-me-up," I answered.

Josh busied himself with the muffin, not answering. That was ok. I was used to Atlas. I could handle long silences. I just leaned on the table and watched Josh eat, trying to send out the calm energy that both Helene and Atlas seemed to have. With enough silence, I always started talking. Maybe the same would work with Josh.

He finished his muffin, wiped his hands, took a drink of his coffee, and then played with the cup, not looking at me.

Finally, he said, "Yeah, I guess I could use a pick-me-up."

"You alright?" I asked quietly.

Josh sniffed, still twirling his coffee cup. Then he shrugged his shoulders, still not looking at me.

I knew he had issues with his boyfriend, and I kind of guessed this was about that, but I didn't really know. He didn't seem to be very forthcoming, either. I tried to channel my best Helene impression. How would she handle this?

"All your feelings are valid. It's ok to be conflicted about how you feel about someone, you know," I said.

Josh kind of nodded his head. We weren't that close, and I thought maybe if I shared something, he would be more likely to as well.

I took a deep breath. "I hated the guy who took me. Hated him. But there were days where I also looked forward to his company. I know that seems weird, but..."

Josh looked up at me.

I shrugged. "Then there's my family. I'm realizing that I love them, but I also sort of hate them at the same time, and that's a weird feeling. I'm angry at them. I'm angry at a lot of things, and I'm finally realizing it."

Josh went back to looking at his cup and twirling it in his hands. I just sat, letting him think about what I'd said.

Finally, he said, "Yeah. I get it. How you can both love and hate someone at the same time. How you can have so many good memories, and be so compatible in some ways, and yet have bad times where you really hate some of the things they do."

"I guess it's a matter of how bad the bad times are, and how frequent they are," I said.

Josh nodded his head, then he looked up at me. "I thought he was perfect at first, you know? He seemed to really get me. I'm sort of a control freak, and he let me... let go. He took care of me. But lately..." Josh just shrugged his shoulders again, his face red.

I got the feeling that maybe Josh was talking about sex stuff. I could see the allure of having someone else who took control—after all, wasn't that what I was just thinking I wanted Atlas to do?

"There's a difference between taking care of someone and being controlling," I said.

"What is it?" Josh asked, looking at me.

I thought about that. I thought about Atlas, and how he took care of me but never controlled me.

"Someone who takes care of you always puts your needs first, even above their own. Someone who takes care of you considers you, both in *and* out of the bedroom. It doesn't stop with just sex. They respect your feelings and your boundaries," I answered.

Josh looked down again.

"Does your boyfriend respect you?" I asked gently.

"Some days, I'm not sure he even likes me anymore," Josh answered, and I could hear the sadness behind his words.

"Then maybe it's time to find someone who does. You're smart, and fun, and funny..." I said, but Josh cut me off with a snort.

I touched his wrist, and I didn't miss the flinch he gave at the unexpected contact.

"Josh, you are worth so much. We all are. Don't ever let anyone take away your worth," I said, and then I drew my hand back.

I heard the bell above the door jingle, and Jude walked in, probably ready to take us home. Josh looked up and noticed him, and probably came to the same conclusion. I could see him physically pull himself together and put all his walls back up in place.

"Thanks, Aiden. It was good talking to you. And thank you for the muffin," he said, looking back in control.

"You have my number. Call if you ever need to, Josh," I said, and then I got up before he could answer. I didn't want him to tell me that wasn't necessary or he was fine, because I knew it would be a lie.

He wasn't fine. I just hoped he would realize his worth. Like Helene said, sometimes we locked ourselves into rooms, and sometimes we didn't even know we were doing it.

I hoped Josh would break free from whatever cage he was in.

The drive home was (thankfully) uneventful—meaning the sheriff was apparently not out patrolling, because Jude didn't drive like a maniac. Liam was doing research, so Q headed into the main house where Liam's office and all his tech was, and Jude walked me to the door of our house and then left with a wave.

Fluffy was inside, and I breathed out a sigh, going to sit down on the couch. He tilted his head at me, obviously sensing something was up.

"I think I want to just talk for a minute, and it's probably easier if you're in this form while I do it, because in your human form you're... distracting," I said.

I swear Fluffy grinned at that.

I swatted at him lightly, laughing, and he only grinned his doggy grin a little wider. I sat and thought for a minute, and Fluffy let me have the time, just being calm and peaceful next to me.

"I think... Well, I think maybe I want to have sex. With you. Well, duh, I mean obviously with you. But... yeah," I muttered, feeling kind of stupid already.

Fluffy just sat there, looking calm as ever, and it gave me the courage to plow on.

"I don't think I can initiate, but I wouldn't mind if you did. Or maybe you could, like, sort of ask me? Or something? I'm not sure I'd be able to say no, but you'd probably smell a no on me anyway, and I wouldn't say yes, either. So I guess not answering means no? And I know that's kind of confusing and probably a little difficult, and I'm sorry," I said, clenching my hands together and looking at my knees.

Fluffy gently licked at my hands, and I looked over. Still as calm as ever. I unclenched my hands and breathed out.

"I want to try sex. Like, anal sex. I've never done that. I liked it when you touched us both, too. I like it when we're skin to skin. Lately I've been... interested in trying more. I guess that part of me kind of woke up? But I'm not sure how to go about starting anything, and then I get in my head, and that never leads anywhere good, so, yeah..." I said, trailing off again.

Fluffy was still patiently staring at me. He tilted his head slightly, like he was waiting for me to go on. Only I didn't really have anything else to say.

"Um, I guess that's it. So what do you think?" I asked.

And then there was a very naked Atlas sitting on the floor. He scooched up next to me on the couch, and I couldn't help a glance down...

And yes, Atlas seemed to very much like the idea of initiating sex. Or of me staring at him. I wasn't sure which, but damn could that thing grow.

And grow.

And grow.

"Yes," Atlas answered.

I looked at him, totally confused. "Yes what?" I asked. Because, yeah, I had asked him a question, but then I had gotten really distracted by his dick.

It was a really nice dick. It was sort of pretty, even. Hard and thick and a pretty golden pink color. I don't think I'd ever looked at a dick and thought it was pretty, but Atlas's was. It was a pretty pink penis.

I almost snorted in laughter at myself.

"Do you want me to put pants on?" he asked.

I looked at his face then, because yeah, I was ogling him. "Um, not unless you want to?" I sort of asked.

Atlas grimaced. "No. Clothes are so... itchy and heavy and *hot* on your skin."

I laughed. "Yeah, well, you're a furnace."

"Do you want to take off your clothes?" Atlas said, and I swear there were flames dancing in his eyes.

It sounded like a really nice idea, but... "Um, Q and Liam might come home."

Atlas grabbed my phone off the coffee table in front of the couch where I'd apparently put it when I came in and shot off a text. There was a vibration a minute later, and he handed it back.

I looked at the text. It was to Liam, and it simply said, *Don't come home.*

The reply made me laugh. *I'm assuming this is the uncultured mutt. Quinton and I will stay here tonight.*

I stripped off my shirt, and Atlas looked at me hungrily.

"Can I kiss you?" he asked.

"Yes," I answered.

He put his arms around me, his skin hot against me. He pressed his lips against mine, and it was soft and gentle. I breathed a sigh against his mouth, and he licked at my lips, moaning.

"You taste so good, mate," he rumbled against me.

I tasted his lips, and our tongues gently touched each other. It was sweet and sexy, and I realized that Atlas didn't kiss anything like...

Atlas pulled back and bit me on the neck.

"Ow!" I grumbled. It hadn't really been that hard, but I hadn't expected it either. I looked up to see him giving me puppy dog eyes, and I couldn't help the laugh that escaped.

He picked me up then and carried me toward our bedroom, tossing me on the bed so I practically bounced. I giggled a little at it. Then he pulled out lube from the nightstand drawer.

My eyes widened. "When did you get that?" I asked.

"Liam gave it to me when I asked him what human how-to videos I should watch about sex," he said matter-of-factly.

I sputtered in laughter again. "You asked Liam about sex how-to videos?"

"Yes. He searched for some, but they didn't seem very practical," Atlas answered. "There were some articles, too, and they seemed more educational."

I could just picture Atlas and Liam ending up on some porn site talking about the practicality of whatever was happening in the video, and asking each other, "Do humans really do that?" I couldn't help the giggle that escaped at the thought. They were so clueless sometimes that it was adorable.

"Can I take off your pants?" Atlas asked, and his eyes were staring hungrily at me, the flames back.

I didn't answer, but I unbuttoned my pants and pushed them, along with my socks and underwear, off. I waved him over, and he climbed onto the bed. Rather than coming straight up to lay side by side with me, though, he started at my legs, smelling along my calf and then giving my skin a soft nibble. It kind of tickled, making me laugh a little, but it was kind of sexy, too.

My cock was rock hard by the time he had sniffed and nibbled his way up my legs, and he nosed at my balls, inhaling deeply and moaning. It was totally weird, but the fact that he liked my smell that much was also a huge turn on.

Then Atlas licked at my dick, and I sat up sharply, looking down at him. He smiled up at me, raising an eyebrow and sticking his tongue out to give another soft lick.

"Yes," I murmured in answer to the unspoken question.

He reached up and placed my hand on his head as he laid between my legs, and I carded my fingers through his hair, which made him rumble against me, shooting little sparks through my whole body when I felt the vibration against my balls.

Then he sucked me into his mouth, and holy shit. His tongue circled around my cock, his mouth moving up and down. It was hot and slick, and the feel of his hair in my hands was soft and familiar. I looked down at him as he made eye contact, and he looked so happy—it was such a turn on. He moaned against me again, like he was the one who was getting off.

I groaned when he licked at my slit, and he moaned when he got a shot of my precum, his hips moving against the bed. His hand cupped my balls, gently holding them, and his other hand was holding the base of my dick, softly squeezing.

I leaned back and closed my eyes in bliss, reveling in the sensations. It was overwhelming. I moaned again as Atlas made needy sounds while he sucked on me. His tongue seemed to be everywhere, and his mouth was moving up and down. I knew my hips were thrusting me deep into his mouth, but he seemed to enjoy it. Then his finger was lightly tickling against my hole, not entering, but just rubbing softly, caressing, and when it pressed gently against my hole, just barely penetrating, I felt my orgasm rush through me.

I cried out, and Atlas groaned loudly as I shot into his mouth. I don't know how long I came for, but it seemed like the longest orgasm ever, and only when the last drop had been milked did he gently pull off my cock, giving my slit one final lick that made me shudder.

He slid up the bed next to me, wrapping his arms around me tightly. Before I could even think about getting Atlas off, he mumbled, "You tasted so good that it made me cum."

My face got hot but I chuckled. "You're a weirdo, but I love you," I murmured, and then I froze.

Because fuck, I'd just told Atlas I loved him.

"I love you, too, mate, even though you aren't a weirdo," he replied, like it was the most natural thing in the world.

Maybe it was. I relaxed into his embrace, warm and sated and comfortable. That had been an amazing blow job, and knowing that Atlas had enjoyed it so much made it even better. His tongue had been magical, and his hands on my cock, and my balls, and... I froze for a second.

"Atlas?" I asked, suddenly a little curious, because last time I'd checked, he only had two hands, so I wasn't quite sure how they seemed to be in three places at once.

"Hmm?" he murmured against me.

"Did you grow an extra hand?" I asked.

"Uh uh," he mumbled. "Just my tail."

Then he snuffled against my neck and sighed in happiness, holding me tight.

Ok then. Just his tail.

I had questions, but Atlas was hot and relaxed around me, and

I was feeling sleepy and cozy, and I figured tail questions could wait until after a little nap.

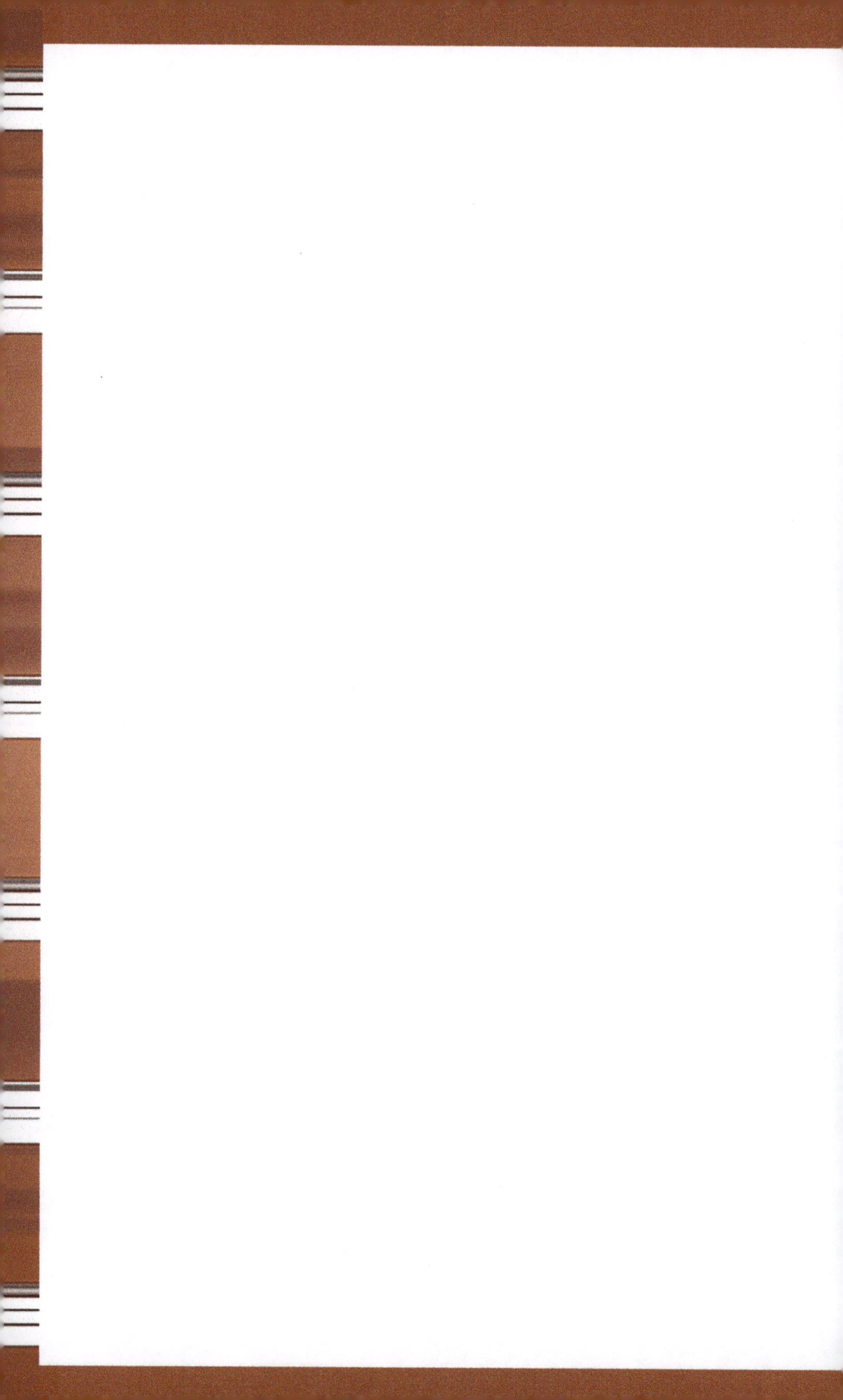

CHAPTER 19

ATLAS/FLUFFY

I had fallen asleep briefly, and Aiden was still snoozing on my chest. The light was fading but it wasn't fully dark, so I knew we hadn't napped for long. I breathed in the soft, warm, happy smell that was Aiden, along with the alluring scent of both our releases.

Would Aiden want to do that again? Or maybe something else? He had said he'd like to try anal sex. We had lube. I'd read how-to articles. I thought I could make him feel good. Or maybe he wanted to be the one to penetrate me?

I mulled that over for a moment. I wanted to be inside Aiden, but the thought of Aiden inside me was certainly an intriguing one as well. I would like him to find his pleasure inside my body.

I shifted slightly, my hard cock rubbing against his stomach. He snuffled a bit, and I stilled. I didn't want to wake him.

He pressed against me, and I felt his hard cock as well. I sniffed at his neck—he was waking up, and he was aroused.

"You like to sniff me," Aiden murmured.

"Mmmhmmm," I murmured, sniffing him again. "Would you like to try something else?"

Aiden leisurely rubbed his body against me, and then he leaned his head back to look at me. He was sleepy and mussed and adorably sexy.

"What were you thinking?" he asked.

"I could suck you again. Or rub our cocks together. Or you said you wanted to try anal sex some day. I'd love to lick you and open you up and make you feel good, then put my dick inside you and fill you up. I'd also love it if you wanted your dick to be inside me," I answered.

Aiden was flushed a pretty shade of red and breathing heavily.

"Fuck," he murmured.

"Yes, I believe that's what it's usually called, but with a mate it's more than just a fuck," I said thoughtfully.

For some reason Aiden giggled at that. Then he hopped out of bed mumbling something about a shower. I got out and followed him into the bathroom, where he had already turned the water on to heat up.

"Would you like to shower together?" I asked.

"No. I mean yes. Just not yet," Aiden answered, blushing again. "If you're gonna... If we're gonna... tasting... yeah, so... I just need... Why don't you go... do something. And I'll shower. And you can join me in a few minutes," he muttered, getting more red with the start of each sentence.

"I would like to taste you just as you are, mate," I said, not understanding why Aiden would want to shower off his natural scent.

He just rolled his eyes, pushed me out of the bathroom, and shut the door.

"Get snacks! And water!" he yelled through the door.

Huh. Apparently humans were shy about bodily needs and functions. I knew they liked privacy for those things, but I figured once mated, that wouldn't be an issue. Humans were an odd bunch, though.

With a shrug, I went about gathering snacks and bottles of water and putting them in the bedroom. Perhaps Aiden meant to den down for a bit. I really had no problem with that idea—I would enjoy being denned in with my mate.

I waited a few minutes and then went to stand at the bathroom door. Had enough time passed for me to join him? Was I supposed to walk in? Did I knock? I stood there for a bit and pondered how long Aiden would want. I could clearly hear him in the shower now.

"I can hear you thinking out there. Get in here, Fluffy," Aiden called out.

I didn't need to be told twice, and I opened the door and climbed into the shower with a very naked, wet Aiden. His face was in the spray, and I wrapped my arms around him, which made him give a little squeak of surprise.

He turned around, wiping the water out of his eyes, and grinned at me.

"I've never showered with anyone before," he said.

"Me either," I answered. "If you must clean off your natural scent, can I wash you?"

He nodded his head, and I grabbed the soap, giving it a sniff. "You smell better," I complained.

Aiden just giggled, so I began lathering up the soap in my hands. I crouched down and began at his feet, gently raising each one as he put his hands on my shoulders. As I soaped up his calves and thighs, I rubbed and massaged each one. He groaned happily as I pressed into the muscles and rubbed.

As I was finishing on his thighs, I leaned in and nosed gently at his balls, smelling the natural scent of Aiden, even though it was diluted by water. I couldn't help giving his dick a little taste, and I sucked him into my mouth and throat until he was all the way inside me.

His hands clenched my shoulders tightly, and I moaned. I hoped my mate left marks on me. I swallowed around him, and his hips bucked, driving him further into my mouth.

"Atlas!" he cried out.

He was clearly enjoying it, but he had given me a task. With more than a little sadness, I pulled off his dick, licking and sucking as I did. Then I used my hands to soap him, gently tugging at his hard length.

"Fuck, Atlas. You're gonna kill me," he groaned.

I didn't think he meant literally, since all I smelled was arousal and pleasure from him. I grabbed more soap and did his chest next, making sure to massage each nipple thoroughly. When I got to his shoulders, I gently coaxed him to turn and face the other way, and he did so with a moan.

With more soap lathered up, I massaged his muscles, kneading wherever I found a knot. Aiden turned and leaned against the side wall of the shower to support himself, and I simply shifted with him, continuing to rub him.

By the time I got to his ass, he was panting, and I could see his cock was hard and red. I wanted to suck him back into my mouth, but there was another area to focus on now. I spread his cheeks and looked at his pink hole. So pretty. I gently rubbed my thumb against him, and he groaned and pushed his ass back.

That certainly seemed like an invitation to me. I leaned in, licking gently along his pucker. There was a faint taste of soap, but with a few licks that was gone, and it was just the taste of Aiden's skin. I dove in, kissing and sucking, licking into him as he moaned and pushed back.

"Oh my god, Atlas," he murmured. "Fuck."

Yes, fucking was a good idea, but I knew I needed to get my Aiden ready. I had read that certain lubricants were best for inside humans, and I hadn't had the foresight to bring it into the shower.

"Yes," I answered. "Good idea, my mate."

I stood up and grabbed the soap, ducking under the water to clean myself since Aiden apparently wanted that. He turned around and stared at me, his eyes glazed over with lust, his scent musky and aroused and so perfectly Aiden.

"I want to..." he started, reaching toward the soap.

I leaned in and kissed him, nipping at his lips. "I won't last if you touch me," I answered, giving myself the fastest cleaning ever.

I rinsed myself, picked Aiden up and moved him under the water to rinse any residual soap off him, and then shut off the water. He was sputtering a bit, but I got out of the shower, lifted him out, grabbed a towel, and gently but efficiently dried him off and then myself.

"Atlas, I can..." he started again, but I picked him up into my arms and carried him into the bedroom, making him sputter with laughter.

"Need you now," I mumbled as I laid him gently down.

I climbed onto the bed and hovered over him, and he leaned up, his hand threading through my hair and his lips pressing against mine. I groaned as I let myself rest partly on him so we could feel each other's skin.

We kissed and licked and nibbled, our tongues exploring each other's mouths. I could feel Aiden thrusting into me, and as much as I enjoyed kissing him, I wanted to make him writhe in pleasure again.

I grabbed a pillow and the lube off the nightstand while Aiden stared at me dazedly. I slid down the bed and put the pillow under his butt.

"What are you..." he started to ask, but he trailed off again.

I liked the idea that my mate was so turned on that he couldn't even think straight. Still, I answered him. "In many of the how-to manuals Liam found, they put pillows under the man's butt before anal sex."

He leaned up onto his elbows, staring at me. "Atlas, where did Liam find these manuals?"

"Online," I answered, and then I spread his cheeks, adding, "You have the cutest little pucker I've ever seen." Then I gave him a lick.

"Atlas!" he groaned, throwing his head back, but then he pushed against my head, and I immediately backed off, looking at him. "Atlas, where online did you read these how-to manuals that called my asshole a 'pucker'?"

Why did he care about the how-to manuals? His cock was hard and throbbing, and he wanted to know about them? Did he want to read them, too, or did he doubt that they were useful?

"Don't worry—Liam read them, too, and although he said some were not as helpful, he only sent me the links of ones he found to be accurate with his own mate. They were very detailed and informative. Some were articles about lubrication and preparation, but he also sent some that described the act in great detail, so I'm prepared," I reassured him.

"Atlas, were you reading porn?" he asked, a little smile on his face.

I cocked my head at him. Had I been reading porn? "Would Liam send me pornography?" I asked. "He said it was informative sexual material."

Aiden fell back onto the bed, giggles erupting from him. I wasn't sure what was so amusing, but I was glad my mate was happy. I looked at his perfect pucker (which perhaps was a pornography term?), and I couldn't help diving back in to kiss and lick him. His giggles soon became moans of pleasure.

I grabbed the lube and squeezed a good amount onto my finger. The bedspread might need to be changed after this, but I wasn't terribly worried. I moved over to his thigh, gently nibbling at it as I circled my finger around his hole, slowly sinking it in.

"Does this feel good?" I asked him, although his moans seemed to confirm that it did. I ducked down and licked gently at his hard cock, tasting the perfect flavor of Aiden on my tongue.

"Yes. Fuck, Atlas," he gasped.

"Not yet, my mate. I need to prep you first," I told him.

He giggled again, but it ended in a gasp as I added a second finger to the first, easing it in. I gently pressed in and out, occasionally reaching my head down to lick and suck at his cock.

I pulled off and looked up at him as I gently felt around inside him with my fingers. I had read about...

Aiden gasped. Ah, that must be it, then.

"I think I found your prostate," I said, rather proud of myself. "I read about it, and many men find the stimulation of it pleasurable. Do you find it pleasurable, my mate?" I asked, although his groans and scent seemed to say that he did.

"I... Holy shit, Atlas. It's like... I can't even explain it. Feels weird, but good weird," he gasped.

Good weird was good, I supposed. I really wanted better than good weird, though, so I thought of the how-to manuals, and I leaned down, sucking his cock into my mouth as I gently pressed my fingers against his prostate, making the "come hither" motion described and alternating my fingers pressing against his gland.

"Holy shit!" he cried out, writhing against me.

I hoped that was better than "good weird." He spurted a bit of precum into my mouth, and I moaned at the taste of him on my tongue, which made him moan louder.

"Fuck, Atlas, fuck. You have to stop!" Aiden cried out.

I immediately pulled off and pulled my fingers out, sniffing the air. He didn't smell distressed. I smelled sex and musk and Aiden, and I looked up at him. He was leaning on his elbows, looking down at me and smiling fondly.

"I love you, Atlas," he said, a sweet grin on his face.

"I love you, too, my mate. What do you need?" I asked him.

"I need you to get up here and get your dick in me before I come," he laughed, and I smiled at him.

Ahhh. That I could definitely do.

CHAPTER 20

Atlas had read porn for me, and holy shit, it must have been some good porn. I was also feeling emotional—in a good way—that he had stopped and checked in the moment I had said something, even if I hadn't meant "stop" in a bad way.

I smiled dopily as he climbed up my body, kissing his way along every inch of skin and stopping to lick at my nipples, making me moan. My ass was still elevated on a pillow, and it was pretty comfortable, although I giggled a bit thinking that I was definitely gonna nccd to wash the pillowcase. Atlas was smiling, and I could feel his hard cock rub against my skin as he moved up to my mouth, giving me a soft kiss.

"I've never done this before," Atlas admitted. "You have to tell me how it feels."

I smiled and caressed his hair. "Of course I will. Although I think the porn Liam sent you must have been pretty good stuff."

I thought I would be more nervous, but it was Atlas, and he was learning right along with me.

I loved the feel of his naked body on mine, and I was suddenly glad that clothing had so often stayed on when...

Atlas bit my neck, breaking my thoughts, and I hugged him to me tightly, kissing at his neck and making him moan.

"I'm just really thankful for you," I said, feeling a little teary, but not in a sad way.

He picked his head up and looked at me. "I am thankful every moment for you, my mate."

He leaned down and kissed me again, our lips soft and gentle despite the urgency I was feeling. Because fuck, Atlas was really good at doing, well, everything. He sat up then, grabbing the bottle of lube, and he proceeded to take the cap off.

"I think it probably has a squeeze top..." I started, but too late.

Atlas literally poured the lube on his dick. I couldn't help giggling again, but he just smiled widely at me, not at all upset that I was laughing at him, which only made me giggle harder. Lube was dripping off his dick, and we definitely weren't gonna be sleeping on this comforter.

"I don't think..." I started again, but then he was pouring the lube on my ass, and I gasped in surprise. "Atlas!" I half yelled, half laughed.

He was still grinning though, and although it felt pretty damn messy, when he started rubbing it in, it also felt pretty damn good.

He pushed a finger in, watching my face as he found that magical spot that felt weird but also sent sparks through me. He leaned down and licked my dick as he rubbed me.

"Holy shit, Atlas," I groaned. I felt a fullness as another finger went in. It didn't hurt, not really, but it felt... sort of uncomfortable? But then his tongue did something on my dick that made my whole body tingle, and suddenly the fingers in my ass didn't quite matter as much.

At some point I think he must have put a third finger in, because there was more pressure, but not in a bad way—it was starting to feel really good. His fingers were gliding in and out, and he was licking around the head of my dick and occasionally mouthing my balls.

190

"Atlas, I want you inside me," I groaned.

I barely blinked before his fingers were out of me and he was leaning over me. He stared into my eyes as he guided himself into me. There were flames dancing in them, and I tried to keep my own eyes open, but the feel of him pressing in was simply too much, and I threw my head back, moaning.

Fingers were good, but this was *Atlas*, and he was *inside me*. He slowly pushed in, leaning down to sniff and lick at my neck, and I wrapped my legs and arms around him. He stilled when he was pressed up against me.

"My god, you're so deep," I muttered.

"I'm inside you, my mate. A part of you," he growled in my ear.

"Fuck, yes," I said, my hard cock jumping against his abs.

"Fucking. Yes," Atlas replied, and then he started moving.

It felt amazing—his skin was rubbing against my dick steadily, giving me pleasure there too. He picked his head up and I looked into his eyes, and all I could see was love and passion.

He grabbed my hips, angling them up a little bit, and then— holy fuck. He hit that bundle of nerves with his dick, and I gasped, warmth and tingles shooting through my whole body.

"There," I cried, and Atlas continued to stare at me as he thrust into me, getting quicker and quicker, pressing against that spot every time. Then something was curling around my dick, tightly holding onto it, only one hand was supporting him and one hand was on my hips.

"Atlas!" I cried out again.

He smirked at me, muttering, "Just my tail."

Not *just* anything, because oh my god. My ass was full, my dick was being massaged by his tail as it gently squeezed and rubbed, and Atlas was everywhere around me. His skin, his scent, his burning eyes.

My eyes widened as it felt like he got... bigger. Thicker. He was suddenly stretching inside me.

"Atlas?" I gasped.

He stopped moving, that thickness just outside my hole.

"Don't stop!" I demanded, pressing him closer with my arms and legs.

His gaze didn't leave mine as he pushed against me, impossibly big, holy shit. I was so full, stretched so wide, and then that thickness was all the way inside me, and it was hitting that spot again, pressing against it, massaging it as he slowly moved.

The sensation was unlike anything I'd ever felt, like my entire body was being massaged from the inside. All that existed was that bundle of nerves, and it was overtaking every part of me, like the rest of my body was just floating and every nerve I had was centered in that one spot.

"I love you, Atlas," I cried out, knowing I wouldn't last much longer. It was too intense, and I felt like I was about to leave my body.

"I love you, my mate, and I want to mark and claim you," he said, his eyes wild and burning.

"Yes," I gasped, because suddenly I wanted that too. I didn't know how he would mark me, but I didn't care—I *needed* it.

He leaned down and bit me hard, just below my neck by my shoulder, and a wave of pleasure exploded outward. My orgasm crashed through my entire body, causing me to spasm and shake and cry out as I was completely overwhelmed.

I heard Atlas cry out as well, and it felt like he swelled even bigger, making my orgasm go on and on as my prostate was relentlessly massaged. He was filling me up, and the idea was unbelievably erotic. I grasped him tighter as our pleasure washed through us, overwhelming everything.

We stayed entwined together, even as the intensity slowly faded. At some point, I let my legs fall away because they were shaky, and Atlas's dick slipped out of my ass. He rolled me over so I was laying on top of him, and though I knew we were probably covered in my cum, I couldn't seem to manage the energy to care.

I rubbed my face against his hot, firm skin, smelling the unique scent that was Atlas. Maybe there was something to this whole sniffing thing, because Atlas smelled like safety and home. I drifted off to sleep with that thought in my head and a full feeling in my heart.

⚮

I was in Helene's office, only I knew I wasn't *actually* in Helene's office, because I was still laying in bed with Atlas sleeping next to me. The whole bed was in Helene's office.

Weird. Maybe I had some emotional baggage that my subconscious wanted to unpack? I sat up, tucking the sheets around me—no need for Helene to get an eyeful, even if it was just a dream.

She was sitting in her chair, her glasses on and her hair in a messy bun. She looked up from her notebook, smiling at me. Only, she didn't look quite... right? Her face was more angular and looked flawless, almost like a statue. Her hair was darker, and it was almost like it was moving gently, and...

"Helene, do you have wings?" I asked.

She took off her glasses, replying, "I always think the glasses make me look more human, but I don't suppose I need them with these in view." She flared her dark, inky black wings out slightly before tucking them back in.

"They're very lovely wings," I said, because somehow that seemed important to mention.

"Thank you, Aiden," she answered, smiling at me. "You've always been so polite and such a pleasure to work with."

I smiled at that, and then I asked, "Am I upset after having sex with Atlas?"

She cocked her head. "Are you?"

I stopped and took stock. I didn't *feel* upset. I felt good. Happy. Warm. Safe. "I don't think so," I finally answered.

"I'm glad you thought about it," she said. "I want you to know that you feel good now, but it's perfectly normal to have uncom-

193

fortable feelings about this later. The most important thing is to talk about them, especially with Atlas. He'll want to give you whatever you need, whether that's space or cuddling."

I nodded my head.

"This also doesn't mean that you'll feel this way every time. Every sexual encounter will vary, but you have a loving and respectful mate who will always honor whatever you need. Remember that communication is the most important thing," she said.

I nodded again. She was just staring at me, so I finally asked, "If I feel ok after sex, why am I dreaming about you?"

She laughed lightly. "Not everything is about sex, Aiden."

Well, no, I supposed it wasn't, but... "Well, I just had sex, and I'm dreaming about you, so I thought the two were connected."

She smiled gently. "You're mated now, so it was easier to access you, and I feel like there are some things we need to talk about."

"Oh. Ok. Like what?" I asked.

"Your family," she said, and she suddenly looked a little... frightening. Not that I was frightened of her, but that she seemed like someone you did *not* want to fuck with. She seemed like a badass, not my sweet, unassuming therapist.

"Are you a hellhound?" I asked her. I knew I was probably stalling on the whole talk-about-my-family thing, but I was also curious. "Atlas doesn't have wings, but he apparently has a tail."

"Hellhounds are not the only creatures who decided to leave the underworld. Afterlifers have forgotten so many of us. Out of sight, out of mind, as the saying goes. We really don't mind that in the slightest—easiest if the afterlifers leave us to our work," she answered.

"Am I your work?" I asked, suddenly feeling a little odd. "I mean, I know I'm your work, because you're my therapist, but am I some kind of... I don't know, experiment or afterlife project or something?"

She smiled gently at me. "Everyone I work with is something of a project. I help those who have been wronged. You were wronged, Aiden, not just by your kidnapper, but by your family as well. You are a wounded soul, and yes, I want to help you heal those wounds."

I nodded. I guessed that was ok, then. But... "How did my family wrong me?" I asked.

She gave me a look. I thought about my family—about their conditional love, my escape from their carefully planned future, and my brother searching for me. Ok, maybe they had wronged me. Maybe they were planning to wrong me even more.

"Your grandfather isn't dead," Helene announced, watching me.

I was surprised, and yet it also seemed like a perfectly reasonable truth. I knew they'd said he was dead, but it hadn't seemed real. It was very hard to imagine my grandfather dead.

"Atlas will tell you when you both wake up, I'm sure. I doubt they'll find out much about him, though. I believe he is beyond their ability," she stated, frowning.

Well, that didn't sound good. "He's beyond the ability of a hellhound?" I asked, confused. "I thought they could deal with anyone."

"They can deal with any mortals," she replied.

Ok then, so she didn't think Grandfather was mortal. Just lovely. "Is he really the one looking for me, then?" I asked.

"No, it is very much your brother looking for you, but I believe it all ties back to your grandfather," she said.

Atlas stirred, grumbling a bit in his sleep.

Helene looked at him before turning back to me. "Not much longer. I need you to think, Aiden. Think very hard. Did your grandfather have a mark? Something on his face or his hands, perhaps, that you always saw on him?"

I nodded my head. He did. I didn't think about it and wouldn't have thought to mention it, but obviously Helene thought it was important.

"You must tell Wilder," Helene said, and then Atlas was growling and grabbing onto me, and Helene was suddenly... I don't even know. She looked like some kind of dark angel or something, all scary and powerful and totally kick ass, and then she was gone, and I was opening my eyes with Atlas leaning over me, growling, flames dancing in his eyes.

"Where'd you go?" he growled, sounding slightly panicked.

"I went to see Helene," I said.

I knew that made no sense, because we were both still in bed, but Atlas's grip loosened, and he looked a little less panicked.

"Helene smells odd, but she's ok," he said.

"I don't think she's human," I said.

Atlas nodded like he already knew that.

"What is she?" I asked.

He just shrugged, like it wasn't important. I almost rolled my eyes, but then I thought about everything she said.

"Atlas, she told me my grandfather isn't dead," I told him.

He pulled me into his arms. "I'm sorry, Aiden. I just found out, and then I got... distracted."

I chuckled a little bit, because I knew exactly what had distracted him, and I wasn't going to complain. I felt... sore, but in a good way. Atlas must have cleaned us both off before he fell asleep next to me, because I wasn't a sticky mess. It felt very late, or else really early—I wasn't sure how long we'd slept, but it felt like a long time.

"I doubt the middle of the night, or the early morning, is a good time to make phone calls, but Helene told me I have to talk to Wilder," I said.

"Ok. Should I see if he's ready now?" Atlas asked.

"I think we can wait until the sun comes up. Besides, I'm kind of starving," I said, and right on cue, my stomach growled. We'd been so preoccupied that we hadn't really had dinner.

Atlas smiled and gestured over to the side of the bed. I looked over, and... holy shit. How had I missed that when we came in here?

There were like six bottles of water and so many snacks that half of them seemed to have fallen off the nightstand. It looked like there were chips, cookies, pretzels, bread, peanut butter, fruit... Was that a can opener? I leaned over the bed and noticed the cans on the floor next to a case of water.

"Atlas, did you bring everything from the pantry in here?" I asked, trying really hard not to laugh.

He just looked at me, all puppy dog eyes. "You said to get some drinks and snacks."

I did laugh then, giving him a hug. I really loved this man, and I was so glad he was in my life, even if my life had gotten a hell of a lot weirder.

Yeah, we had to figure out my crazy family, but we could feed each other snacks in bed before we went and made some phone calls.

CHAPTER 21

ATLAS/FLUFFY

"He's WHERE?" Aiden shrieked.

I had the urge to flatten my ears against my head, but since I was in human form, that wasn't really possible.

After lots of food, drink, and more cuddles with a bit more sleep, we had showered together and gotten dressed to head over to the house where Wilder, Jude, and Corbin were staying. Aiden had made a comment about calling Wilder, and I had told him a phone call wasn't necessary since Wilder was at the house.

Now my mate had stopped right outside the door, staring at me and looking somewhere between panicked and pissed off.

I really didn't want him to be either of those things.

"Uh, he's at the house?" I questioned, because I knew he was at the house, but I didn't know why that was a problem.

"Oh my god. He's *here*? What am I even wearing? Do we smell like sex? What the hell, Atlas?" he said, starting to pace back and forth.

I was... confused.

"You're wearing jeans and a sweatshirt, and we showered, so we don't smell like sex," I answered.

He just gave me a sour look. "Does Q know?" he asked.

I held out my hand, and he stared at it a moment before he handed over his phone.

I dialed Liam, and as soon as he picked up, I said, "Aiden is upset."

"About his grandfather?" Liam asked.

"I don't think so," I answered, staring at Aiden, who was muttering to himself. "I think it's a human thing."

"Did you ask him why he's upset?" Liam said.

I heard Quinton mutter in the background, "I can't with you guys. All fucking hopeless." Then he grabbed the phone, because his voice was clear when he said, "Put Aiden on."

I held the phone out to Aiden.

He grabbed it, saying, "Did you know Wilder was *here*?"

"What?" Quinton screeched. "Here, as in *here*?"

"Yes!" Aiden said, still sounding panicked. "*Apparently* he's at Jude and Corbin's." Aiden shot me a dirty look with the first word.

"Fuck! Liam! Why the fuck didn't you tell me Wilder was here?" he demanded.

I could hear Liam mutter about Quinton meeting him at breakfast, but based on Quinton's growl (it was a rather impressive growl for someone who wasn't a hellhound), he didn't like that answer.

"Fuck," Quinton said into the phone. "We'll be right there. Don't go without us. It'll be fine. We'll be fine. Right?" Quinton asked, sounding sure then totally not sure.

Aiden breathed out, like Quinton's panic was somehow calming him down. "Yes, we'll be fine. He'll like us."

"He'll like *you*. You're fucking nice. I'm an asshole," Quinton muttered.

Aiden smiled. "Get over here so we have each other for moral support," he said, then he hung up the phone, glaring at me.

I was still confused. "Wilder won't hurt you," I reassured him.

Aiden rolled his eyes and scoffed at me. It seemed like Quinton's attitude had rubbed off a bit, because he usually wasn't quite this sassy.

I walked over and hugged him. "I'm sorry, my mate, if I somehow distressed you, or if Wilder's presence upsets you. We can leave and not see him if that's what's wrong," I assured him. I had no idea why Wilder would make him nervous, but my mate's happiness came first.

Aiden leaned back and gazed at me, suddenly looking less angry. "You are the sweetest man I have ever met, Atlas."

I grunted. I didn't think many people, or hellhounds, would agree with that assessment.

"Wilder raised you. He adopted you guys. He's really important to you. Of course I want to meet him, but it's also really nerve-wracking to meet the parents, you know," he said, leaning into me. "I was just really surprised. I thought we'd just talk on the phone. I didn't know I was gonna meet your dad today."

I liked the sound of Aiden calling Wilder my dad, even if it wasn't biologically accurate. I also found the idea that he was nervous somewhat odd. "Wilder will love you," I reassured him.

"How do you know?" he asked.

"Because you're my mate, and I love you," I answered.

It must have been the right thing to say, because Aiden was leaning up for a kiss, and I was only too happy to comply. We leisurely kissed until I heard Liam and Quinton walk up.

"Fuck, parents never like me," Quinton mumbled, and Aiden went over and took his arm, patting it. They both started walking toward the house.

Liam and I just looked at each other. He shrugged, and then I shrugged, and then we followed our mates.

Humans were *weird*.

⁕

Despite Quinton's scowl and Aiden's obvious nervousness, Wilder greeted them like he'd known them forever, giving each one a hug that picked their feet off the ground. Jude had music playing and was cooking breakfast, and Corbin, Toby, and Dexter were already there. When they spotted Toby, they seemed more reassured, and I wondered again at this weird nervousness over meeting the parents.

What usually happened when humans met the parents of their mates? I'd have to ask Jude. Perhaps humans had some barbaric customs that needed to be performed that I was unaware of. I couldn't figure out why else both Quinton and Aiden would be nervous.

Whatever they expected, they seemed reassured as we all sat down and ate breakfast together. There was all the general chatter that usually accompanied breakfast when everyone was present, and Wilder sat and looked happily at all of us, smiling and throwing in comments here and there. His ease seemed to put Quinton and Aiden at ease, and I felt my mate grow calmer as we finished eating.

Dexter and Corbin cleared the dishes, and Wilder slid over and looked at Aiden and Quinton.

"I'm so glad to finally meet you both. Welcome to our pack," Wilder said, a gentle smile on his face.

"You don't even know us," Quinton grumbled, even as Aiden elbowed him.

Wilder just chuckled. "Of course Liam would need someone who was spunky. Someone who can drag his attention away from his computer screens. Someone who won't let him always take all the responsibility. You're perfect for my boy," Wilder said.

I think Quinton actually got a little teary, and Liam picked him up and put him on his lap.

Wilder turned to Aiden then. "And you, my boy. I don't think I've ever seen Atlas last so long with all of us together, and I definitely haven't seen him so at peace. You're the reason for that."

"He's the reason for my peace," Aiden responded quietly, reaching out and grabbing my hand.

Wilder smiled at us both. "Perfect for each other," he said.

"I hate to break up the love fest, but we do have an FBI agent in the basement," Dexter announced.

"Ohhh, do you think he could answer some questions about being a crooked FBI agent?" Toby asked, looking excited.

Dexter looked thoughtful, but Jude and Liam both answered, "No," at the same time.

I agreed. Toby was a bloodthirsty little thing, but I didn't think he needed to see the agent. I also didn't think the agent would be very cooperative in having a little chat to help with Toby's next book. Hellbound souls generally weren't the helpful type.

"So, I had this weird dream about my therapist," Aiden said.

All the hellhounds got quiet and stopped what they were doing, looking over at Aiden. He, Quinton, and Toby looked around.

"Oh, is this like some pack mentality thing?" Toby asked.

"It's fucking creepy, is what it is," Quinton replied.

Then Toby started looking around for his notebook. It broke the stillness, and Dexter helped him find a notebook and pen.

Aiden looked at me, and I explained, "Your therapist isn't human, and I'm not sure if it was really a dream."

"Huh. You mean the wings and badass vibe were real?" he asked.

I blinked in shock. "An angel or demon?" I asked, looking at Wilder. "She didn't smell like either."

"No," Aiden answered before Wilder could. "She said something about hellhounds not being the only ones who left the underworld, or something like that. She said she was helping me heal because I had been wronged."

Wilder hummed thoughtfully at that, then he looked at me.

"She's pure. I sensed no rot or evil intentions on her," I told him.

Wilder nodded, then looked back at Aiden. "What did she tell you, son?"

"She said she thought my grandfather was beyond your ability, or something like that. She didn't think he was mortal? I think? She asked about my grandfather having a mark on his face or hands," Aiden told him.

Wilder was very still. "Does he have a mark?"

"Yes. Like this kind of scar or something on his hand. He's had it for as long as I've known him. His brother died in a fire when they were little, and he tried to save him. It's a burn mark from that, apparently. My mom told me the story. The family really doesn't talk about it. I didn't even know my grandfather had a brother," Aiden finished, shrugging.

Wilder leaned back, obviously thinking.

"Helene said he wasn't looking for me, though. She said it was definitely my brother," Aiden added.

"Your older brother?" Wilder asked.

"Yeah," he responded.

Corbin's crow cawed, ruffling its feathers, and I felt a sudden chill.

Liam was typing away on his computer, and he said, "Mark of the beast? That comes up in a search, but that's Revelations, and I don't know how..." Liam trailed off, then he looked at Wilder.

Wilder nodded his head, like he knew what Liam had found.

"Mark of Cain?" Liam asked. "But that's... It can't be."

"It makes the most sense, and it explains why his older brother is looking for him," Wilder answered.

"I wasn't big on church, so can someone please fill me in here," Quinton snapped.

"Cain killed his younger brother, right? Out of jealousy or something?" Aiden said. "But my brother isn't jealous of me. He has everything, and he doesn't even know where I am."

"There's a bit more to it than that," Wilder explained. "Cain killed his younger brother out of jealousy, and god cursed him for it, telling him the ground would no longer yield crops for him and he would be removed from god's sight. But it doesn't end there. God, being god, was forgiving, and when Cain worried over being killed for his actions, god gave him a mark. This mark protected him from being killed."

"Well why the hell would god do that? Cain was an asshole who killed his brother," Quinton grumbled.

Wilder smiled at him. "I can't pretend to know what upper management is thinking, but most afterlifers think it was so that Cain could eventually be redeemed if he so chose. It was a free will thing—giving him a chance to be sorry for his sins and not end up in hell. There's always been speculation that after a few decades Cain did end up remorseful and found his way to purgatory. Others think he wanders Earth still, unrepentant and cursed."

"You don't think my grandfather is Cain?" Aiden asked.

"No, not Cain. But a descendant of Cain is likely. The curse would run in the bloodline, and if an older brother killed a younger brother, with a bit of ritual, probably, then they would receive the mark of Cain. It sounds as if your grandfather has that mark," Wilder answered.

"Why the fuck would he want that?" Quninton asked.

"Eternal life," Toby answered, distractedly writing in his journal. "Oh, that's such a good villain idea. I love it. And obviously your brother is looking for you to kill you so he can get eternal life, too, since he must have figured out that your grandfather has eternal life from killing his younger brother. Because I bet it wasn't an accidental fire. I bet he murdered his brother and used the fire to cover it up."

We all stared at Toby. He must have noticed, because he looked up, then he blushed.

"Ah, yeah, I mean, sorry that your brother is trying to kill you," he said. "Do you want, like, some juice or something? Or a drink? It's early—maybe a mimosa? Family sucks sometimes. Sorry."

Aiden gave a slightly hysterical giggle at that, and Quinton stared at Toby.

"Only you would offer someone a mimosa when they find out their brother is trying to kill them," he said, rolling his eyes. He looked back at Wilder, asking, "But why would he want eternal life at the cost of his soul or whatever?"

"Are you saying I'm descended from Cain?" Aiden asked, interrupting Quinton's question. I could tell my mate was a little disturbed by the idea, and I pulled him into my lap to give him some cuddles.

Wilder waved his hand dismissively. "A huge chunk of the world's population is descended from Cain. Most people say the flood killed them off, but Cain was still around and still fornicating after that. I don't know exactly how the curse gets passed on, though. Perhaps only firstborn sons inherit that bloodline—that would limit it to a much smaller number.

"As for why, eternal life is a great motivator, but there's also the wealth and power on Earth. The ground would no longer yield to Cain, but he did go on to build a city. Obviously his ability to amass and accumulate wealth wasn't inhibited."

"Shit," Aiden said. "Wealth and power definitely sums up my family. And my grandfather used to brag that he was from a long line of firstborn sons. It's why I always felt like he favored my brother, not that he was ever mean to me or anything. I just wasn't his favorite."

"So we kill them," Dexter said matter-of-factly.

"I don't think we can," I growled. Helene had told Aiden that he was beyond us. I hugged Aiden tightly in my lap. I wouldn't let anything happen to him.

Wilder nodded. "Aiden's therapist is right—someone who bears the mark of Cain is beyond our ability. They are no longer mortal, and we only send hellbound mortal souls on. Aiden's grandfather is beyond our reach, but he would also have no reason to hurt you."

"But my brother doesn't have the mark. Not unless he kills me," Aiden said.

"That's right," Wilder answered, reaching out to place a hand on his shoulder. "And we can't let him do that."

Aiden leaned into me, breathing a sigh out.

"So either he kills me, or we kill him," he said.

I hugged my mate tightly. I could tell how distressed he was, but there was no way I was letting anything happen to him.

I would protect my mate no matter what.

Chapter 22

Aiden

My brother was planning to kill me.

The guys finished cleaning up breakfast, and Atlas just sat on the chair and held me as I tried to absorb it all. At some point, Q looked over at me, huffed, and announced that we were going home.

Atlas picked me up, and I halfheartedly declared I could walk, but he carried me anyway. I snuggled into him, pressing my face against his chest.

My brother wanted to kill me.

I thought about one Christmas when I was a teenager. Caleb had gotten me a cookbook from a famous pastry chef, and he'd gotten it signed for me. I'd been so thrilled. I had cherished that book. When I'd been so excited after opening it, he had smiled at me and said he knew I liked to bake.

I remembered a family party where he had come over and snuck me a champagne, and we had joked about how horribly boring it all was. We laughed about all the stuck-up people who were there, making up little stories about them.

I couldn't think of a time when he'd been mean to me. He

hadn't teased or made fun of me. He hadn't been around much, that was true, and most of the time we sort of ignored each other. Our ages were so far apart. But we still had a few moments, times when we connected.

He was my brother.

We had both grown up with my parents, and even though he was older than me, we could give each other looks across the room when they were doing something particularly annoying. When my father started talking about politics, we always gave each other a look, because he could be on the topic for hours. When my mother started on about influencers (she hated the idea of them), we would just smirk at each other.

We hadn't shared much, but we shared a past. A family. Growing up with wealth and privilege and the rules that went along with that.

No one else in the world knew what it was like to grow up in my family. He was the only one.

He was my brother, and he wanted to kill me.

I rubbed my face against Atlas's chest, wiping away the tears that had come to my eyes. We were sitting on the couch at home, although I wasn't even sure when we'd gotten there. Atlas was just quietly holding me and rumbling gently against me.

Eventually I picked my head up. I could hear Liam and Q talking quietly and the clack of computer keys, so they were obviously doing research.

Atlas took one hand and cupped my face, leaning in to give me a soft kiss. He moved back and raised his eyebrows then. Did I want to talk about it? Was I ok? I knew Atlas well enough to know exactly what he was asking,

It was just that I didn't know the answer. I shrugged, and he hugged me tightly again.

"We weren't close, but I still have a few good memories, you know?" I said quietly.

Atlas nodded against me.

"If I kill him, aren't I just as bad as Cain?" I asked.

"You wouldn't kill him, my mate," Atlas answered.

"I know. You guys would do it, but you'd do it for me. So in some ways I would be responsible. I'd feel that way, anyway, even if it doesn't make sense," I answered.

Q came over and sat by us. "Listen, I know you don't want to feel responsible for your brother's death, but if he's a hellbound soul, then a hellhound would kill him no matter what."

"But they wouldn't know about him if it weren't for me," I answered.

Q took my hand, squeezing it. "I can't lose you, Aiden. I know your mate certainly can't lose you either. We're kind of invincible after we're mated to hellhounds, but this whole Cain thing is another level of fucked up, and Liam doesn't know if we're protected from that or not."

"Could they be in danger?" I asked, feeling panicked at the very thought.

"No," Atlas answered. "Your brother is still just a mortal. Not until he kills you and takes the mark could we be hurt."

"But," added Liam from over at the table, "if there's some ritual that allows him to get the mark, I'm not sure afterlifers would be protected from that. Of course, it wouldn't work on hellhounds, because none of us are descendants of Cain. But it could possibly work on you, and even Wilder isn't sure if you'd be protected. This is an old curse, and Wilder said something about the universe being 'unbalanced.' I'm not sure what that means, but we shouldn't take chances."

"I don't even think my brother is evil," I announced.

Q snorted. "Honey, he's trying to kill you. That makes him evil."

I shrugged. "Maybe. But we're making a lot of assumptions. I can't see my brother get killed over assumptions."

"Oh, no," Q said, shaking his head. "Whatever idea you're cooking up is not happening."

I turned to look at Atlas. I knew he was the one I needed to convince. "He's my brother, and we don't know anything about him. Liam can't even find out much. We don't even know if he's hellbound. I have to talk to him. I have to find out for sure. People have free will. Maybe we can change his mind. Maybe that isn't even why he's looking for me. Maybe it has to do with grandfather and protecting me. We just don't know, and we should find out."

Atlas was growling steadily beneath me, and I knew he didn't like the idea.

"Please," I whispered.

He leaned his head against mine. "I can't see you get hurt, mate."

"You'll be there to protect me. I won't go anywhere without you. But I need to talk to him," I answered.

Finally Atlas nodded his head against mine, and I breathed a sigh of relief.

It looked like we would be making plans to meet up with my brother.

⁓⁂⁓

The guys decided they'd have a meeting and strategize, and Q and I went into work, because we were both scheduled for a later shift. Q shot me dirty looks all afternoon, but I wasn't changing my mind. I needed to talk to my brother. I couldn't effectively condemn him to death without knowing for sure. It would haunt me if I did that.

Cass grabbed my arm at one point and announced that I would be ok, so I figured that was a good sign. Otherwise I lost myself in baking, trying not to think about it all. Ser, the woman from yoga class, came into the shop towards the end of our shift, and Q called me out to say hello.

We made some plans (despite Q's general groaning) to meet up for yoga again. Ser said she was thinking of getting certified to teach yoga, and she said I should do it with her. It was tempting, and it was nice to think past all the shit with my brother. I told her I would think about it, and then I was back in the kitchen until the end of our shift.

Liam and Fluffy came to pick us up, and despite Cass's general scowl (Fluffy usually waited in the car), he didn't say anything. One of the customer's commented, but Q just snapped, "Emotional support animal."

We piled into the car, and I cuddled up to Fluffy in the back.

Liam sighed. "I love how he gets to be a dog so he doesn't have to explain everything."

Q said, "You better have a good fucking plan, because I do *not* want Aiden so much as getting a scratch."

Liam reached over and grabbed Q's hand. "Aiden is pack, and we'll all protect him."

I got a warm feeling at hearing that. My biological family may have been shit, and maybe my brother was trying to kill me, but I had these guys. I chuckled a little thinking of Liam telling me he'd hunt me down "in a nice way" and find me if I ever ran away.

Fluffy cocked his head at me, but I just smiled. I'd told him the story already, after all. "I want to hear the plan," I announced.

"So, it was actually quite easy. Much simpler than we thought. We found the contract for Aiden on the dark web, and Jude took it. Apparently he has an assassin identity on there," Liam explained.

"Jude is an assassin?" Q questioned.

"My little hellcat, we're all assassins of a sort," Liam answered.

"Yeah, but he's, like, on the web? Like he's fucking comcast or some shit, taking out ads and going door to door and asking if you might need someone killed?" Q asked. "What the hell?"

"He grew up with humans," Liam answered, like that was somehow an explanation. "At any rate, his prior activity made the fact that he found the mark so quickly much easier to explain. He said he'd seen the photo, and he'd happened upon Alden in the course of his work. He refused to divulge the location, insisting on handing him over in order to be paid. Things aren't really done that way anymore, but assassins don't usually deal with live exchanges, either, so it must have seemed like an acceptable idea to your brother."

"When?" Q asked.

"Tomorrow night," Liam answered. "I asked Cass if you could both have off work for the next few days, and he said he had already planned for it."

"I'm going," Q announced.

"No, my little hellcat, you aren't. And neither am I. I'll conduct surveillance, and you'll help me. We'll keep Toby with us as well. Dexter, Corbin, and Wilder will be near the location in case they're needed, but the exchange will only take place with Jude, Aiden, and Fluffy. Anything else would look too suspicious," Liam answered.

I hugged Fluffy tighter to me. I was kind of dreading it, but I also kind of wished it was happening right away. I couldn't imagine the wait until tomorrow night.

We pulled into the driveway, and Q announced, "You have to show me everything about the exchange point. I wanna know where all the cameras are. Can we put one on Aiden, too? Or Fluffy? Who checks a dog's collar? And we'll need to track their cell phones..."

"Who is the sexy stalker between us? Of course I already track their cell phones. I like the idea of a camera in a dog collar, though," Liam said, opening his door and getting out of the car.

Fluffy growled, and I laughed thinking about him wearing a dog collar. Q and Liam were discussing surveillance, and they were obviously heading toward Liam's place. As much as I wanted to cuddle with everyone tonight, I also wanted some time with Atlas.

I got out of the car, clearing my throat. "So... You guys are gonna be working for a while, right? Maybe we can call you to come back and sleep later? Or for a late dinner?"

Q looked at me and winked.

"Yes, we'll call before we come over, and then we can all have cuddles tonight," Liam stated.

I tried not to laugh at Liam talking about having cuddles, because it was kind of ridiculous, but it was also what I wanted. Liam and Q headed toward the big house, which I guess was kind of their house. Although they still lived with us, too, but we all had private time if we needed it this way.

Fluffy huffed and grabbed my sleeve, and I laughed as he led me toward the house. We got inside, and I looked down to slip off my sneakers, and when I glanced up there was a very naked Atlas standing there.

"Hi," I said, and I knew it was sort of dumb even as I said it. He was just so damn gorgeous.

"Liam said that sometimes when humans are stressed they may want cuddles. He also said they may want sex. He even said sometimes they liked a hot bath. What would you like, my mate?" Atlas asked.

I was staring at his dick, and yeah, that thing was growing as I was staring. I remembered the feel of him inside me, and I started stripping off my own clothes. Atlas growled in approval.

I took his hand and led him into the bedroom, pushing him onto the bed. He stared at my hardening dick, but he still asked, "Does this mean you would like sex? Because cuddles are excellent as well."

God, I loved this man. He was so willing to give me everything I needed, and I really wanted to give him everything he might need.

I crawled my way onto the bed, stopping at his dick. It was a beautiful cock, so hard and jutting up so proudly. I wrapped my hand around the base, squeezing lightly and sliding it up, thrilled when a drop of precum appeared at the tip. I did that for him. I made him feel good.

He'd sucked me more than once, and I had never returned the favor. It was a beautiful dick, and it didn't even look like the other one. It would probably taste different, too. It would probably be a whole different experience. I used to like sucking dick—a firm cock on my tongue and in my throat. I could do this. I could lean forward, and I could take him into my mouth. There was a roiling sensation in my stomach, but it was ok. This was Atlas.

Hands gripped my shoulders and hauled me up, and suddenly I was looking into Atlas's eyes. There were flames burning in them, but it was like I could see the love there too. Then he leaned down and bit my shoulder.

"Ouch!" I grumbled, because it had *not* been a sexy bite. It hadn't *really* hurt, but it hadn't felt nice either. I stared down at him grumpily, but he just smiled when he looked at me.

"Grumpy Aiden smells much nicer than sad or worried Aiden," he declared, and I couldn't help the little laugh that escaped me.

He pulled me down onto his chest, cuddling me close and growling softly, but in an almost pleasant way.

"I want to give you the same pleasure you've given me," I mumbled against his chest.

He actually laughed, and I lifted my head to look at him.

"My mate, your presence gives me pleasure. Sucking you and tasting you gives me pleasure. Feeling your mouth on mine, feeling your body against me, feeling our hard cocks against each other, feeling inside of you and hearing your moans—it all gives me pleasure. Knowing that you're enjoying yourself is pleasurable for me. Knowing that you're sad—that does not give me pleasure. I don't want you to do anything you don't want to do," he said, then he leaned his forehead up against mine.

I sighed. "But I do want to suck you. I want the idea of it, at least. I want to reclaim it or whatever. I want to replace the bad memories with good ones."

Atlas pulled me close again, so I was almost smothered in his chest. I kind of didn't mind. He was an inferno against my skin, hard and hot and yet somehow still comfy.

"I want that for you, too. But there's no rush, my mate. We

have eternity. You don't have to push yourself. Maybe you start with just staring at my dick. I don't mind. Then one day maybe you give it a lick. Just a lick, like a lollipop. Then maybe one day you lick it a little more. Then maybe one day you'll want a whole taste for just a moment," Atlas said.

"Like exposure therapy to your dick?" I asked, laughing. The idea sounded kind of absurd, but also kind of... fun?

I slid down Atlas. We had both gotten softer when we first started talking, but I had hardened up again as Atlas had described all the things he enjoyed, and as I stared at his dick, it went from half mast to full hardness. I looked up at him, and he was smiling at me, flames dancing in his eyes.

"You really do have a pretty dick," I murmured.

Atlas actually blushed, which made me giggle. Without too much thought, I leaned down and gave a long lick from the base of his dick up to the head, getting a taste of his precum. It was sweet, not sour like I expected, and I barely had time to process it, never mind worry about doing more, before Atlas was dragging me back up and rolling on top of me, kissing me frantically.

His tongue was in my mouth, his teeth were nibbling on my lips, his hips were pressing down into mine, and the surge of arousal that ran through me was intense. I pushed my hips up, my tongue frantically dueling with his. I felt out of control in my need, and I bit down on his lower lip so hard I think I tasted blood. Before I could even pull off, he moaned and clutched me tighter, letting me know he liked it.

I ran my hands along the muscles of his back, which were flexing as he moved. I moaned, feeling how hard and strong he was. Our dicks were rubbing against each other, sending tingles through my whole body. It felt amazing, but it wasn't enough—it only made me more frantic. I wanted to be closer to Atlas. I would climb inside his skin if I could.

I wrapped my legs around him, and I gasped as I felt something slick rub lightly against my hole.

"Atlas?" I gasped out, pulling our mouths apart.

He smirked at me. "Just my tail."

Holy fuck. Just his tail. He leaned back down, his lips pressing against mine, our breaths mingling together as "just his tail" slowly entered me. I groaned as it slipped in deeper, finding that spot that made sparks shoot through my body.

"Oh god, Atlas," I groaned, then his tongue was sliding against mine and our lips were pressing together, and his tail was working in and out of me, hitting that spot on each thrust in.

"Do you want my knot?" Atlas asked as he broke our kiss, and he must have meant the overwhelming fullness I'd felt last time.

Suddenly that was all I wanted. I craved it. "Yes. Now, Atlas. Please," I moaned.

His one hand reached down to pull my hips up. The other was supporting him, and I grabbed onto his arm with my hand, the strong, flexing muscle so sexy beneath my fingers. That fucking tail must have guided his dick in, and I didn't even know where the hell the lube came from, but he was wet as he pressed in, slowly stretching me.

He was definitely bigger than his tail. I panted, closing my eyes, but his low growl had me opening them again, staring into the flames as he pressed in, and I got fuller with each second. It was slow, and it was so intense I almost couldn't tell if it was pleasure or pain as he filled me up.

"Breathe, mate. Breathe me in," he murmured.

I gasped, and all I smelled was Atlas—that strong, musky, fiery smell, and then his hips were against mine, and his mouth pressed to mine, gently licking at my lips as I gasped and grew used to the sensation of him inside me.

It wasn't long before it wasn't enough. I wiggled my hips, and he groaned in pleasure. I thrust again, wanting him to move, and he understood and did exactly what I wanted. He pulled almost all the way out, then slowly slid back in, rubbing my channel and gliding over my prostate.

He was slow and patient, even as I moaned and gasped underneath him. His tail came up to slide around my dick, squeezing and caressing just below the head. It was glorious, and then it was torturous, because I needed *more*. I pressed my legs and feet against him, urging him to go faster, but still he kept up that lazy, slow pace. I looked up to see fire dancing in his eyes, his forehead furrowed in concentration, like it was just as excruciatingly hard for him to go slow.

I wanted him out of control, and I reached my head up and bit into his shoulder, hard. Atlas growled, and his hips stuttered and then picked up speed. I cried out, even as I tasted the coppery tang of blood on my tongue. I had broken the skin, but I couldn't even care as Atlas pounded into me.

His dick was growing bigger inside me, and his tail was jerking my cock, wrapped around it with the tip caressing the head. My orgasm slammed into me from nowhere, cum spurting out between our bodies.

I cried out, and although his tail loosened, it held onto my still hard dick, and he continued to thrust into me. My god, it was too much. I was mewling, the painful pleasure overwhelming every sense.

"Do you want me to stop?" he panted.

I barely had the words to cry out, "Don't stop."

He was still growing thicker, and every movement was caressing my prostate, rubbing against it. He was impossibly big, stretching me wide. His tail was wrapped lightly around my dick, but even that was almost too much.

He was barely thrusting now, his thickness making only small movements possible, but each one was a massage on my insides, intense and overstimulating. He bit into my neck, and the line between pain and pleasure disappeared, and it was all pleasure. I cried out again, a second orgasm pulled out of me as I felt Atlas growling against my skin, his own orgasm making his body twitch above me and his dick twitch inside me, emptying into me.

We came together for an eternity, and when the pleasure passed and we were just two sweaty bodies lying together, I felt exhaustion pulling me under.

"I love you," I managed to murmur.

"I love you, my mate," I heard Atlas whisper, and then I closed my eyes and surrendered to sleep.

CHAPTER 23

ATLAS/FLUFFY

I cleaned Aiden up, and then we both had a little nap before we called Liam and Quinton to come over for a very late dinner. We ate and chatted, avoiding the topic of tomorrow, and then we all piled into bed, a happy puppy pile.

Keep mate safe, Fluffy growled, and as we all cuddled, I clutched Aiden tight as I fell asleep, determined to do just that.

We slept long and hard, and the morning found us all at Jude and Corbin's house, eating breakfast. We managed to keep things light, everyone joking around and teasing each other. Jude and the sheriff were the center of quite a few comments, and Wilder said he would need to meet this sheriff, which made Jude blush, strangely enough.

When breakfast was cleared, we started planning. Liam and Quinton showed off all the cameras near the area, the map tracking our cell phones, and then they gave me a collar—which Fluffy grumbled relentlessly about in my head—which also had a tracker and a camera.

They put a tracker in Aiden's shoe, and Jude had trackers on him as well. We hashed out everything multiple times, and then there was nothing to do but wait. I changed into my hound form, and

Aiden and I took a long, leisurely walk through the woods. He was thoughtful, and he talked a lot about his brother. He went through all his memories, good and indifferent. He talked about all the times his brother was nice to him, but also all the times his brother was absent, if not physically, then emotionally. He talked about his brother's family, and I knew he felt bad thinking about them.

I simply walked beside him, licking his hand or leaning against him as needed. My mate was strong, and this wouldn't break him. I had no doubt that his brother aimed to kill him, but I understood his need to speak to him and to find out for sure. He needed closure on this. My Aiden had a good heart and soul. He could wish people dead—he had certainly been happy when his kidnapper had died—but he'd had ample proof of that man's evil. He couldn't align the two versions of his brother in his head, though.

We got back, ate another meal, and hung out with the pack until it was time to go. Wilder, Corbin, and Dexter left first, but eventually it was time. Jude drove, and Aiden and I stayed in the backseat, his arms wrapped around me the whole drive. It was a couple hours' drive, but it went by quickly, and then we were pulling up in front of a warehouse in an industrial part of town.

"How very mobster-like," Aiden muttered. "It could be straight out of the movies." He almost smiled. "Caleb would go for movie-like, though. He always liked movies."

I could smell two people inside, one rotten and one almost rotten, along with the stench of a gun. I really hated guns. Jude had brought one as well, though. He led us both inside the warehouse, which held rows of plastic-wrapped pallets. It was filled, but the area the men were in looked like it was under construction, with some of the flooring pulled up behind where they were standing. There was a folding table and some chairs scattered around as well.

We came to a stop a few feet away, and Aiden's brother stepped forward. I was surprised to smell that he was *not* the rotten soul.

222

The other man must have been an assistant or hired muscle—he certainly didn't look old enough to be the grandfather, and he didn't bear a family resemblance. It was obvious that Aiden and Caleb were related, though.

Caleb being morally grey rather complicated things. Jude's stride broke for a moment, then he continued walking, obviously sensing the same thing I did. We couldn't kill someone who wasn't hellbound.

"Caleb?" Aiden asked, sounding surprised. He was gripping my fur tightly, but when I looked up, he acted confused and not nervous. "What are you doing here? Did they get you, too? Are we here for ransom?"

Aiden had said that would be the conclusion any of them would have drawn, and he wanted to see what his brother would say.

"Alden," he said, smiling. "I've been looking for you. I'm so glad to have finally found you."

Jude cleared his throat, stating, "I'm due payment."

The other man drew a gun. He was quick, but Jude was quicker, and he fired a shot off a moment before the man, hitting him in the forehead. Jude then crumpled to the ground, although I didn't smell blood on him. I guessed he was playing dead. It hadn't been part of the plan, but it made sense for him to seem not to be a threat.

"Jude?" Aiden cried, starting to rush over to him.

I grabbed his hand lightly in my teeth, and he looked down at me, stopping in his tracks. I licked his hand, hoping he would know that Jude was ok. He seemed to, because he looked back at his brother.

"What the hell, Caleb? What's going on?" he demanded.

"That man kidnapped you. He couldn't live," Caleb answered. "As for my man, well, he knew the risks. He wasn't a very good person, either. I'm just sorry you had to see that, Alden. You were always a sensitive person. But you can come home now, and take your proper place in the family."

He started forward, but I growled menacingly, and he stopped.

"An attack dog? I do approve, but call him off. I want to hug my brother," Caleb announced.

Aiden looked at him, and his face twisted. "You have never wanted to hug me once in our lives, Caleb, so cut the shit. I'm not going anywhere with you. I'm not going home. I'm not getting into a car with you. I will drive off and disappear, and you will never look for me again if you have any love for me at all."

Caleb grimaced. "I'm afraid that isn't possible, Alden. Grandfather is dead, and you're needed for inheritance purposes, or else all the companies will suffer. Mother and father will lose everything. You don't want that, do you?" he asked.

Aiden stared at him before replying. "All the companies went to you, the firstborn son of the firstborn son. And grandfather isn't dead."

Well then, I guess we were laying all our cards on the table. I sat down next to Aiden, which seemed to reassure Caleb a bit. He walked over and picked up the gun from the dead man. I let him. I could block a bullet if needed.

"Grandfather told you?" he said, the gun loosely pointing toward me. He kept it carefully away from Aiden, which was fine with me.

Aiden just gave a shrug.

"Huh. I'll have to have words with him about that. It does make things rather more difficult. I was planning to make it very simple and painless for you. You never would have even known, Alden. I'm not a monster, after all. You would have just gone to sleep and not woken up. I wouldn't have been so awful as grandfather was, keeping you awake and conscious for the ceremony," Caleb said.

"How long have you planned on killing me?" Aiden asked. "I remember that you were nice to me. You were kind."

"Of course I was. You're my brother. You're my passage to eternal life and endless power and riches. I love you for that, probably more than I love mother and father. I'm thankful for you, Alden. Father didn't have the option since our grandmother died before she could have a second son, so grandfather never even told him about the curse of Cain. You can rest assured our parents will know nothing of this. They'll think you're happily out there living your life," Caleb said.

"And I'm just supposed to be ok with being killed in some ritual?" Aiden scoffed.

His hand was gripping my fur hard enough to hurt, but he could pull all my hair out if it got him through this moment. I knew he had been hoping his brother didn't mean to kill him. I just didn't understand how his brother wasn't hellbound, because that obviously was his plan.

"I'll still knock you out, Alden. Then it's a simple ritual where you'll bleed out into the ground, and I'll receive the mark and the protection that comes with it," Caleb said.

It was insane how perfectly reasonable he sounded. He walked over, still pointing the gun at me, reached into a bag that was sitting on a folding table behind him, and grabbed a syringe and a knife. The knife was black, and it was obviously a ritualistic blade.

"I love you, Caleb. You're the only brother I'll ever have. You'll condemn yourself to hell and to being removed from god's sight if you do this," Aiden pleaded. "Don't do this. For your own sake."

Caleb actually laughed. "Being out of god's sight is not a bad thing, Alden. It allows us to do whatever we need to without fear of retribution. And I have no worries of hell if I never die," he said, shrugging. "It's good I'm the older brother. You're too soft to claim the birthright yourself."

"What grandfather told you was lies," Aiden said, trying again.

I could smell the rot seeping into Caleb, though, and I realized that Aiden probably wouldn't be able to convince him. Free will meant he wasn't hellbound yet, but doing this would rot his soul.

The tricky part would be the timing. I couldn't let him harm Aiden, obviously, but his intentions had to be clear enough that he became fully hellbound and worthy of death.

I huffed a sigh, and I saw Jude flash a smirk at me before his face looked peacefully dead again. The jerk. He knew waiting was not my strong point.

"Grandfather showed me that he cannot die. When he faked his death, he gave me the ritual, and then he left everything to me, taking enough wealth to do some traveling," Caleb answered.

"Cursed to roam the earth, you mean," Aiden snapped. Then his face turned soft. "You're my brother. Please, Caleb. Please don't do this."

He looked genuinely regretful for a moment, and then he fired the gun into me, saying, "I'm sorry, Alden."

Fuck, that hurt. Motherfucking guns. At least he didn't get my head, because those were *really* a bitch to heal.

"Fluffy!" Aiden cried, falling to his knees beside me and taking his attention off his brother. He leaned into me, tears already falling from his eyes. I licked his arm to let him know I was alright, but I'm not sure he got the message.

He was turned toward me, so he didn't see his brother coming up behind him with the syringe and the gun.

"You shot Fluffy," Aiden said, finally looking up at his brother.

"It's alright, Alden," he said calmly, and he pressed the syringe to Aiden's neck, pressing the plunger down. I reached my head up and bit him, making him back off before he could fully drug Aiden. A drug couldn't kill him with our mating, but I still didn't want him to get the full dose.

Aiden pulled the syringe out of his neck as Caleb cursed and shot me again. Fuck. Fucking hell. Two gunshots. Aiden cried out, but his eyes were drooping, and I licked his hand.

Let go, mate. We've got you, Fluffy whispered.

It was like Aiden heard him. He fell on top of me, and he managed to whisper, "Fire Fluffy," before the drugs claimed him.

Well, I figured that was permission, which was good, because his brother wasn't leaving this room alive.

Caleb came over, carefully avoiding me, and dragged Aiden off of my body and over to the patch of the warehouse where the floor looked like it wasn't complete. He began muttering then, holding the knife, and the smell of rot was suddenly all consuming. He had made his choice, and he was hellbound. Jude and I rose at the same time, but I was quicker. Fire Fluffy was on Caleb before he could even get a scream out, the knife knocked from his hand.

"Well, he's out cold," Jude said, checking on Aiden. "Fine, but sound asleep." He looked over at me, then at Caleb, who was whimpering beneath me. "Probably for the best. Our Aiden is soft," Jude said to him, "and I'm afraid he wouldn't like what's about to happen to you."

I changed into my human form, and Caleb squeaked in surprise. I looked around, smelling the air. "Thank you for the location, though. No one will hear you scream."

He did scream, then. And those screams continued on and on.

It's a good thing Aiden slept through it all. He was too good for what his brother deserved.

<hr>

"How do you feel?" I asked my mate. He was groggy but awake, and we were home, snuggled in bed.

He snuffled against my chest. "Numb," he answered.

I didn't think he meant his body, and I squeezed him tightly.

"He's dead, isn't he?" he asked.

"Yes," I answered. "He had a choice when he went into that warehouse, and he chose the path that led to death. You did everything you could to save him, Aiden," I reassured him. I didn't outright tell him that his brother hadn't been hellbound at first. Jude and I both agreed we didn't want him second guessing everything he had said and wondering if there was some way he could have changed his brother's path.

There wasn't. Jude and I both knew that. The choice was his alone, and he had made it. Aiden couldn't have saved him, and he didn't need the burden of wondering if he could have.

"He said my parents didn't know," Aiden said.

I grunted in response.

"I just wonder, then, why they named us Caleb and Alden. Kind of close to Cain and Abel, isn't it?" he commented.

I grunted again, kissing his head. "Perhaps it was your grandfather's idea," I assured him.

He nodded. "Grandfather never talked to me. He showered me with gifts, but he never got close to me. I just thought Caleb was his favorite."

I squeezed him again, letting him know I was listening.

"I don't want to talk about them anymore, though. I don't want to see them again or think about them. They're not my family. Not anymore. You're my family now. You and all your brothers, Q, and even Toby and his weird friends. And Cass and Kushiel and the people at the coffee shop. That's what family is, and it's better than all the riches in the world or eternal life."

"Yes," I grumbled.

"Maybe if my brother had known love like that, he wouldn't have made the choices he made," Aiden mused.

"Eh, that's bullshit," Quinton announced from the doorway.

He climbed into bed next to Aiden. Liam followed him and cuddled up on the other side of his mate. Quinton wrapped his arms around Aiden, and for a moment we had a bit of a tug of war that led to me growling. Aiden was *my* mate, and I got the biggest cuddles.

Aiden somehow snuggled into both of us at the same time.

"You would've given him love, Aiden, but he chose money and power. That's on him. But you're right, we are your family, and you're fucking stuck with us," Quinton said.

Then he slapped my hand, the little shit, trying to hog more of Aiden. I growled again, lifting my head up and showing my teeth, which made Liam growl from the other side of the bed.

"He's hogging my mate," I snapped.

"Learn to fucking share, Fluffy," Quinton snapped.

Aiden just giggled between us, and Quinton and I looked at each other, both relaxing at the sound. Our Aiden would be ok. After all, Quinton was right—he was fucking stuck with us, and we'd make sure he was happy.

EPILOGUE

AIDEN

"And how do you feel about your brother's death?" Helene asked me.

I stared at her. The glasses and mussy bun were in place, and no wings were in sight, but once I had seen her in a different form, it was like I couldn't unsee it.

I shrugged, trying to focus. "I mean, I feel sad, but it kind of doesn't feel real? And I'm ok with that. I'm ok with remembering the kind but detached brother, and not the one who was planning to kill me in a warehouse. I'm ok with not really thinking about him at all, honestly. Maybe that seems harsh, but I've survived a lot in life, and weirdly, him drugging me in a warehouse isn't the worst of it."

Helene nodded. "I'm glad this trauma didn't set you back on your journey of healing, Aiden. I'm also very glad you won't need to worry about your family anymore."

I tilted my head at her, reaching to pet Fluffy, who'd come with me. It occurred to me that the head tilt probably looked like Atlas, and I almost chuckled. She seemed to understand the gesture, though.

"Yes, you really won't have to worry about them anymore," she reassured me.

"But what about my grandfather? All the guys are talking about him. He's a definite loose end," I said.

"He's not your loose end, though. He has no interest in you, and he isn't your responsibility," she assured me.

"Is he your responsibility?" I asked, curious about her.

She took off her glasses and looked at me. "I feel like our time together is almost done, Aiden. You've grown so much and come so far."

I nodded, but there was a lump in my throat. "Are you leaving?" I asked, sad at the thought.

She looked off into the distance, as if she was thinking. Hell, maybe she was seeing the future. I didn't know.

"What are you?" I asked, unable to help myself.

She looked over and smiled. "Fury," she answered.

I was confused for a moment before I remembered my ninth grade mythology lessons. "Like the furies? Weren't they all about vengeance and punishing those who broke oaths or hurt family members and loved ones?"

"Aiden, what better way to achieve retribution against someone who harms you than to go on to heal and live a full, rich life? That is the best vengeance against the monsters in the world—to not let them win," she said.

Huh. I had never thought of it like that. Maybe she was right. Every day I wasn't afraid, and I got out of bed, and I loved Atlas, I wasn't letting my kidnapper win. I was defeating him, even in death.

"But no, I'm not leaving just yet. My work here isn't done. This is such an interesting town, after all. We'll see each other again, Aiden," she assured me.

I breathed a sigh of relief and stood up. Our time was up, and I was expected for a "gathering" at Toby's house. Oh boy.

As Helene walked me to her office door, I could almost swear I saw the woman from my dream, wings and writhing hair, and she said, "Don't worry, though, Aiden. Helping people heal isn't the only way I achieve vengeance."

Well, that was a scary as fuck thought. I just smiled, though, and left the office, taking a deep breath when we got outside. Corbin had driven us, and he was sitting in the car with a crow perched on his shoulder.

It was a quiet ride back, and we were pulling up to Toby's before long.

We got out of the car, but Corbin stayed in the driver's seat and stared at the house for a moment, almost like he was in a trance.

"Coming inside?" I asked.

He shook his head and looked at me. "Not yet," he said. "It isn't time."

With that cryptic statement, he pulled out of the driveway and drove off.

"Ok then. That was weird," I said.

Fluffy just shrugged, which was a bit weird in dog form.

When we got inside I may have clutched onto Atlas a bit, mumbling, "I like how you get to be a dog so you don't have to talk to anyone."

I looked down, and he panted up at me. The smartass. I smiled, because it was still easier to be here with him by my side, whether or not he talked.

"Holy shit, that's a huge fucking dog!" Sebbie exclaimed, coming over. He held a hand out, but of course Fluffy turned up his nose, like the very thought of greeting someone like that was offensive. I chuckled.

"Come have a drink!" Sebbie gushed, leading the way in.

Jude, Dexter, Liam, and Q were all sitting at the table, and they were staring at Toby, Josh, Cass, Kushiel, and, surprisingly, Ser. Apparently she knew Cass and Kushiel, because they were chatting away. Toby and Josh were chatting, too, and Wilder was nowhere to be seen at the moment.

"Why am I getting middle school dance vibes with two separate groups?" I murmured to Atlas.

Jude must have heard, because he snorted in amusement. Wilder took that moment to come in the front door, and he stopped to look at everyone, eyebrows raised.

He came up next to me, sniffing the air, and he draped an arm around my shoulder. It made me feel good that he was so casually affectionate, like I was just part of the family.

I mean, I guess I was, but I still didn't feel like I knew Wilder all that well, and his unconditional acceptance was... just not something I was used to.

"This is like a bad joke. An angel, an oracle, a Nephilim, some hellhounds, and... huh... that's interesting..." he said quietly, sniffing and trailing off.

"Well, they aren't walking into a bar, but a bloodthirsty writer's house may be an even better punchline," I said. "And I don't want to know who's what. I already found out my therapist is a fury, and that's enough for today."

Kushiel and the hellhounds all looked over at me, varying degrees of surprise on their faces, but they must've quickly realized how odd that was because they all went back to their conversations.

Hellhounds and their good hearing. Apparently Kushiel fell into the good hearing category too. I still didn't want to know. Head in the sand—that was me.

"Huh," Wilder said, squeezing me a bit with his arm. "This town really is so very interesting. I had forgotten about furies. She's right, there were more than hellhounds that chose to leave hell. My boys have picked up quite the interesting mix of afterlifers and almost-mortals."

"Almost-mortals?" I asked, then I held a hand up. "Never mind. I don't want to know. I like just thinking of everyone as just... everyone."

Wilder laughed, and Josh looked over. Wilder seemed to sense it, because he looked directly at Josh, making him blush and look away quickly.

Interesting.

My eyebrows were up when Wilder turned back to me, and he smiled softly. "Not time yet, I think," he said.

"Corbin said the same thing," I told him.

"Did he, now? That's interesting. Very interesting, indeed," Wilder said. "This town is really going to be an adventure, I can already tell. The universe may be unbalanced, but this place is working to fix things. It's a good choice."

He patted my back then and walked off toward the table, avoiding Josh, despite Josh sneaking looks at him. I pet Fluffy's head. Very interesting, indeed.

"I think our pack might get bigger," I murmured, and Fluffy licked my hand in agreement.

With that, we waded into the fray, ready to socialize. I could manage an hour, at least, before Fluffy and I snuck off for some peace and quiet.

<hr>

Unfortunately, it wasn't even a half hour before Jude looked utterly ecstatic and we heard a car coming up the driveway.

"Well, shit," muttered Liam, and I figured we were about to get a visit from Sheriff Paul.

Since my brother was gone, I didn't feel the same level of panic or dread about him, and he had really proven himself to be a good person. He had warned us about the photo, after all.

By the time he was at the front door, Jude was already throwing it open. Thankfully we hadn't all crowded around the door like movie characters hiding something this time.

"Walrus! Come in!" Jude announced, and then he was leading the sheriff in. The sheriff glanced around at the group, blinking twice.

"I'm sorry, I didn't realize you were having a party. I can come back another time," he stated. Then his gaze found Ser.

"Seraphina Caelius?" he asked, looking at her.

She strode over, smiling. "Well hello, sheriff," she said flirtily, and I think Jude actually growled at her.

"I've been looking for your brother, Michael Caelius. He was on the force before I took over as sheriff, and I've been hoping to speak to him," the sheriff stated.

"Ah, yeah. Michael and his partner are hard to pin down. They're out causing chaos most of the time," she said, and for some reason that made Cassius snort in amusement. "I'll tell him you're looking for him, though," she said.

"What can I help you with, sheriff?" Jude asked, and even I couldn't miss the suggestive tone.

Ser obviously didn't either, because she rolled her eyes and walked back over to chat with Q.

The sheriff looked at me, though. "How are you, Aiden?" he asked.

"I'm good," I answered, feeling a little weird.

I could tell pretty much everyone was watching us while pretending not to watch us, which was kind of weird. The sheriff looked around, and he must have noticed it, too, but he didn't comment.

"I wanted to check in on you. I heard something rather concerning," he said.

"Aww, isn't that sweet, you looking out for our Aiden," Jude said. I swear he actually fluttered his eyelashes at the man.

The sheriff just blinked at him, then he looked at me and added, "I'm glad you're ok. The agent who circulated that photo is... no longer with the FBI," he said. "And apparently the man in the photo was found and... acquired, and I worried that perhaps someone else had mistaken your identity for that man's. The person looking for that man seems to have disappeared as well."

"Ah, yeah, we killed him in a warehouse because he was planning to kill Aiden to achieve immortal life, and we obviously couldn't let that happen. But don't worry, because he was evil, and we got rid of the body and didn't even take him to the torture basement. We still have to track down the evil, immortal grandfather, though," Jude said.

Everyone literally stopped what they were doing to stare at Jude and the sheriff. The sheriff stared at Jude.

"You're lucky I don't drag you down to the station one of these times," he finally muttered.

"Oh, Walrus, I thought you'd never ask. Would you like to use handcuffs on me?" he asked, holding his hands out and winking.

"Where's my notebook?" Toby mumbled from the other side of the room. "I think there was a meme about this, and you know, it's a great story idea…" he trailed off as Dexter handed him a notebook and pen.

"Sheriff, ignore my idiot brother, and why don't you have a snack while you're here," Liam said, coming over and smacking Jude upside the head. "Aiden's cookies are really the best."

He led the sheriff off to grab a cookie, and Jude sighed dreamily next to me. I just looked at him, shaking my head. I had a feeling he wasn't going to stop throwing himself in the sheriff's path. Either he'd end up arrested or mated—I wasn't sure which way I was leaning on that one.

I looked at Fluffy, and he licked my hand, smiling. I took that to mean he was voting for mating.

We managed another half hour after that, but only because I'd promised myself an hour of socializing. I loved people, especially all of these people. Heck, even Josh, Sebbie, and the sheriff were growing on me, but it was still a lot, and Atlas was all too ready to head out when I gave him a look.

I snuck out without any goodbyes—they all knew where to find me, anyway, although I did walk by Josh and give him a nod. He looked like he was having fun, but I could see the shadows beneath his eyes. I didn't know him well, but I still worried.

Fluffy and I headed out, taking the long way home through the woods. We walked silently for a bit, just decompressing after all the people.

Finally, I said, "You know, I may have lost my brother, but I gained all of you. That whole crazy crew in there is like family, or they could be, at least. And I know they aren't all pack, but they still all feel like family."

Fluffy licked my hand in agreement. I guessed that they didn't need to be mated to a hellhound to still feel like family. After all, Cass and Q had been my family way before I was mated to Atlas.

"We make our own family," I announced. "I guess you know that, because that's what you did with Wilder and your brothers. I'm so glad Wilder found you, Fluffy. I'm so glad you didn't have to be alone. I feel sad thinking about you without them."

We reached the door of our house, and Fluffy turned into Atlas as we walked in. He grabbed me and kissed me, his lips firm yet soft beneath mine. It was a gentle kiss, sweet and slow, and I sighed against his mouth.

He lifted his head and pressed his lips to my forehead, holding me.

"I don't regret the time before Wilder," he said softly. "I learned what unconditional acceptance in a pack meant before I ever had to deal with people. It was lonely, yes, but it made me more thankful for what I later found."

"Still, I wish you were never lonely," I said.

"I wish you were never raised the way you were, and that you were never kidnapped," he said. He gripped me tighter. "But I also understand that those things made you who you are, and you're the strongest, bravest person I know, and I love you just as you are."

"I love you too, Fluffy," I said, feeling teary.

"If I hadn't been lonely and learned how to be a wolf, then I never would have gotten to know this strong, resilient man who liked to take walks in the woods," he continued. "You fill all the lonely parts of my soul, my mate."

I leaned up and kissed him, then I snuggled into his bare chest. Atlas didn't talk much, but when he did, he really said the best stuff ever. I breathed in the smell of my mate, and I felt his naked body against mine. He breathed in as well, and I knew he could smell the arousal running through me.

I wasn't dead, after all, and Atlas was all naked and hugging me and saying romantic stuff. I only had so much willpower. I thought maybe I'd like to try taking a lick of his lollipop again (and god, wasn't that corny—I almost grimaced at myself).

I didn't worry about what would happen next, though. I purposely cleared my mind and just breathed in the warm, comforting scent of Atlas. We'd get to the fun stuff, and we'd do it at whatever pace worked for us.

After all, I had forever with my mate. There was no rush. The joy was in the journey, and we were taking it together.

Afterword

If you want to find out more about Josh and Wilder, preorder the next novel in the *Hellhounds of Paradise Falls* Series from Shannon Mae on AMAZON.

Author's Note

Dear Reader,

This book was an amazing experience, and I really didn't want to say goodbye to Aiden and Atlas. Aiden's trauma was heavy to deal with, and I drew from my own past as well as many other people's stories in order to write his character. I want to reiterate what Helene said, though—everyone deals with trauma differently. Aiden is in NO WAY meant to represent what is "normal" or even typical when it comes to dealing with trauma and healing. The journey is different for everyone. If you or a loved one have experienced trauma, there are resources available, and please do use them. It's very hard to be on a healing journey by yourself—find someone you trust to help you through it. (And I cannot stress enough that if you are in therapy, you should trust and like your therapist. Not every therapist will be a match. Find your own Helene.)

There was a lot of heavy stuff, but I also loved the light moments in this book. The hellhounds are, as usual, clueless about humans. Atlas was just so amazingly adorable with Aiden, too. I expected him to be this badass character, but he really was Fluffy when it came to Aiden. They were so sweet and cute together, and I loved writing them. I also loved all the side character development—Helene and Ser were especially fun to have show up in the book. I hope you enjoyed their presence as much as I did.

If you're looking for more of Toby and Dexter, they were featured in <u>How to Flirt with a Hellhound</u>. Liam and Quinton got up to their own trouble in <u>How to Hack a Hellhound</u>. If you want to read Cassius and Kushiel's story, they are from the Demonic Disasters and Afterlife Adventures series, and their story is in <u>A Beginner's Guide to Ghosts, Fallen Angels, and Other Afterlifers</u>.

Ser is also a side character in the Demonic Disasters series—she is Michael and Gabriel's sister, and she couldn't help butting her way into this story as well. Paradise Falls is never dull, that's for sure, and of course Ser would find all the excitement.

Josh is up next, and he'll finally get away from that boyfriend we've all been worrying about. Eventually Sebbie and the sheriff will get their books as well—they're all chatting away in my head, anxious to be written.

If you enjoyed this book, please leave a review. Every time one of my books is recommended or I hear from a fan, it inspires me. None of this would be possible without all of you. Thank you!

Happy Reading!
Shannon Mae

About the Author

Shannon Mae began her journey in the M/M romance world as an avid reader, then a beta reader, and eventually an editor who works with the unparalleled Tammy B. PA from Aspen Tree E.A.S.

When a dear friend suggested she should write her own book, she decided to do just that. She gravitates to writing paranormal romance, since that genre is her first love, and her books tend to be low-angst and filled with happily-ever-afters.

She is an unfailing optimist with a side of snark and sarcasm. When she isn't editing, writing, or working her day job, which she loves, you'll find her on some outdoor adventure or embarking on a hands-on project (that is probably slightly more complex than she thought it was).

She lives in a small, seaside town on the east coast, and she spends her free time with her eye-rolling, sassy teenage daughter and her adorably loving dog.

Life is a place full of mysteries and wonders, and she hopes to capture that joy and fun in her writing. Adding some fun, sexy times makes it all complete.

Shannon Mae loves hearing from readers!

Join <u>Shannon Mae's Menagerie</u> on Facebook for updates and all kinds of fun things!

 Visit Shannon's website at <u>shannonmae.com</u> and sign up for her newsletter! You'll get teasers, free chapters, and all the latest updates!

Also By Shannon Mae

Demonic Disasters and Afterlife Adventures:
(Paranormal Romance)
A Beginner's Guide to Death, Demons, and Other Afterlife
Disasters
A Beginner's Guide to Mistakenly Summoned Demons and Other
Misadventures
A Beginner's Guide to Revenge, Chaos, and Other Absurd
Escapades
A Beginner's Guide to Ghosts, Fallen Angels, and Other Afterlifers

Demonic Disasters and Afterlife Adventures Novellas:
A Beginner's Guide to Christmas Miracles (A Holiday Novella)
A Beginner's Guide to the Care and Feeding of Pet Demons (A
Novella)
A Beginner's Guide to Demonic Possessions (A Novella)

Collections:
Demonic Disasters and Afterlife Adventures Collection 1

Hellhounds of Paradise Falls: (Paranormal Romance)
How to Flirt with a Hellhound
How to Hack a Hellhound
How to Tame a Hellhound